CARPE
NOCTEM

CARPE
NOCTEM

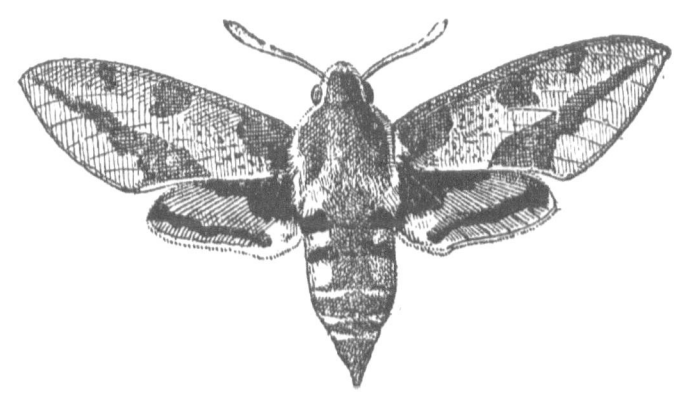

EDITED BY

MEGAN FENNELL
LESLIE VAN ZWOL

TYCHE BOOKS LTD.

CARPE NOCTEM
Copyright © 2024 Megan Fennell and Leslie Van Zwol

The publisher does not have any control over and does not assume any responsibility for author or third-party websites or their content.

This is a work of fiction. All of the characters, organizations, and events portrayed in this story are either the product of the authors' imagination or are used fictitiously.

Any resemblance to persons living or dead would be really cool, but is purely coincidental.

Published by Tyche Books Ltd.
Calgary, Alberta, Canada
www.TycheBooks.com

Cover Design by Indigo Chick Designs
Interior Layout by M.L.D. Curelas
Illustration 163070204 © Patrick Guenette | Dreamstime.com

First Tyche Books Ltd Edition 2024
Print ISBN: 978-1-989407-67-7
Ebook ISBN: 978-1-989407-68-4

For Mom and Dad:
All those years of "I-had-a-nightmare-can-I-sleep-in-
here?" should at least get you a book dedication out of
the deal. Love you!
—Megan

To the night owls, the insomniacs, the moonlight
dreamers, and those who burn the midnight oil, all
bleary-eyed at it's-too-damn-early o'clock.
—Leslie

TABLE OF CONTENTS

CONTENT WARNINGS

The following pages will outline any content warnings for the enclosed stories. This is intended as a guide for readers who wish to be aware of potential content in navigating these wonderful works.

Only works with warnings are listed (and may contain mild spoilers).

Your mental health and reading experience matters, and there are plenty of literary delicacies within to enjoy.

O, Nyx/ Ὦ Νυξ
Child abuse/child violence; Animal cruelty/Animal death; Death or dying [implied]

Sustainability
Paranoia/anxiety [direct]; Violence [implied]; Missing loved one [mentioned]

The Dark Backward
Paranoia/anxiety [direct]

Out on the Fringes, Down in the Weeds

Psychological abuse/coercion, Mental illness, Body horror [direct]; Suicide, Kidnapping and abduction, Poverty, Bigoted language, Sexism and misogyny [implied]; Death or dying [mentioned]

White Lies Cast Dark Shadows

Paranoia/anxiety [direct]; Kidnapping and abduction, Death or dying, Stalking, Violence [implied]

Chekhov's Gun is Screaming

Murder, Violence, Imagery of war/conflict, Gore [direct]; Child death/murder [implied]

One Dead Petal

Brief physical violence, Debilitated children [direct]; Harm to children [implied]

Owl Hoots Four Times

Paranoia/anxiety, Strigiformophobia (fear of owls) [direct]; Death or dying [implied]

Nothing But What You Bring with You

Animal cruelty/Animal death, Kidnapping and abduction, Violence [direct]; Death or dying, Non-consensual drug use [implied]

Grampire

Murder, Stalking, Violence [direct]; Ableism, Ageism [implied]; Spousal death [mentioned]

Held in the Shadows

Poverty, Paranoia/anxiety, Drug addiction, Chronic pain/illness, Car Accident [direct]; Death or dying [mentioned]

Midnight Man versus the Long Night

Psychological Abuse/coercion, Kidnapping and abduction, Death or dying, Murder, Body horror, Violence, Gore [direct]; Torture [implied]

Limbo of Sun and Shadow

Sexism and misogyny, Drug addiction [implied]; Death or dying [mentioned]

Mormolykia

Drug use, Murder, Violence, Gore, Possession [direct]; Physical Abuse, Intimate partner violence [implied]

Red on White
Gore, Violence [direct]; Animal cruelty/Animal death [implied]; Murder [mentioned]

The Tiyanak
Body horror [direct]; Sexual assault, Murder [implied]; Parental death/loss [mentioned]

Digging for Bear in the Evernight
Cannibalism, Romance between cousins [implied]

A Healthy, Happy Holiday
Animal corpse [direct]; Animal cruelty/Animal death [mentioned]

Love Like the Moon
Body horror, Being restrained [direct]

Impact City
Mind control [implied]

Corinne's Carousel
Intercourse [direct]; Death or dying [implied]

THE SMALL HOURS

Maxwell Lander

What lies ahead is a game. It's also an experiment, and it asks you to do things with your real human body in your real (presumably) human life, which means it could have real world consequences. Take care of yourself. The game is not more important than your comfort or safety, break it for fun or need.

The goal of this game is to be a bridge between you and this collection of stories. It can be daunting to open a new collection of stories and decide on where to start. This game is intended to help. It asks you to craft a small story, or at a minimum some small details of a story. When it speaks directly to you, it means "you" as you exist in the fiction of your playthrough. There are no wrong answers.

If you haven't played a solo roleplaying game before, it can be a strange experience. You don't need much. A single six-sided dice, a pen and a small piece of paper, or a willingness to write in your book (it's better this way!). The game asks you to "reflect on what you know", and this can be interpreted how you wish; through journaling, sitting and thinking, speaking aloud, etc.

Remember though, you're making a fiction. The game is not asking you to be realistic, it's asking you to craft a little, creepy story, to make a little, creepy character, and maybe creep yourself out a little in the process.

When you're done with it, you'll be given a page number where your story really begins.

I hope you enjoy it.

One of these stories is not like the others. One of them is for you. One of them is about you. You're a monster, really. In one way or another, we all are, but someone knows about you and has made record. I know this may be shocking, but it'll become clearer with time. Trust the process.

The System

There are 12 hours till dawn.

Each passage comes with three questions. They are the same questions. This is a ritual; it is intentionally repetitive.

For each question you answer yes to, roll a d4 and add it to your remaining time.

For each question you answer no to, roll a d4 and subtract it from your remaining time.

Choose 4 main passages in any way that feels good to you. Read them, roll them, let the drippings from your candlelight guide you. When you complete your 4 passages, or your time reaches 0, move to the final round and complete your ending passage. Which ending you complete depends on the time remaining.

If your time reaches 0, proceed to *Dawn Approaches*

If your remaining time is at 12 or more, proceed to *The Night Stretches Out Before You.*

If your remaining time is between 0 and 12, proceed to *You are Doubtful of the Light's Return.*

The Passages

Darkness
It's normal, being afraid of the dark. Find a comfortable place to sit. Turn off the lights, go outside, pull the blanket over your head, close your eyes. Something shares this darkness with you. It's possible you can just make out its shape. Focus.
Does it scare you? Do you resist it? Do you recognize it?

Cold
You're reminded that the flesh needs warmth as the last dregs of the sun's heat fades. Your skin prickles as if someone is running icy cold fingers along your body. The hands close around you, holding you in place. Your muscles stiffen and ache. To move now would be to release what little remaining heat you have stored, to invite those hands up under your skin into the darkest parts of you.
Does it scare you? Do you resist it? Do you recognize it?

Silence
It's not really a thing, is it? The thing we describe as silence is just a different level of awareness. No matter how quiet it gets, there's always new sounds to hear. Deeper sounds. Hums and buzzes, clicks and scratches. Find a silent place and listen until the chorus retreats. Something remains—breathing, maybe.
Does it scare you? Do you resist it? Do you recognize it?

Shadows
We can't ever really know what exists in the shadows. Limits of our biology and all that. Any attempts made to illuminate or uncover, make plain to our eyes, just destroys them. The best we can do is to catch glimpses, movements in the corner of our vision. Figments, we call them before dismissing them. Too often. To confront the reality of what is there could be world shattering. Try not to focus on them, the shadows, let them occupy the periphery of your vision. There's something there.
Does it scare you? Do you resist it? Do you recognize it?

Sleep
It is meant to be restful, our nightly withdrawal into our own

minds. A sanctuary for our bodies to recharge and recover from the ordeals of the day. Lay down, get comfortable, close your eyes. What is a waking dream called if it's not in the day? You are not alone, something is in here with you, occupying your most personal space. You might wonder, if you're paying attention, what else it could control of yours if it already has your mind.

Does it scare you? Do you resist it? Do you recognize it?

Solitude

At this time of night, the streets are all but deserted. Go outside. Maybe for a wander. Keep your eyes on the shadows. Beneath the trees and down the alleys. Under the awnings and lurking in the grass. It's tracking you. Interrupting your solitude.

Does it scare you? Do you resist it? Do you recognize it?

The Ending

The Night Stretches out Before You

The sun has only just receded behind the horizon. The light it reflects out basks everything in hazy oranges and purples. A long night extends out ahead of you, filled with potential. Your time is just beginning. Reflect on what you know of yourself. What do they find scratched in the dirt after you're gone?

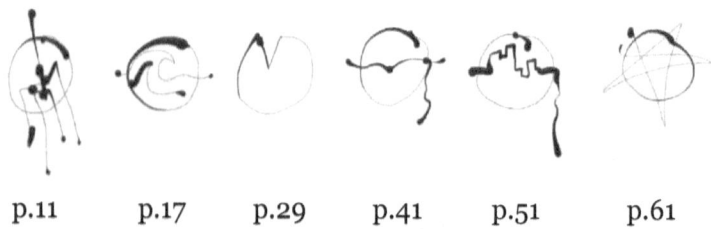

p.11   p.17   p.29   p.41   p.51   p.61

You are Doubtful of the Light's Return

There's a moment, in the deepest part of the night, where it becomes difficult to imagine the day returning. Even in the city, surrounded by the living. The cold gets too cold, the dark too dark. The absence of comfort becomes almost unbearable. This is where you live, straddling the line of bearability. What do they paint in the streets to mark your turf?

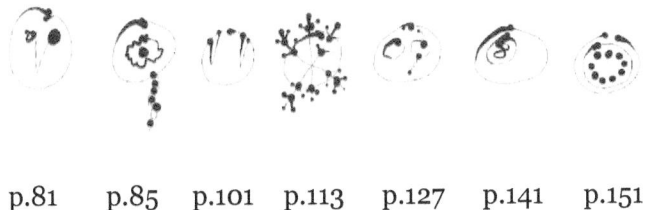

Dawn Approaches
   When dawn arrives, reflect on what you know of yourself. You're stranger than the rest, unsettling and surreal. Your kind are as old as any, possibly older. You are of the land and sea, and the fog that sits between them. The people have developed a symbol for you, a way to warn away the youth, though they do not always listen. Which is it?

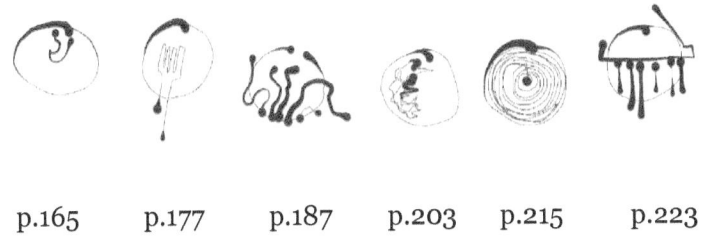

DUSK

THE HUNT BEGINS

O, NYX / Ὦ ΝΥΞ

AVRA MARGARITI

The months trailing the winter solstice
bring solace, a longing to be.
Each day waning, a relief
for children weaned on darkness
the soothing dark within
shielding us from harm.

Nights pulled long and languid now
through the omphalos of the world.
The owl and bat hawk screeching gratitude,
nourished by nocturnal visions
as they snatch the sleeping rodent.

Sylvan stones and springs gathered under
Stygian firmament, I've found, are the most
Potent when placed inside talismanic phials
gracing the bedside of lovers
sleeping fitfully with dreams
of traumas past.

I walk through paths lit only
by moon silk.
Like a spider I teeter over earth
and cobblestone,
ferns and flowers unfurling in my wake.
Shivering dew.

The night blooming Cereus will open
for a matter of hours once a year
and only bathed in darkness.
I will be ready for it, caressing
petals white and fragile. O,
how they only feel free to flourish
away from the sun's accusing glare.

SUSTAINABILITY

RICHARD LAU

 The campfire is very beautiful, isn't it? An abstract splash of reds, oranges, yellows, with hints of blue and white. As if painted by an orchestra conductor's brush, the flames leap and twirl in a flickering ballet, pulling reluctant, wallflower shadows to dance along with them.

Along with the physical heat the fire provides, you're wrapped with a warm blanket of nostalgia. Memories of youthful summers, thoughts of simpler and better times slacken your jaw and clear your airways. You are tempted to sing an old-timey campfire song your father taught you on one of your many joint excursions out here. But even now, alone in the wilderness, you shyly just manage a slight, barely audible hum. But we can hear it.

You sigh. Are you wishing your father was here? We are, too. Some of us are very old, and we have long memories. Your features, even in the erratic, ever-changing glow of the firelight, remind us of your father when he was younger, camping out here with his father and his brother.

Your family has camping in its blood. We know. We have tasted it.

You shiver. It cannot be because you can hear us. Not yet.

It must be the cooling in the air as the sun is going down, a fiery casket lowering into yet another freshly dug grave. The sanguine sky ushering the death of the day; the stars brightly heralding the cold, sterile birth of night. Your imagination spreads with the growing dimness. The fear is far from blinding, quite the opposite. You start seeing things that cannot possibly be.

"A well-tended fire is your best friend," your father had instructed you on one of your first outings into our environs. "It cooks your food. It provides light. It keeps the animals at bay."

But we're not animals. But never mind that. Enjoy the wilderness.

That's what you want, right? Getting away from the hustle and bustle of urban life. Away from the goddamned city. Back to nature. The way it was meant to be. The way it's supposed to be. The way that doesn't seem to exist in too many places anymore.

You enjoy the taste and smell of the fresh air with its musty mixture of pine, mould, and dampness. The peace and quiet, as different and unnerving as that may be. Even the solitude can be rejuvenating. Taking the time to focus on yourself. Slow your thoughts. Contemplate something greater, larger, more significant, something other than bills, traffic, and the nine-to-five. No television. No cellphones. No unwanted intrusions, human, electronic, or otherwise. Or so you think.

Even here, as with everywhere, there's the circle of life.

Yes, I am speaking of predators and prey. Nature doesn't care and knows no boundaries. Survival of the fittest. Eat or be eaten. Sometimes both.

Life and death are two sides of the same tree. So, if the wilderness is abundant with one side, why not the other?

As I mentioned, there are plenty of living things in the immediate area, us included. However, for the sake of genetic variety in nutrition, it is a fruitful benefit to have something different once in a while. A nice treat that is so convenient.

One that treks along on long, winding, lonely trails, stepping off said trails, until it finds that perfect little area to set down its heavy gear and camp. Like you did today and have done so many times before. Here is a small clearing, as open and welcoming as the mouth of a Venus flytrap. Perfect for you. Perfect for us.

Dead animals occur naturally in the wilderness. Their corpses are rarely seen. If they are noticed, they are usually ignored, unless a scientist or researcher is doing a study or a ranger is looking for off-season poaching.

But you humans are a different matter. Your corpses attract special attention. Especially from other humans. Which could cause a problem and expose us for the predators we are.

Fortunately, when your bodies are found before we're finished with them, depending on what we've done and how far along we are in the digestive process, these remains are usually attributed to accident, exposure to weather, or a large predator like a bear. Only on the rare occasion will the death be classified as "cause unknown" or "unsolved homicide".

Metal like backpack frames and canteens are indigestible for us. But even when these are discovered, they are deemed abandoned trash or lost. These inorganic remains take more time to conceal than your organic ones. But due to our nature, if you pardon the intentional pun, time is the one thing we have plenty of.

That's the way we have evolved. Slowly and surely. Hiding in plain view. Watching as a conveyor belt of delicacies slowly goes by. Delicacies alert to other delicacies, but never to us.

We don't move a lot. But we don't have to. When food comes to those such as us, why should we waste precious sun-given energy stalking and hunting it? We just need one lightning-fast moment to capture it. The flick of a frog's tongue. The strike of a snake. The bite of a venomous insect. To put it in terms you can understand, the fast, sudden hook-sinking jerk of the fishing line. And then, the predator can take its time, enjoying the triumph of the catch.

But don't make the mistake of thinking just because we don't often move on our own that we can't move at all. You may see us shifting slowly and slightly and blame the movement on a light breeze that you can't feel. You might catch us after we move and think you've confused your path and are in an area you haven't been in before. Or you might not notice anything at all. That is our greatest strength. You literally can't see the trees for the forest.

And you feel safe with that fire, don't you?

We're not afraid of fire. We don't like it. We try to avoid it. But we and fire have co-existed for longer than humans have been on the Earth. Long before there were careless campers or drivers throwing cigarette butts out their car windows, there were lightning strikes.

We accept fire as just another part of that circle of life. We understand that one day we may be blocking out the blazing sunlight, and on another, we may be burning up like the sun's surface. If one is lucky, one is fed to live another day. If one dies, the death provides space and nutrients for other things to grow, including any remaining seedlings. Our children will continue in our stead. We are satisfied with that. Are you?

So, flood, drought, mudslide, wind, storm, illness, fire. It makes no difference to us.

Speaking of fire, have you noticed your campfire is dying out? We see your eyelids droop, growing heavier after the exhaustive efforts of a long, long day. Distracted by random thoughts settling slowly to the ground like dry leaves and the seductive lure of sleep weighing on your shoulders like a family of raccoons. The time is almost here. Our roots reach out, unnoticed, underground.

As the fire burns itself down to a barely glowing ember and darkness closes in from all sides, the clearing seems to shrink. If you notice, you will blame your imagination.

You might look upwards and wonder why the starry night is now obliterated by a leafy canopy that wasn't there earlier in the day. But you'd blame your imagination for that, too.

You marvel about how beautiful your surroundings are, even though you can barely see any of it. You renew a vow to protect us, to do all you can to sustain us. And you will. We will help you keep your promise.

Fortunately, we have other sources of nutrition and don't require much. Like a bear in hibernation, we store our energy, digest slowly, and a little goes a long way. So, as long as there are nature-lovers like yourself, we will sustain ourselves.

It is so touching, so very human, so perfectly ironic that you are concerned about our sustainability when you would take immediate action to destroy us if you knew what we really are and everything that we do and are capable of. And even though you don't, you're still doing a fairly decent job at controlling our population.

And in the same literal vein, we try not to thin out your kind too rapidly, as well.

Once, when you, your sister, and your dad were camping out here, we heard him talking about your uncle. How he had lost touch with his brother. How he didn't even remember what they had argued about to cause such a break and the resulting years of silence.

Your father didn't know his brother had brought a companion out here. That was the last time the two of them were seen. Their bodies were never found. Her family probably labelled your uncle as her murderer and presumed that he was on the run.

You humans can be so creative when explaining the missing. A child that just wandered away. A tragic attack by a wild animal. Teens spontaneously escaping their parents' oppression with their runaway lovers. An entire family deciding civilization was not for them and choosing to live in seclusion.

Your father came up with a pretty good one himself. Remember when he described how he and your grandfather came out here, on that last tragic outing? How they had just set up the campfire, how they had just started cooking dinner when your grandfather wandered off into the woods. How the old man never returned?

Your father suspected dementia as the cause for the disappearance. And he never got over the guilt of waiting too long to go looking. We watched his fruitless search in silence. We shed not a tear of sap, but we felt his very primitive pain.

On subsequent visits, it was clear he still expected the old man to suddenly appear like nothing had happened, like no time had passed. We know, for he called out to the missing man at every twig that snapped, every branch that fell, every leaf that rustled in the still air.

"Is that you, Pop?" We can hear his voice now.

Is your father still alive? It's been a while since we've seen him. Is he too old or too ill to come out here anymore? If so, it's a shame. And especially unfortunate for you. You see, his absence has sealed your fate.

He was always one we let go.

We, too, care about sustainability. We always leave some humans alone. It's good for preserving our concealment, reducing the risk of discovery. But such behaviour is also good for keeping your numbers sufficient for future needs. Our future needs.

It is important that the humans we spare return home, raise offspring, and introduce them to the outdoors life. When they come back, little ones in tow, some of them won't be returning home the next time around. Some of them will.

And that is mutual sustainability.

You sit there, almost dozing. Unaware of your fate.

We are patient. You should be, too.

After all, you have that fire, don't you? Or had that fire. It seems to have gone out.

We have you surrounded. But you either don't notice or don't care. Or to repeat myself, you literally can't see the trees for the forest. You can't see us leaning toward you, inching closer, centimetre by centimetre.

By the time our roots spring up from the earth, quick and sharp, like the steel teeth of your spring-jawed hunting traps snapping shut, you will know the truth. The truth that has been around all this time, all of these years, throughout your lineage and that of humankind.

But for now, just relax as my branch caresses your shoulder.

THE DARK BACKWARD

Paul McQuade

 He expected the ring at the door. He had, after all, returned the call from the police to arrange this visit. And yet, looking at it, some precipice wells up inside him. It is as though a floor has suddenly fallen away. He finishes his chilled jasmine tea and places it down on the table. He has drunk nearly the whole carton waiting for the police. He had wanted cold, clarity. None is forthcoming. An unstable energy pulses in him. Why fear the door, the answer on the other side?

He moves to the genkan of the apartment, calling for the officers to come in, beginning to bow before they even open the door. The two officers introduce themselves as Suzuki and Tamura. Ryūtaro invites them in past the threshold. They place their shoes at the threshold, meticulously, before entering the upscale *manshon*. He draws the detectives to the Western-style entertainment space with a high table on parquet flooring. He pours what's left of the jasmine tea into tumblers for the officers. His hand doesn't shake as he pours. He is surprised at that.

"How can I help?" Ryūtaro asks. On the phone, the police had simply said it was important they talk to him to assist with an ongoing investigation.

The officers watch him, implacable. Every infraction, every failing, every wrong and every piece of shame seems laid out in front of them. Their gaze seems to say: *We know. We know everything you've ever done.*

They stare at the tea in their hands in unison, as though rehearsed. The tea is crystalline, a strange topaz.

"It's about your friend Hideyoshi Aomori," the one on the left says. What was his name? Tamura, Ryūtaro thinks, though already the two are indistinguishable to him.

"Hide? Why do you want to know about him?"

The officer, who may or may not be Tamura, looks up from the tea. "Because he's missing."

In Gunma, when he was younger, Hide would lie in the long stalks of the rice field and watch the stars. The weird green of the paddy, the undiluted starlight, and the earth, soft, recovering from the flooding of the planting season. The memory of those nights has been revised as an adult, something of the original magic pulled out of it: when he thinks of it, he feels as though the ground would float up to meet the sky, that his body, pinned to the earth, was weightless. How much sweeter these things are with time and distance, with absence. There are no stars in Tokyo and there is no dark either. Outside the window of his apartment on the forty-second floor, the city pulses. Stardust clots the hubs of Shinjuku and Shibuya, clusters of light along the stops of the Yamanote circle. The city floods with neon. The night sky above it is dull, blank, suffocated. No matter how long he has lived here, it is always strange to see it: all this light under a sky without stars.

He is sitting in jinbei striped dark grey, drinking barley tea by the window where he has laid his futon. A little way away, a coffee table with short legs, suitable for tatami floors like this, holds his laptop, some documents, and a cracked paperback of Shakespeare's *The Tempest* he had picked up at a used bookshop near Waseda. He has been charged with producing a new translation, something more modern than the antiquated things produced by Tsuneari and Tsubouchi.

He never should have taken this commission. He had

protested when the agency sent it over. He works primarily with technical translation—dentistry, so much dentistry—and his experience with literature is confined to one or two "light novels". Who is he to translate Shakespeare? But the client had insisted: it had to be him. Had they said why? That they were impressed with his work? No, no, not that he can recall, but they must have, surely, otherwise why insist? He hadn't questioned it at the time. The money was too good.

Why is it we only think to question things when it is already too late?

He is stuck at the beginning, where Prospero speaks to Miranda about blindness and forgetting. Hide can summon a tooth from its very root but he cannot make it past this one, simple question: *What seest thou else in the dark backward and abysm of time?*

An abyss is difficult to render in Japanese, let alone an *abysm*. Prospero is referring to a gap in his daughter's memory, a gulf where she cannot recall the shipwreck that brought them to their magic island. In Japanese, there are two words for time. Which of the two holds this abyss? What kind of darkness is it that obscures the past?

In the interest of sanity, he has settled for: *Toki no wareme.* It doesn't quite call forth Prospero, but it will do. He has had to make peace with it.

This metaphysical question put to bed, he had thought, maybe the rest would flow. But it is the simpler part, the first, that is giving him the most trouble.

The dark backward.

Shakespeare is using *backward* to refer to what is behind, that is, the past. That it functions as an adverb is an accident, surely. *Dark* cannot be a verb. And even if it were, what is it that would do it?

He has written on a notepad next to his laptop: I dark, you dark, he/she darks, they dark, we dark. Backward? It darks me, it darks you. We are darked. It darks us.

Several circles, in different coloured pens—as though this might change things—around the word "it".

The lights flicker then die. Only the light of the city remains. The window darkens. He cannot see the slow climb of cars or the images that float above the city, promising cup noodles, pop idols, discount air travel. At the window, something swells, trying to bring itself into existence beyond the glare of the city.

What light there is barely penetrates. In the room, he can make out only the outlines of things. Pale slips of books on the floor next to the desk where he has been working. It seems, in its shadow, abandoned to human devices but not distant or lifeless so much as differently inhabited. The scene unsettles him. It unseats his reason, this primal fear—that something is with him in the dark.

It darks me, it darks you. We are darked. It darks us.

The translation lies on the desk, unfinished. It is only when a dishwater dawn slips over the city that he finally finds the courage to move.

"How was he the last time you saw him?" Tamura or Suzuki asks. No matter how he tries, Ryūtaro cannot get either fixed in his mind. Just when he thinks he knows who is who, one folds into the other. It is as if they are swapping features as they talk. Picasso distortion, all noses, eyes, and triangles. The lines of the face, smudged, rewritten, appearing again on the other. "Asano-san?"

"Sorry," Ryūtaro says. "I'm trying to remember. He was stressed about some assignment he had been given."

The two exchange a look. For a moment, their faces slip. One eye changes into another. Then a nose. Why won't their features stay still?

"Did he tell you anything about the assignment?"

"He had to translate Shakespeare for some new publication. You know how it is, the kids in school these days can't read the Japanese people wrote fifty years ago, let alone a hundred. They're always bringing out new editions of things."

His niece had been studying an edition of *The Tale of Genji* the last time he visited. He had asked to see the book, to look at the pages that had tormented him in school. Not a word of it was familiar. This new translation read as though it had been written by someone his age, not the ancient voice he remembered. He had asked Hide about it afterwards. For Ryūtaro a translation should be done once and for all. There is one *Genji*—why should there be more than one translation? Because, Hide explained, while the text of *Genji Monogatari* may be fixed in time, the language of the translation is not.

Was that the last time he had seen him?

"You look troubled," the detective on the right says. Suzuki? "I was just thinking of something strange Hide said. Not about the Shakespeare translation. Just something he said."

"Tell us," Tamura says. "Anything might be helpful."

"He said that only a translation is ever truly alive," Ryūtaro says. "That the original is already dead. That recently he had found himself wondering why he spent his life trawling the dark with all these dead things."

"I see," the one on the left says. Ryūtaro has to fight the urge to think of them as one being, temporarily suspended. The egg and its white. "What exactly was it that was troubling him about the translation he was working on when he disappeared?"

"One line," Ryūtaro says, "just one line he couldn't seem to get over."

Hide wakes late. There are emails. There are always emails. Someone always wants something. They want him to buy things, to subscribe to things, to watch things, to send money. Among them is an email from his boss. He wants answers. He wants a timeline. He wants to know, most of all, why the client had insisted on Hide. *Do you know why they picked you?* It's so strange. He wants a timeline. He wants to know how much progress Hide has made with the translation.

Hide ignores the emails, and, after a moment's hesitation, changes into a pair of sweats and a loose t-shirt. At the *konbini*, the familiar chime, the sudden wash of light. These convenience stores possess a quality of light that is designed, he had heard, to emulate daylight. So people will shop longer. He selects the last spicy miso pork onigiri, two tuna mayonnaise, and a can of Yebisu. As he walks out with his ramshackle meal, he looks up at his apartment building. At this time of day—he savours the English word *crepuscular,* for which no Japanese comes close— he doesn't expect lights on in many of the units. But the windows of his apartment are pitch black. Looking there, at the dark window of his own apartment, he feels something watching. That *it* that lives there, in the gap between things.

It darks me. It darks us.

Something is moving within. Like a squid rolling in its own ink.

He sits down on the edge of a flower bed outside the *konbini*. His apartment is next to a subway station on the Marunouchi line, so it's not uncommon to see people sitting here, waiting for people, or maybe like him, just afraid to go home. There are so many people in Tokyo. There is so much light. And yet what waits for so many people at the end of the day is a small apartment ironically called a *manshon*, a meal warmed up at the *konbini* on the way home, and the long dark.

No wonder we're always going out, he thinks. The dark backward and abysm of time. *It darks me. We are darkened.* Like the night sky. Sometimes, it seems, all the stars in us are extinguished by this other dark, this darker dark, in the neon flux of this place.

He gets out his mobile and messages Ryūtaro to see if he wants to go out for a drink. He goes back into the *konbini,* buys two more Ebisu, and, after a moment's consideration, a packet of Super Seven Ultra Lights and a lighter, so that he has company while he waits for a response. He hasn't smoked in years. He doesn't know why. It is a whim. Some want is pressing itself up against his skin, in the dark behind his eyes. He hesitates, briefly, at the threshold of the *konbini* by a case of steamed buns, but the clerk says *mata okoshi kudasaimase,* which means it's time to go, though literally she has just asked him to come again. The words don't mean what they say. He wants the *konbini* light. Its mindlessness. But he goes out, opens the pack of cigarettes, and lights one. When was the last time he smoked? His twenties, must be. His lungs constrict at the pull of the cigarette. The past moulders in his lungs. A thin shred of the dark backward. A little word he can't quite render in Japanese but that pulls at him.

The past is not enough, he thinks. It must involve the sense of movement. Of being dragged into the dark.

He looks at his apartment again. Something is there, watching. He's sure of it.

He jumps when the phone buzzes. Ryūtaro is almost done with his work at the office. His train will be stopping at Takadanobaba before he switches lines on his way home. He could stop there for a drink.

Hide leaves the convenience store and goes to the subway entrance, walking a little way along the corridor until he comes to the stairs down to the platform. The light from the overhead strips fails at the first step. He stops. It is the same dark, if dark has a quality, that is waiting for him in his apartment. It does not feel like a hunt. It is an invitation. There is something there. Something that yearns for him. What is worse is that, somehow, from somewhere, he yearns for it too.

He backs away, his eyes on the shadow in front of him. He finds his way to the wall and walks backwards, toward the stairs, and backwards still. The shadow follows him as he moves.

Once outside, there is the light of the convenience store, the pachinko parlour, the sign for the karaoke bar. He has always found this kind of light inhuman. Neon blue, relentless. But he feels safety in it, tonight, and something human, too. What could be more human than that simple wish to hold back the dark?

He gets on his bike and, sticking to the strip of sodium lights along the way, relishing the wash of car headlights on his back, he cycles his way to Takadanobaba, not once letting himself stumble into shadow. Not daring to face something he knows is waiting there.

"Tell us what happened after that meeting?" maybe-Suzuki asks.

"Nothing special," Ryūtaro says. "We went to an izakaya. We drank beer. He told me he was stressed about his assignment. He didn't want to go home, he said. We went to a karaoke box. I fell asleep. When I woke up, he was awake, sitting there with the lights on eating some onigiri he had brought with him. He went home after that."

"And were you in contact after that?"

"Yes," Ryūtaro says. "I was worried about him after we met, so I phoned each day."

"But you never saw him?"

"No," he says. "Just on the phone."

"What did he say?"

Ryūtaro stands on the platform of the Yamanote line. He has time before the next train so decides to call Hide, as he's done every few days since the karaoke. Something about him had seemed unsettled. The phone connects. There is breath, no voice.

"Hide?" Ryūtaro says. "It's me."

"Teeth," Hide says to him.

"What?"

"You can always count on teeth. There are different words for them," Hide says. "Much better than Shakespeare. Teeth can be trusted. *Kenshi, kyūshi, monshi.* And their counterparts: canine, molar, incisor. It's so much simpler. Teeth can be trusted. There's no dark there, nothing running backward. Not even words, sometimes, just numbers. Upper 3. Lower 32."

Ryūtaro remembered one time when Hide showed him a diagram of the teeth and he was nearly sick. A small arc of them behind the front ones—the milk teeth. In another diagram, they were visible in the X-ray of a child's skull, undescended. A whole line of teeth just below the eye. He shuddered.

"It's simpler with the numbers," Hide went on. "They collapse everything. Infinitely collapsing. No shadow. No shadow there."

"You need to take a break," Ryūtaro says.

"No," he insists. "I like the dentist stuff. The teeth. It's simple. I try to get the words right. But there's no back to them, anymore. Numbers are better. Teeth. Words. Words look out on to something. There is space behind them. A dark . . ."

"And what?"

"And something's there."

"What?"

"I don't know," Hide says. "I just feel it there, pulling . . . It's like it knew there was an opening. For just a moment, I think, my mind was opened to something. When I was thinking about that text. And I keep wondering—Why did they insist I do it? Who sent this to me? I think they knew. I think they knew this would happen."

"You're just overworked," Ryūtaro says. "You're overthinking it."

From the receiver, no response. The announcement for the train comes. People begin to line up.

"Look, I need to get on the train now. But tell me you're okay, first. At least say something."

"We're never really alone in the dark, you know," Hide says.

The line cuts out.

When he gets a seat, after changing to the Hibiya line, Ryūtaro places his tongue against the ridge of his gums. Tongue against palate. Flesh against flesh. The press. He tells himself that he knows they are really there. Hide is just overworked, he tells himself.

When he gets off at Nakameguro and begins to walk back to his apartment, he tries not to look at his own shadow. It is his shadow. Of course it is. It is a trick of the night that it seems to follow at a step behind him. That it seems larger than him. That its dimensions are distorted. That its hand has such sharp fingers.

When he finally gets home, he kicks off his shoes, showers, and goes straight to bed. He has turned off the lights in every part of the house, but not the lamp beside the bed. His hand lingers over the switch. He cannot bring himself to turn it off. He needs something this light offers. Some guard against the dark. That thing behind things. He lies there, in the light, and runs his tongue over his teeth. Sleep is not forthcoming.

"And you're sure you never saw him again." He cannot tell which one says it. The voices are shared, too, now. A resonance that makes Ryūtaro feel nauseated.

"Positive," Ryūtaro says.

"Only, we have a report of you visiting. There are CCTV cameras. The landlord is the one who recognised you."

The landlord. He had met the man once, maybe, but he has remembered Ryūtaro better than Ryūtaro did him. A strange feeling, to think that strangers know more about you than yourself. But then, he doesn't remember the visit to the apartment so well either.

The door was unlocked. From the genkan you could see straight through to the tatami where Iide worked and slept.

"Was there anything odd? Anything out of place, anything that gave you cause for concern?"

"No," Ryūtaro says. "Only . . ."

"Yes?"

"The lights were on. All of them. In the *washitsu*, that's the room he spent most of his time in, there were stand lamps and table lamps and even smaller lights, things with batteries, toys." He remembered that very clearly: a little lamp in the shape of a dumpling, its face smiling unfathomably. The light turned its skin translucent. The bulb inside looked like a glass organ. The smile. The lifeless eyes.

"But you never saw Aomori-san again?"

"No, I never saw him after that."

"You never visited," one of them repeats, as though this will change the answer.

"No."

He does not tell them that, though there were hundreds of lights in that apartment, it didn't feel bright. He doesn't tell them that he sensed something press itself against that light. And that, with that feeling, came also the knowledge that this pressing must one day give, that the light must one day yield to this thing.

"I think we have what we need," the police say.

He walks them out. They put on their shoes and open the door. When the men stand close together, their skin starts to slide, slowly, as though detached from the bones beneath. A trick of the light, he thinks.

"If you think of anything else, please give us a call," someone says. One of them says. It says.

"Of course," Ryūtaro says, as though everything is normal.

When the police are gone, he goes to lie on his bed, under the window, in the strange mix of neon and sunset, in that time when things are not quite. He turns on the light. He needs it. He needs to see the red flush of his own skin. Eyelids, blood. These things are real, he tells himself. Nothing else. This he can trust. He tries not to think of something behind the words. Some darkness that can't be held back.

He still can't sleep. He can't get Hide's words out of his head. He should have called again, after the last time, but he'd gotten busy. No, no that wasn't quite right. He didn't want to talk to him after the last phone call. Ryūtaro had been avoiding calling. And now Hide is missing. And he can't stop thinking about that last phone call, what he said. *We're never really alone in the dark.*

The doorbell rings. This time Ryūtaro has to mute the variety show he has been half-watching while looking at his phone. It is Saturday afternoon. No plans. He looks at the door. He moves to the peephole. On the other side is only blackness.

He hesitates. Then opens the door.

There is a postman standing there in his uniform, holding out a letter in both hands.

"Registered mail," he says. Ryūtaro offers his ink seal and stamps the official form before being handed the envelope, on which his name has been written in an ink that is remarkably black. There is a postmark on it that says the letter has been delivered from Gunma.

"Thank you," Ryūtaro says absently, as he is closing the door. The postman gives the letter a strange look, puzzlement almost, as if he does not recognise the thing he has just handed over. The door closes over his face. An eclipse.

Ryūtaro goes through to the other room. For a moment he stops, then turns on all the lights.

He opens the letter at the table where he had spoken to the two policemen. Inside, there is nothing except one piece of paper with scant writing on it. When he looks for a return address, he finds it obscured by a thick smear of black. The liquid is darker than ink. It is a kind of black that leads out of the world itself. The message inside is written in this substance, too. His hands tremble as he takes it out of the envelope. On one side is written: *It darks me. It darks you. It darks us.* And on the other:

The dark backward
時の割れ目
It is here.

and abysm of time.
逆の闇と
In the dark. It is here and it lives in the dark.

OUT ON THE FRINGES, DOWN IN THE WEEDS

JENNIFER LESH FLECK

Last leg of our drive ahead—miles of piney woods, oil refineries, and forgotten swampland. You're tired. It's getting dark. And I've asked too many questions. Sometimes, in my eagerness to know someone, I do that. So relax and let me drive. Ask me anything. Close your eyes if you need to. I won't be offended, promise.

Where'd I grow up? California.

No, no Hollywood glamour there. No surfboards. What I mean is the forgotten region, a dry, white-hot valley. Runs down the middle like a skunk's stripe.

Strongest childhood memory? Ah, *there's* an origin tale never told. And being deeply known and understood—isn't that what we all want, deep down in our pits? Very well. Picture me a child, then. Born late in my parents' lives, all their bright hope bound up in me. Small and clingy, so I seemed carved from my mother's waistline.

Still, I'd managed to make this one little good friend. That's what my parents called her: Janie's one little good friend. Fifth grade was well under way—alliances formed, allegiances declared—when her family arrived, up to work the wine grapes.

"Say hello to Yolanda, class."

And Yolanda was pushed in front of us all, her eyes dark as a mink's and mouth clamped like a vise.

But at recess, I was the one she sought out and tagged, sending me back to home base with a smile and a "sorry."

And that was that: we were friends.

There's a photo of us I've kept. Her hair in precise braids, mine unruly, we face each other at the harvest dance. Even though we look nothing alike, we seem coordinated: gingham dresses, knee socks. But try-hard dress shoes on her. And on me, dusty black boots like a goat's hooves. Our hands are linked. We're poised, ready to begin the Virginia Reel. She's taller, so I'm beaming up at her like she's the sun. Years in storage have tinted the photo a permanent autumn. So that's how I remember that time in my childhood. Fall-coloured, like it's viewed through a jar of honey. Golden, but uncomfortable, too, like looking sideways through a beam of sunlight and dust.

Outside of Yolanda, school was dull. Picking glue off my fingers like dead skin, a clock with hands that dragged. Though at recess I'd come alive for our invented game. I was a cat and Yolanda my owner. I mewed for her, winding between her gangly legs. I hissed and scampered, unexpectedly lunged to make her laugh.

Sometimes she wanted us to join the friendly girls who had a jump rope. I'd clown, redouble my efforts, pretending it was all play. But what I really meant to do was have Yolanda to myself, cut like a calf from the herd. Something was already askew in me, a streak of clasping greed. Love situated on the dial too close to loathing.

I tried to join the fun; mask my weakness. If I could forget I was being observed while I jumped, focus on the words, the rhythm, I was better at it. The jump rope songs were the usual ones, only strange if you consider them now. Cinderella kissing a snake she mistook for her fellow. Burglars knocking at your front door.

If I realized I was being watched and the rope hit me—if I missed a step—hot humiliation. Then as now, I played best in a pair, heads together, secretive.

Each day, Yolanda and I were squired home from school by my mother. It was, my mom said, to keep me safe. She didn't mention Yolanda, but I assumed she meant her, too.

Yolanda's street was not far from ours, but had a kind of split personality. One side of the block matched ours: new houses and postage stamp lawns. The other side was something different. Decades older, stucco boxes built right after the second World War and painted optimistic pastels, now bleached and drab. Alterations made over the years gave each house a homely distinctiveness: a ramshackle carport there, a breeze block courtyard here. Dogs streamed through yards without collars or tags, earning my mother's frown.

Some houses, like Yolanda's, lacked paved driveways. Cars pulled off the street and parked in loose clutches, the evidence of would-be mechanics tinkering—or having once tinkered—all around: rotted spare tire, hunk of carburetor, crushed beer cans.

Looking back, I'm surprised my parents ever let me spend the night at Yolanda's. They didn't know her family. I'd never been inside her home.

It happened only once.

My parents were hawk-eyed and protective, but maybe they needed a night to themselves. So on a Saturday, I was dispatched with my flowered suitcase and a reminder for good behaviour.

Yolanda's house smelled of tortillas and bleach, and was tidy, aside from two dead flies on a windowsill. We all piled onto a velvet couch with jouncy springs—Yolanda, little sister Rosa, big brother Enrique, me—our bare legs sticking out straight, theirs well-shaped, mine pale, giving strong hints of the bones inside and marked with three faded bruises of unknown origin. For two solid hours, we watched soap operas in Spanish. Yolanda and her siblings sat slack-jawed, falling into the show. Anguished tears and black mascara streaked the actresses' cheeks. Yet quick as the flick of a lighter, these women turned flawless again, resuming their seductions and cold scheming.

Too proud and too timid to ask for a translation, I let my fidgeting and huffs speak for me. Eventually, they got the hint. We spilled outside to a yard narrow and deep, an alley behind it. No lawn, only lashing foxtails and goat's head stickers. A massive mulberry tree littered the hard ground near the house with berries. We trampled them into stains with our bare feet, pretending to make wine. I'd never been allowed to run loose in the dirt, no shoes. A merry joy to it, a glory in the filth we created.

After our messy jig, Yolanda took me to see the chickens. She passed me a hen—soft, glistening, impossibly light—and studied my face for my impression, which passed wordlessly between us. A jungle fowl from Southeast Asia—a ripped page from the encyclopedia flashed before me. The scaly legs paddled, claws grasping. The eye was cold and reptilian. It would kill me if it could. I released it with a shove to scatter, take up its unhappy clucking elsewhere.

We poked the ground with sticks, at loose ends, until Enrique found us.

"Well . . . Have you shown it to her yet?"

Yolanda's eyes widened. "We're not supposed to."

"She's too scared." He gave me a winning smile. "But I'm not. I'll show you. You wanna see the hole? Then you better come on."

Without hesitation, I followed the boy, watching his shoulders move under his thin T-shirt, its black-striped fabric faded and worn. I was—am—someone up for just about anything if it promises to be off-kilter, off the beaten path, down in the weeds. Like a dutiful soldier I tromped by a sun-rotted car seat, heading back to an area I'd already passed through with carefree indifference.

It was a desert-scape in miniature: burning sand, a scatter of wild seeds, ants impossibly busy with their affairs. Chips of mica and quartz flashed up, the minerals I sometimes gathered as gold and diamonds for my private games. My hungry eyes scanned the dirt, seeking something novel, something of value, a relief from the day-to-day.

"You have to promise never—ever—to reveal what you're about to see to another living person. Swear now on your mother's grave." He paused, considering. "Your dad's too."

I shrugged. Pacts were easy. Mere words.

He held a finger in the air, as though trying to pinpoint a lost thought or test the breeze. "Okay. It's there. Right there."

Disappointment filled me. "That? It's nothing. It's from a gopher or a rabbit." Only a hole an animal had scratched out, just large enough for my arm to fit into. Nothing spectacular, nothing dazzling. Something you'd find in any unkempt yard for a hundred miles in any direction.

A dark, scolding look from Enrique. "It's not from any old damn gopher. It's not from an animal at all. If that's how you're gonna be, well. Then I'm very sorry I showed you." He couldn't hold my challenging look for long, though, and cursed under his breath.

I felt sorry for him and squatted to examine the hole, feigning interest.

A hiss escaped from Enrique. He bit his knuckle. "Would you watch it?! Please!"

"It's an animal burrow," I said flatly.

"Listen. The thing that lives here, under the ground . . . there was one like it where we lived before, in Tamaulipas. It got my uncle. He couldn't leave it be. He never was right again. It's cursed soil. We're not supposed to go anywhere near it. You're not supposed to be back here. This place, Janie . . . is not for you."

"Then why'd you show me?"

"Because. Okay, listen." His eyes were wild. "This is where a devil lives. Not *the* devil. *A* devil. There are many. This one lives right under the ground, around there—" He gestured broadly, as though afraid to be more specific.

I knew then that he was playing with me, the way older brothers tease their sister's friends. The idea of the king of hell—horns, pitchfork, and lashing tail—curled up and cramped. Ludicrous.

I went right up to the burrow. Frowning, I squatted and inspected the hole with an almost scientific intensity. Light seemed to die at its mouth, becoming a cool and velvety darkness. I kicked dirt into it.

Only a gopher's hole, right? I'd seen my share.

"Let's just go. I'm sorry I showed you this. Please, Janie, forget about it."

That evening, we piled around the table, stuffing ourselves with carnitas and tortillas—greasy, crisp, delectable. Yolanda's mom asked questions about my family, what we did, what we ate, the animals we kept. All from behind her hand, hiding the winking gold tooth I found beautiful. Yolanda translated with a burnished pride. They called me *flaquita* and *nina blanca*, for I was so skinny and so pale. Later in life I'd have other nicknames spat at me, but what was said here was said affectionately and with a twinkle.

At bedtime Yolanda and I stretched in the dark, the day's heat flattening us like an iron. Irregular gaps in the metal blinds let street light bleed in. My gaze roved, taking in indistinct shapes, naming them to myself. Books, bears, dollhouse that listed to one side. Her sister Rosa's tightly-made bed. Yolanda's voice went drifty with sleep. It reminded me of sliding, shifting sands, the desert on *Mutual of Omaha's Wild Kingdom*. She fell asleep mid-sentence.

If you were born an insomniac like me, then you know how terrible it is to spend the night with someone new, even someone you like or love or trust. Stuck awake, marooned in consciousness. The bedding smelled of a different soap than the one my mother used. Around us, the house snapped and creaked. "Just settling its bones," my mom would have said.

Yolanda's mother had turned off the bedroom fan. I missed the comforting noise, the caress in the air. But to rise up and turn it back on seemed like crossing a boundary.

Worse still: my good friend then did something I found unthinkable. With a jerk she turned, throwing an arm and a leg over me. The unwelcome surprise stung me. Mine was a family of words and ideas; we rarely touched unless necessary. Now I was pinned on my back, nearly half Yolanda's body weight on me.

Back then, my first impulse was to avoid offense or inconvenience to others. Eons of suffering passed as I made tentative squirms to disentangle us. Small communications of my distress that could—were she to awaken, cross with me—be construed as blameless natural movements made in my own slumber. She sighed, muttered an obscure word. A fitful hand wrapped in my long hair. On her fingers, the smell of mulberries.

My secondary nature rose up. I revolted. I violently shook her loose. Her eyelids never fluttered. I was up and out of the bed, plastered in sweat and brimming with irritation.

I could have simply crawled into her sister's bed, it's true. Instead, I pictured myself home. My father would be up watching Carson. I'd walk the short distance, back to the security of the known. Stepping lightly, I passed closed bedroom doors. Little Rosa curled on the velvet living room couch, blanket fallen to the floor.

I'd seen Yolanda's father bolt the front door, but the back was unlocked, unlatched. A push, and it opened.

The moon was fat and full, the edges of everything fuzzed. A rattle of chain in the distance, the bark of a dog cut short. The chickens made soft, concerned sounds from the safety of their coop. The night air felt fresh.

Then a white owl passed overhead, carrying silence in its wings. I'd seen this bird before haunting the neighbourhood, or one just like it. And for the first time ever, I felt how utterly alone each of us is. My parents could have been a single street over, or oceans away, or nowhere at all. I could have been on an alien planet.

Alone and unwatched, I could do whatever I wanted.

So back I went toward the ripe-smelling trash in the alley. Stopping short, where I knew the hole was, I fell onto my knees before it. I both wanted to believe the story I'd heard in plain daylight, and desperately hoped it was untrue.

I'm not sure how long I crouched there, my mind unspooling under a dark, pitiless sky. What felt like years was probably minutes. Only minutes before what happened to me began.

I get the sense you're a skeptic, but I'll plunge on regardless. I told you I've always been one to seek the strange side of the road. What would happen in that backyard didn't change that, as I was born this way, I'm sure of it. But it did—how do I put this? It sealed the nascent trait in, underlined it, made it permanent. Life's not been easy due to this peculiarity of spirit. I've pushed away the few who loved me with trueness and sweetness. Turned them aside in order to cleave to those who stumble and swerve, trending towards brokenness.

A man in particular I'm thinking of now. From my time in Seattle—not so long ago but several people back. That is, if time is measured in serial affairs.

Beautiful, arrogant, snobbish, exacting. This man had a cruelty I sensed I could coax forth. I saw M. was trouble and turned toward him like a needle finding true north. Soon I hated M. and couldn't get enough of him, both. We'd sever our relationship several times, but the break was never clean.

M. was a talker, liked to call and talk, his voice loaded with alternating scorn and sugar. I pretended to be his gentle listener.

Wrapped the receiver with the bones of my hand and stared at the window, my reflection dissolving into the black and lapping night. I played his bitch, his fix, his mistake, gentle as a mother, an angel desperately needed. When the telephone rang in the early hours, sometimes I'd ignore it. Yank the plug from the wall, toss the phone in a drawer. Other times I'd wait for his call with dread and hunger. Shaping my evening around this expectation, coiled and crouched like something with teeth. I rarely called him—wanting to see if he'd come to me.

He always did. I knew what to say and do to keep him calling and showing up at my door.

"You're not good for me," M. said. "We're not good for us." I'd play hurt and sad, so he'd then work to argue the other side, convince me otherwise.

Things got worse. There were drugs, some legal and meant to fix him, some not. Hypnotics, dissociatives. He said he saw things loom up from the roadside. Or lurk in the shadows, beckoning with a curled thumb. Horrible dreams or visions, M. wasn't sure. I did not partake of his substances, nor discourage his ideas.

That dark, veering part of me wanted to find out how bad it could get.

One night M. begged me to meet him on a certain bridge near his home. He wanted to give me his dog, his 12-string, his books, and both the monstera and the split-leaf philodendron he cherished. All of it, he said, for temporary safe-keeping. He'd be going away for a while. He would not say where.

In this hour of need, I refused him. Not that I couldn't meet him or was afraid to, but that I *wouldn't*. He sat silently, my talker, stunned and letting it all sink in.

"I always believed we'd end up together," he said.

We hung up on what felt like peaceful enough terms. The calls stopped. My relief at gaining this portion of my life back was an uneasy freedom.

Weeks passed. I thought about checking on him. I never did.

When his sister phoned me, I realized I'd been holding my breath. She described M.'s disappearance. The unpaid rent, his dog left with a neighbour. The plants dead in the apartment. The bridge, the crash, his car pulled from black water. Waterweed tangled in the steel strings of his guitar.

So, what I did that particular moonlit night as a child was this: I accepted a kind of handshake. A handshake that was in truth an agreement. And by agreement, I don't mean I signed a contract. I mean I found a harmony, an accord. Something like-minded, like-souled, attuned and in sympathy. Where our boundaries overlapped, we agreed to share. Though at the time, I knew all this dimly, like something from an outdated book I'd skimmed, full of big words.

All my waiting and aching while kneeling in the dark finally paid off. I heard a rustle of sands shifting somewhere beneath me. I flashed again to the desert, to the way a sidewinder moves and its shadow bends and moves with it, drawing out the S-shape. The way the sand stirs, sliding under its scales.

Human eyes can play tricks at night, but what I saw was glimpsed with a different set of eyes, truer ones. I had been patient and I had waited courteously. So when it came, I was ready for it.

A hand pushed up out of the ground. And when I say a hand what I really mean is a paw. Or not a paw, exactly. A paw makes you think dog or cat, maybe monkey. Let me get this right for you. A hoof. A pig's hoof held aloft in a tentative greeting.

Even at night I knew its colours and textures. I saw with the eye you use in a dream. The hairless skin pink-grey, like something half-living or only recently dead. A slaughterhouse shade. The wrist bent the wrong way. Where fingers should be was instead a rough cleaving, the skin tough as horn. The look of that chitinous cleft was obscene, but that's my adult self reminiscing. What I saw as a child, I saw with a child's mind.

Where there should be a thumb on a hand there *was* a thumb. This hoof-hand was painted red, a chipped and coy enamel. The thumb, too, tipped in scarlet. I recognized the shade, Cherries in the Snow. The toe polish my mother's friend Ollie wore. Her one little wiggly wine-drinking friend, who was never invited over when my father was home.

Ridiculous as it might sound, this familiar detail comforted me. Though this was not a fresh and smooth manicure, but spoiled, chipped. The kind of blemishes that might happen if something—someone—dug themselves out of a hard place.

The devil's hand waited on its wrong-bent wrist like a question. It didn't seem right to leave it hanging there unanswered.

So I reached down, fitted its rough weight into my little kid hand. And I felt it move, alive, thumb closing on me in a grateful clasp. I pressed and returned the pressure, the hot dryness of it, feeling agreeable, floating in a pleasant enchantment.

It was just a passing small fancy, a friendly exchange under moonlight.

I woke in Yolanda's sister's bed and stumbled to the kitchen. The morning gleamed like a magazine page: window streaming with sunlight, Yolanda's bowl with its repeating marigold, her glass of orange juice.

"Sorry I pushed you out last night," Yolanda said. "Thought you were Rosa. She comforts me when I have bad dreams."

She smiled. We smiled. All seemed forgiven. We passed a basket of *coyotas* and *cochinitos*, some honey the colour of lamplight, and sat contentedly chatting until my mother fetched me.

That evening, my mother interrupted my bath. She gasped. My fingernails and feet were filthy and stained red. Scratches marred my pale back. I hugged my knees as she examined the dozen raw red marks that would heal to faint cicatrices.

"Flea bites," she pronounced with an absurd finality I didn't dare contradict. Her horror slowly shaded to a grim-mouthed purpose. With a yellow bar of Dial, she scrubbed me, her gripes coming fast and sharp. Houses were filthy these days. Others couldn't be trusted to care for me. I'd been a victim—here her lips quivered with disgust—of neglect. The object of her blame was unclear: Yolanda's family or the world at large.

I could not mention the monstrous thing in the ground. How could I tell her how wrong she was? That her own precious daughter had wallowed willingly in sand and thorns, clasping hands with something who made her darkest thoughts a viable and permissible territory?

"Look at you. Eaten alive," she said. "Who lives this way . . ."

The soap stank and stung. I hung my head in shame.

At dinner, my parents exchanged grim looks, and I knew. I was now expected to make all new little friends.

At school I turned my head and refused to meet Yolanda's eyes. At lunch I hid in a bathroom stall, perched on a toilet so my scuffed toes couldn't be glimpsed. She came looking. She called my name, and the hurt and confusion in her voice tore holes in me. Inside my heart, I screamed.

"I know you're in there, Janie." Her last words to me.

Soon enough Yolanda was out with the jump rope girls, the sun in her hair. And honestly, better off for it.

Never again would I let someone that good get this close. Y. would shrink to a tiny bright spot in my memory. A pinprick star.

The following autumn my mother decided I was old enough. I'd have to get myself to and from school. I peeked in on Y.'s old house from the alley from time to time. But they'd moved. And eventually the backyard was torn apart, a pool put in. The thing that once dwelled there became my private artifact. A faded map, velvety at its creases, secrets in its edges.

Years passed and the pool was neglected, then drained dry. Kids I met in high school—the same ones who cut eyes at me in the quad, who had mouths and hands for me in the dim smoky corners of parties—rode skateboards along its rim and dipped out of sight. I listened to their music, smelled their sweet smoke, quivered with curiosity, and was drawn to the worst of them. If they had someone else already, I'd only double my efforts. I loved blooming in the dark for the lonely and damaged. I left home to seek a world full of dark corners to explore.

Occasionally, over the years, a troubling thought occurred. What if I was still back there, crouched in that blighted backyard, stuck in time? And all this since—a child's fantasy? On a lark, I sought a professional's advice. After less than an hour, having sussed out what he called personality instabilities and toxic cravings, he proclaimed me borderline and scribbled something on a prescription pad, case closed and feeling satisfied with himself.

"You're not familiar with the same borders I know," I said. Later, I tossed his pills in the toilet, watched them circle the hole and disappear.

No saving me, anyhow. The monster was in me. This singular devil among devils *is* me. Whether it's always been this way, or if the handshake changed it to be so—does it matter?

Now it's been many years and people and miles since. My

mother's gone and father too. My wings are wide and silent—I'm flying free.

Oh, I wasn't at all surprised I found you outside that truck stop, thumb out and your big hopeless grin already dying at the edges. Good to finally tell someone these things. In the dark like this, side by side, candidly speaking. All the while, thinking ahead, toying with possibilities. It could be lovely, you know? The two of us—you and me—getting up to no good. Going on the lam, thick as thieves. I do better in a pair, until the wheels fall off and it all goes sideways. A sine wave reaching its natural conclusion, a Gaussian peak and crash.

Ah. We've reached the Basin Bridge—New Orleans isn't so far off now. I'll have you home and safe soon. This long bridge, first: a parallel set of twins shooting fast and narrow through the night, held aloft by steel and concrete pilings running hell-deep into the ground. Fleeing crimson taillights on our side, head-on brights on the other. Eighteen miles plus we'll go over vast and nameless oily black. Down there, it's nothing much: only cypresses, creeping aquatic things with curved jaws that make them look like they're smiling.

Hundreds like me or you cross here every day, nearly all of us without incident. Mostly alone. Or in pairs, which is the same as being alone.

Sometimes, though, if you're anything like me—and I sense that you are, or you were, or you will be soon—then this incredible pressure behind your eyes starts to build, like tears, like pain. Your fingers tighten around the wheel—the skin grey as the hems of ghosts, the red nails chipped. You wonder if you'll make it to the city, or even the next town.

For the world is black and enormous, moon above broken by bars of cloud, a sense of endless water below. And it feels like we may as well be the very last living things alive. Our destination pulls us like a charm as the road unravels ahead and behind. We can always keep going, you and I—despite all risks and warnings. And that's what most do.

Or we can turn the wheel hard and see where it takes us.

WHITE LIES CAST DARK SHADOWS

STEWART C BAKER

 This time of year, the sun sets early.

I tell myself that's why the shadows are darker. Why I can *feel* them stretch toward me the instant I look away.

Deep down, I know it's not true. That it's just another lie I've told myself and those I love.

Maxine is the only reason I know about the shadows.

Not that she told me herself—she was always too private to share anything about her life. About what she'd been through.

But there was the way she disappeared, and the changes in how she acted when I moved back home. The way she carried herself in the presence of bright lights, how she would start to speak only to trail off and go silent. The way she kept looking over her shoulder.

I'd been away ten long years, and we'd arranged to meet up at a coffee shop in the city's crumbling old downtown—although in my absence it had gentrified. The coffee shop itself was proof of that, all exposed wooden walls that had been polished to a shine, with huge picture windows that looked out on a city park filled with greenery and people. The last time I'd been through here, this had been a decaying antique storefront, and the park was mostly gravel. I had a hell of a time finding parking, and by the time I walked into the shop Maxine was already inside, perched in one of the tall chairs by the windows, shoulders hunched as she stirred her coffee in little stop-start motions.

She was so absorbed in the view she didn't notice me come in. I set one hand on her shoulder and she jumped, then closed her eyes and let out a breath when she saw me.

The lavender-and-rose scent of her drink hit my nostrils, sickeningly sweet. "You're drinking *herbal tea*?" I asked. "Little Miss 'Caffeine or Death' herself?"

She gave me a wan smile and scraped the chair back to stand and give me a hug. "You've been gone a long time, Jordan. We're neither of us little anymore."

I grinned. "Hey, I get enough of that from my nutritionist."

She laughed and held me at arm's length, brushing the one hand absently along my sleeve. "You *do* look good, Jordan. And it's so good to see you. I wasn't sure I'd . . ." She trailed off, then shivered and turned sharply back to the window.

I swallowed the joke I'd planned about a decade in the California sun making anyone look good. "Everything okay, Max?"

Her grip on my arm tightened, and I gave it a little shake. "Max."

She looked back to me, eyes unfocused, then blinked a few times and was back from wherever she'd gone. "What did you say?"

"I asked if you're okay."

Another one of those smiles. "Oh, you know me. Nothing interesting *ever* happens to me." She slipped back into her seat with a sigh. "My doctor said I should cut back on the coffee, that's all. The caffeine was making me jumpy." A little half-laugh. "Guess it hasn't helped."

As lies go, it wasn't convincing, but I did what I always did when Maxine bottled up her feelings. What I had learned to do from the time we were kids and she wouldn't let me in. I smiled and let it go.

I don't remember, anymore, what we filled the rest of that evening with.

Meaningless chatter. Empty platitudes. Neither of us daring anything of substance, although I would have been willing to listen, if only Max had opened up a bit.

I *do* remember how she left. It was still summer then, if only barely, and the late September sunset poured through the foothills like treacle gone molten, revealing the fluorescent streetlights that flickered on during its fading glory for the tawdry, garish toys they were. As soon as Maxine realized it was evening, she mumbled something about the time and ducked out the door, scurrying down the street like a frightened mouse in an alley full of cats: head down, never breaking her stride even when I stepped out from the shop and called her name.

At the time, I wondered if she was in a bad relationship and afraid to get home late.

Now, of course, I know better.

Now, as the shadows lap and pool beneath my bedroom door, I try to shake off the sensation that something is *watching* me. That whatever it is laughs quietly from the edge of my hearing.

The next time I saw Max was in the library basement.

I'd been back in town about a month by then but kept making up reasons not to see her: I was busy. I was trying to find work. I thought I'd caught a cold and didn't want to pass it along. It's not that I didn't *want* to see her. I did. But at the same time, I couldn't shake the feeling that once I did, there'd be no avoiding disaster.

My excuses ran out in the sci-fi section, in the space between Lawrence and Le Guin.

The gentrification that had come to the downtown area had visited the library, too. The lobby upstairs was like one of those fancy hotels you see in movies about rich people, so full of plush chairs and nice art it was easy to forget you were in a library at all. They must have run out of money before they reached the basement, though, because it was even dingier than I remembered. The books were decades out of date, and some of the lights were out, casting half the floor into gloomy darkness.

I was squinting at the titles on the books as I walked, and I nearly bumped into a skinny teen in a dark hoodie crouched down in the aisle. I stopped so suddenly I nearly fell over, but when I got my bearings again the kid was gone. I'd nearly run into a book return cart.

I rubbed my eyes, checked again. I was *sure* I'd seen someone sitting there, but either I needed more sleep, or the poor lighting was playing tricks on me.

That's when I saw Max, sitting at one of the grungy tables behind a pile of books with titles like *The Psychology of Lying* and *Real Ghost-Hunters of America*. She had one of those portable camping lanterns on top of the pile, the brightness turned up to full. It might have made reading easier, but the light was so intense it hurt my eyes.

She looked like a beacon in the dimness of the basement. Like the signal in a lighthouse that warned ships of danger. I wet my suddenly dry lips with the tip of my tongue and went over. "Hey, Max. How've you been?"

She was so involved in her reading that she flinched when I spoke. "Oh! Jordan. Um, it's . . . How are you?"

I blinked into the glare. "I'm okay. Doing some research?"

"Yeah. Hey, that reminds me. I, uh . . . I need to tell you something."

My throat tightened up. "Sure. What's up?"

"It's just . . . We . . ."

Her words were replaced with a soft rustling, like paper brushing up against itself. With the lantern between us, she looked like a living shadow. I couldn't see her expression. Couldn't see what she was doing with her hands.

"Max? Do you think you could turn this down a bit? I know the library doesn't have the *best* lighting, but—"

"I have to go," she snapped, so loud I swallowed the rest of my sentence. "It's going to be dark soon. I can't be . . ." Then, after a pause, in a whisper: "I'm sorry. I can't do this."

I tried to ready my usual forced smile, but I needn't have bothered. The light swung away from my face and Max brushed past me, striding from the building with her lamp held high like she was re-enacting a bizarre parody of *Liberty Leading the People*.

I'd come to the library just after lunch, so I fished my phone out of my pocket, surprised to hear Max say that it was almost evening.

It was only 1:15 p.m.

Shadow people.

The hat man.

Red eyes.

The hooded monk.

Watchmen.

And those are just the names in English, for just one type of being. Do you know how many stories there are about creatures that dwell in the shadows?

I know.

I've spent too many hours on websites, trying to dredge the truth out of the crap people share to get more followers on social media. The librarians won't answer my requests and go on sudden errands when I walk up to the desk. Even the local UFO fanatics have stopped returning my calls.

On the worst days, I want to give up. Want to believe this is all just in my head, paranoia from the shock of an old friend's kidnapping and likely death at the hands of an unknown assailant.

But I know what I saw. What I heard. I know what I've *seen*, since she vanished.

I know there's something watching me, there in the shadows. Judging me for all the lies I've ever told. Waiting to make its move.

About a week after she ran out on me at the library, Max gave me a call.

It was close to midnight, but I hadn't been sleeping well lately, so I was half-awake on the sofa with the TV on and all the lights turned up when she called.

"Hello?"

"Jordan." Max was breathing fast and hard and heavy. "Jordan, we have to meet."

"Max?" I rubbed grit from my eyes. "What's wrong? It's late."

"I've figured out a way to stop it, Jordan. A way out. But I need you there to do it. I have to . . . I *have* to tell you something."

I wanted to tell her she wasn't making sense, that whatever it was she was trying to stop could wait until morning, but her voice was as urgent as I'd ever heard it. As I'd ever heard anything. It made me uneasy.

"You know I'm there for you whenever. Where do you want to

meet up?"

"Waffle House, over on Ninth. See you there in ten."

"I was asleep," I said. "Can you give me . . ." She'd already hung up. *Be there when I can,* I texted her. *Have to get decent.*

Maxine was nowhere in sight when I arrived, so I ordered some hash browns and a coffee and took a seat in a window booth. I'd finished both before I spotted her outside the window, walking down the street with a flashlight in her hands and a harried, frantic quality to her movements. She would pause beneath each streetlamp and look behind her, then take quick strides to the next. It wasn't until she was nearly at the Waffle House that I noticed a stranger keeping pace across the street, on a sidewalk abutting the part of town that wasn't as well lit.

I was curious to see who she'd brought with her, but she came in alone, her companion just standing there beneath the eaves of the next building over, staying out of the light. Not a fan of social situations, I guessed, and gave it no more thought.

Max lit up when she saw me. "Jordan! You came!"

For a moment, she was her old self. Bright and outgoing, full of cheer. So much so that I felt guilty for avoiding her all this time. If I'd known I could lift her spirits that thoroughly just by being close, I would have come back sooner. Might even have stayed home instead of going off to California.

I shook the thought away. "What did you need to see me about?"

She sat opposite me, a nervous grin on her face. "I don't know if you remember," she said, "but when we first met, I said we'd just moved here from Okinawa."

"Sure, I remember. Your dad was in the military, right? Is he all right?"

"My dad?" She blinked. "Oh, yeah. He's, uh, fine. But . . . he was a gas station attendant."

"In Okinawa?"

"No. No, that's what I'm trying to tell you," she snapped. "Why aren't you listening? We never went to Okinawa. My dad was never in the military. I just wanted to make a good first impression. I *lied.*"

Her dad had never seemed military to me, but I figured it took all kinds—and anyway it wasn't any business of mine what her family did. What they'd done.

"Okay. No big deal."

"It *is* a big deal," she said, that panic in her voice that I'd heard over the phone. "Don't talk down to me, damn you."

I wanted to smile, to repeat that it was really fine, but instead I put my hands up in a placating gesture. "Okay, sorry. But I mean, we all said stupid stuff back then, all the time. I forgive you, if that's what this is about."

She nodded, the grimace on her face relaxing a little, and then took a deep breath. "My cat didn't die when I was seven—I never even had a cat. I didn't draw any of the pictures that I sent while you were in California—I copied them from a website. I wish you'd stop sending me Jane Austen stuff because I think *Pride & Prejudice* is the stupidest book ever written. I only said I liked it when I saw it in your backpack senior year. I . . . I . . ." She glanced outside.

I followed her stare. That guy was still there, in the shadows. Not moving. Not doing anything, so far as I could tell. I wondered if he was the reason she'd dragged me out here. The reason she'd been acting so weird. Maybe she was on one of those TV shows where they make people do outrageous things for money and record it all on a hidden camera.

I shifted in my seat. We'd been friendly enough in high school, and we'd kept in contact after, like old friends always do. But this sudden unburdening made me uncomfortable. Why did it matter to Max so much that I knew all this about her? What did she want me to say, if she wouldn't accept that I didn't care that she'd lied to me?

The questions made my stomach clench, so I asked her one instead of answering them. "Why are you telling me all this now?"

"I have to," she said, voice breaking on the second word. She put her hands to her face, sobbing.

"Whoa! Max, hey, it's all right. It's okay." I reached out and touched her elbow, let my hand stay there when she didn't push it away. I still didn't know what was going on, but I knew that when someone needed comfort you offered it. "I'm here. You're here. Everything will be fine."

"I *love you*," she wailed. "I always have. Ever since we met. But I was so afraid. So afraid you'd . . ." She broke off, sniffling.

I froze. I couldn't help it. All these years and I'd never so much as suspected. Never thought she'd seen me as anything more than a friend. To have it thrown at me all of a sudden robbed me of my thoughts. Of what I could have—should have—said in return.

Her shoulders tensed up. "I knew you'd react this way," she said, low and tremulous. "That's why I never told you. Why I never dared. But now—"

"Is that guy outside doing this to you?" I channelled my confusion and distress into anger. Into blame. "You don't have to tell me anything you don't want to, Max. You *never* do. That's how it works. How it always has."

It was the wrong thing to say.

As soon as I said "guy outside", her eyes widened and the colour in her face drained. "Oh no. Why isn't it working?" Max snatched her arm away from my hand and dashed into the bathroom, slamming the door behind her.

One of the servers came over, eyeing me suspiciously. "Everything okay?"

Everything obviously wasn't. "Uh, yeah. She's just having a rough time. You know how it is."

"Well, let me know if there's anything we can do. Nobody needs to go through that kind of shit alone."

"Actually, there's this guy across the street. I think he might be bothering her. Do you think you could call the cops or something?"

"Sweetheart," she said, "there's nobody there. You and your friend there are the only people I've seen since I started at eleven."

The hairs on the back of my neck stood up. Dreading what I'd see if I looked outside. But I made myself turn to the window. The space was empty, and the rest of the parking lot too. "Yeah. Long day. Guess I'm seeing things."

"We've all been there."

At least the guy was gone, I thought, as she brought me another two cups. Whoever he was. Maybe now Max would chill out a bit. Maybe she'd give me time to talk to her, as well. About what she'd said. About what I never had. I thought about what I would tell her, when she came back out, pouring cream into both our cups, then stirred until the darkness within them faded to a milky, frothy white.

Max didn't come back out. I sat there for nearly half an hour, staring at the bathroom door and waiting, before I found the courage to go to her.

By then it was too late. There was nobody in any of the stalls. No sign of Max. No sign of a struggle. Not even blood.

The only unusual thing was the dark pool of shadow underneath the sink, which burned away like fog as I stood there, telling myself the pounding in my chest was just too much coffee and too little sleep.

It's early November now, and the last scraps of fall are giving way to winter. Bands of shock-cold rain stripe the park downtown with mud and dead leaves, and the sunlight they let in is weak, as feeble as my hopes and every bit as quick to dim.

The days are getting shorter. The dark nights, longer.

The police really grilled me after Max disappeared. I tried not to hold it against them when they wouldn't accept that she'd "just disappeared". At last, exhausted, I told them about the person I'd seen outside the Waffle House. Eventually, they let me go.

I know they'll never find the truth, even if I suspect it myself. And I'm safe, anyway. Safe as I can be. I have my growing bay of lights, each brighter than the last. They illuminate every nook and cranny of my bedroom, surging into the corners and under my bed, tangling in the pile of dirty sheets, spreading blessed survival to places that have probably seen nothing but shadow since before I moved in.

I sleep worse than ever. Every few hours I jolt awake with the sense that someone's just left the room. That there was someone whispering in my ear. That the shadows recoiled back to their normal places just before I opened my eyes.

I spend hours when I'm awake reciting all the truths I've never said aloud: I never wanted to move to California. I hated my job there. Hated the endless sun-bleached warmth. I'm glad I'm going to disappear. I deserve it. I'd loved Max with every fibre of my being ever since I met her, but I was always too afraid she'd leave to let her see what lay within my heart.

It doesn't help. Nothing helps. My only comfort is that soon, whatever came for Max will get me too.

I'm sitting in the corner opposite the door when I find a new post on one of the websites I frequent, titled SHADOW PEOPLE -

REAL PROOF.

I click the link with shaking fingers and it takes me to a fifteen second video. It's a shot of a woman I don't know, walking down a street in a city I don't recognize. The video is some kind of security footage, grainy and low-res but just good enough that I can tell it's raining in long, endless sweeps. The woman hurries along just like Max did on that summer evening that seems so long ago now, her hands wrapped tight around her shawl, until she comes to the edge of an alley.

She stops—just like Max did—and looks over her shoulder. The camera isn't good enough to make out what expression she wears, but I can still see Max's unfocused eyes from the coffee shop. The way her lips, which used to be so soft, were chapped and bloodied.

By this time, I'm leaning forward, face inches away from my phone, breathing so heavily I could almost believe I'm alone. When the video flickers off and turns to static, I jump up with a curse. But it's just part of the footage missing. A glitch in the security camera, maybe.

When the video returns, there's no sight of the woman. No proof that she was ever there.

I load the video again and again, until my hands are shaking so badly, I can barely see the screen. Until I can feel that presence in the room with me again, can almost hear the quiet breathing that's timed perfectly with mine.

This is the worst it's ever been.

There! In the other corner, a flicker of shadow!

I flip my phone over and turn on its flashlight, shine it as quick as I dare around the edges of the room. Then again, in broad, sweeping arcs that make my eyes water.

It helps a little, but I know it isn't going to save me. My phone charger's out in the hallway and as soon as the battery dies there won't be enough light remaining. I'll have to get up. I'll have to crack open that door. I'll have to go outside.

And the instant I do, the shadows will be waiting.

CHEKHOV'S GUN IS SCREAMING

BARRY CHARMAN

We met during the opening night of *The Cherry Orchard*. Soon to be proclaimed the finest play of the twentieth century. It was 1904.

We were strangers, sitting next to each other in the stalls, when she yawned it; "Chekhov's gun is *screaming*."

I think I knew from then that our proclivities, our dark inclinations, were the same. We married the first time in Paris, before their first war. Perhaps we were chasing Madame Ranevskaya's ghost.

The trenches became our honeymoon. We loitered. We inhaled. Death's song had rarely been so sweet. Mankind invented this violence, it was only fitting it be exploited. They should have known something would be drawn to the fire, even if they couldn't name it.

We parted when their second war ended. It was so disappointing. Two mushrooms only, so much left to be said. It was hard to be patient when they showed such reckless devotion.

Over the decades we caught traces of each other. We played a game where we married and killed our lovers, leaving messages for each other in their epitaphs. Often, I'd stalk a cemetery at night, and find some sign of her. Her words lingering in other lives. *We made a heaven in hell. She loved me till the end. Love is a higher form of death.*

And so on. Ashes and confetti are everywhere, if you look properly. Diligently.

Finally, we found ourselves drawn once more to the same conflict. Over time their wars all blurred into one, which was tedious. Here was another mosaic of craters, another map of flesh carved up by would-be cartographers. But then I caught her name while listening to two soldiers bickering as they filled graves. They called her the hollow woman. A fascinating choice. She gorged on misery, they said, like she was some kind of tourist. They did not know that the company misery sought was at hand.

Inira. I could hear the quickening of pulses as they met her. The sudden ends that came. Heartbeats like birds falling out of the sky.

Grave and lover both, I wanted to be buried inside her. After all these ants had been dismissed, we would have a banquet, she and I. Uninterrupted, sated, would we feast on each other? Would we become animals?

Become?

In a chapel, burning like a beacon in the night, I caught her laugh. I found her drinking at the altar, accompanied by a ragged group of drunken soldiers, all too young to know better. They laughed when she did, then fell silent when she scowled. She was playing them for the fools they were.

They had little time left.

She passed around a flask; I recognised its black obsidian gleam. She'd told me about it one night. How she'd dug it out of the oldest coffin she'd ever found. The thing that had taken it to its grave had hugged it tight. Not tight enough.

The men drank. She became bored so she drank them, pouring their blood into the flask when they'd emptied it. I applauded the elegance of it all, and she turned to look at me.

Had lips ever been so red?

"Khader."

"I've had many names since that, Inira."

She smiled slightly. "I've never felt so many graves beckoning.

Centuries have led to this. It's always beauty that brings us together."

I joined her at the altar; we stood over the young soldiers. "You'd think they'd learn. Do you ever feel sorry for them?" She giggled lightly. I almost passed out for love of her. We were together again.

Hand in hand, we wandered through the shadows. We indulged the killing fields. Pulling back barbed wire, we exposed the fragrant bone beneath. It was the courtship we'd never had.

We passed time together, *made up* time. I cut the throat she drank from, and vice versa. When the stars came out, we sat on a rock and studied them. When day turned to fire, we applauded the spectacle. The wars used to be in odd little pockets, secluded nightmares, now they were rolling over the towns, the villages. All to ruin.

I asked her how she'd spent the last decades.

Throwing hair over her shoulder, she pursed her lips into a bleak kiss. "I got bored. I stopped myself from partaking for some time, just to want it again."

Partaking. I laughed at the phrase, but I understood. "I walked," I said. "Just walked." In truth I had been searching. Even shadows, given enough time, will wonder what freakish shape first cast them. I had looked for our people in history, but found nothing. No mention, no depiction. No trace in any painting. Any story. Any song. We were not even folklore. The world had given me no reflection. This was an oddly liberating thing. I was not bound, constrained, by any law, any philosophy. I was my own thing, apart, separate.

Alone.

I thought of that night at the theatre, becoming aware of her presence close by. How my world had suddenly expanded.

If there was only us, it was enough.

I followed Inira as dawn lit the way. We were sifting rubble when we came upon a family living in the dust. They were not afraid. Indeed, the father offered to share some bread. I exchanged a look with Inira. Seeing her amusement, I gestured for her to lead, and she made the dawn redder still.

I watched as their brief lives were quickly spent. At least they had lives to end. This curious thought had been with me for some time. A low murmur, at first, a dull voice. Over the years though, had it not become louder? They were insects, yet their small existences were somehow realer. *Fuller*. It was a difficult notion. Grotesque.

And yet.

It was difficult not to look at the overturned crib, the wall covered in photographs, the bodies reaching for each other, and not witness something I did not know.

I remembered Matilda. She'd spent years tracking me down, after one bloody night. Apparently, I'd taken her world and put it under the ground. At first, she'd wanted some kind of justice, some measure of revenge. She found me living well, in a loft apartment in New York. Patient, I put a chair between us and asked her to sit. I wasn't a savage. I'd eaten, so I had no desire, no need, to harm her.

I was curious to note that I was supposed to be a monster. Was she a monster for washing the germs off her hands? I think she didn't know how to accept what she'd found. "You just look like a man," she'd said.

"Of course. What else?"

Numb, she'd sat, and listened. I talked of the centuries I'd known. The extraordinary things I'd seen, the distant cities I had walked in. Expanding, I mentioned the invigoration of blood, the dreamers I could still taste. The exaltation of hunger. When she was unable to see beyond simple deeds, I left her sobbing and found a child to drop at her feet. "Here, something for you to look after."

I was being pleasant. True, shoving two things together that you'd broken was a graceless solution. She'd asked where the boy's mother was. I asked if she really wanted the answer, and off she went. The expression on her face stayed with me. That confusion, of what horror and fear could unmake, could allow.

These small lives . . . Grains of sand caught in the rush of the hourglass as it leisurely gave thought to turning. I wondered if Inira had ever had any such meeting? What would she say if I expressed even this passing concession to their frailty?

From a hill, we sat and watched as rockets thudded into the city below. Normal days had long abandoned these people. "Wars used to be on battlefields," I murmured.

"This is progress," she smiled. "The wars are coming to us."

We drank to that. The sun descended. Stars dotted the sky like a constellation of butchers, speaking just to us.

Down in the city, they were wailing.

"Before dawn," Inira said, softly, "we'll take what's left."

I nodded. Next to me, her eyes glinted like silver shards. The night was a layer, a veil we wore as well as discarded. I watched as it grew thin, and her face became paler, skull shining like a song of bone.

Patches of moaning broke out below us. A dog barked. A child was calling, though no one answered. All of this drifted into a deadening silence. Soon, there was only birdsong, emerging slowly with the smoke. Broken sonnets, both.

"Nights like this," she murmured. "I want only nights like this."

I reached for her hand and she pulled me towards her. We shared a kiss full of teeth. Her lips were warmer than I remembered. We lay together for a while, exploring the silence. I tried to stroke her hair, but she pulled away. Some intimacies were too much. I wondered what she did when she felt lonely. Perhaps she never had?

When the sun duly returned, she sat up, and nodded at the city. "We should be quick. Let the war take the blame."

The blame for whatever we left behind. I knew what she had planned. My heart quickened as the corners of her lips tugged up into a brutal smile.

Gorging on the darkness we brought, almost reckless with appetite, we made our way down. My fingers outstretched to catch wisps of smoke. I watched one tendril curve around my finger, such a tender image.

"Khader, come." Inira darted ahead of me, climbing through the tumbled wall of a collapsing house. She'd caught a scent. I heard a brief wet cry, and then she reappeared, wiping blood from her mouth. Her excitement excited me. Oh, I felt young again.

I took the next house, finding an old man huddled under a table. It had protected him from the debris that thickly covered its surface, but did nothing to hinder me. I threw it up into the wall, then took his arm back to Inira. A foolish gesture, but I liked feeling foolish.

"Silly." Smiling, despite her dismissive expression, she accepted the arm and took a chunk.

"Seasoned," I said, "with many years."

She laughed.

A low light coming from a battered building caught her eye. I followed as she hurried to a house that had survived the last bombardment. She had broken through the door by the time I reached it and was already up the stairs. Such a fever she had, such a want.

I paused on the stairs, letting her wallow. There was a single scream, harsh, like hope being flayed from a heart. Here was a new horror at the door, finding them after they had survived another. They were so fragile. So pointless.

Was it wrong to analyse the screams? I sometimes felt the need. They were nothing to us, brief moths that never knew the fire till it burned them. Yet sometimes I wondered; if they meant nothing to *us*, who would ever give them meaning?

When I first arrived here, I'd followed the cries to this once civilised bowl of dust. At the heart of the conflict, I settled briefly in a small house, still partly on fire. Inside, I realised I was not alone. There was a boy, face the same colour as the ashes.

He'd rocked on the floor in shock, mother's shawl wrung in his bony fingers. Staring at nothing, he talked about killing. About redistributing his pain. Sometimes I had time for their children. Their young were somehow wiser, less fixed in their notions, their knowledge of the world.

"But then violence will never end," I'd told him.

"They'll be dead, though."

"Then what has death made of you? What will the death *you* sow make of another?"

The boy had frowned. I could see him attempt to unravel this new thought. Seeing it all go round and round, he'd looked nauseated. Haunted. Eventually he'd looked up, with that strange solemnity of youth. "How does it end?"

I gave him no answer. Most likely, no one ever would. It was interesting, to see the blankness begin. To see the emptiness take root.

Inira appeared at the top of the stairs. Seeing me paused in thought stopped her. "What?"

I tilted my head, uncertain of myself. "Nothing, I thought I heard something."

Uninterested, she went to a window and looked out. The glow

from a fire below lit half her face. "Why can't it always be like this?" she asked.

"Fire has to fade," I said.

She turned to me, the sudden anger in her eyes would have blinded most. "*Has* to?"

I shrugged. It was difficult to put into words. "Crops must always be allowed to regrow. You want to rip them out by the throat . . ."

Her voice was soft, lethal. "But we'll never run out of throats."

We. The smallest word. Not as small as *I.* I wondered if she heard a difference in my heart. She smiled faintly, then turned away.

We walked down and back out, criss-crossing the city, picking at the houses. Bodies could be left in the street, or even in the rubble of their homes. Not even an unexpected bite mark would raise a question, not here. The dogs were hungry, the people mad. After sunset, all was expected.

"War allows," I murmured.

She nodded, looking down at a couple we'd arranged in the dirt together. "Yes. I like that. *War allows.*"

Then we heard a baby cry.

Inira was gone from my side before I could even comment on it. I followed her through narrow winding streets, past leaning buildings and crooked walls. The sun was above the horizon. Large, ripe, swollen—as if corrupted by our thoughts. I found her in a large clearing. These had probably been houses once, but there was nothing now save the flattened shapes and angles of what must once have been. Inira was leaning over something swaddled in linen. It cried, and she suddenly stepped back.

Something about her reaction made me freeze. I had never seen her uncertain. Never that.

Joining her, I crouched down and pulled back the fabric, studying the child it exposed. A boy. I stood back, overwhelmed.

"It's like us," she said.

It was pale, horribly so. I recalled my own skin, before it settled, altered. I had never known anyone like myself, just her. And here was an impossible thing, just lying in the rubble.

I looked around. There were bodies nearby. Face down, sprawled out, not long dead. Had they run with the infant, trying to keep it hidden? I inhaled the blood spilled all about. Some conflict had passed through here, interrupting lives.

The remains of a house sheltered us from any who might have watched. Its surviving walls were pockmarked with bullets. Contemplating the devastation, the bodies, the boy, I was struck by this seed of life, found in a valley dense with so much that was now rotten.

"Sometimes death's hands are too full and it leaves something behind."

Avoiding the infant, Inira looked at me, unsettled. "What?"

"Just a thought."

She sneered. "Leave it for the animals."

Inira began walking away. I couldn't move. "It's like us."

"So?"

Startled, I watched her go, but I simply could not move. "You were a baby once. Someone didn't walk away from you."

Inira paused. For the first time I saw hesitation stab at her. Like me, she didn't remember her childhood. It was so long ago, so far away. Who had found us? Nurtured us in that brief time when we were vulnerable?

Did it all mean nothing?

I continued. "I was raised by people that didn't understand me. I remember little but the little love they spared for me. Imagine if we'd been found by one of our own?"

She turned and laughed. "You want to keep it?"

I didn't know. Somehow, impossibly, we had found each other, and now there were three of us. "Do you remember where we first met?"

She frowned. "The theatre?"

"I sensed you long before I saw you . . ." I paused, tried a smile. "We could call him Anton."

After a moment's confusion, she smiled. "Chekhov's gun as love at first sight."

Love. I didn't know she knew the word. "That's how it was for me," I said. "I thought our path was simple, perhaps it isn't. Perhaps there's *more.*"

Refusing to respond to that, she turned her back and began walking briskly through the rubble. I waited a while, in case she returned. Then I picked up the baby, wrapped it up warm, and carried him away.

We hid for the rest of the day and I found food. He was cold, but he was not weak. He could endure a hard journey. My mind refused to settle, it was like another piece of the terrain, unsettled by the war. I didn't understand myself, my actions, my thoughts. Nonetheless, I had known since I met Inira that the world was larger than I'd understood, and I'd always hoped it would be capable of more.

I just hadn't known what that meant.

How many of us were there? How many did there need to be? Perhaps three was the perfect number. I'd thought it was two.

At nightfall, I followed an unused trail to the edge of the city and heard movement behind me. Inira. I could smell her blood, could hear the thudding of that dangerous heart. She had begun circling us soon after we took this path. Was she angry? Was she following us, or the road?

The boy was cradled at my chest. I thought of the mother that had carried him, kept him, nurtured him. I liked to think we could be loved, somehow.

Any of us. All of us.

"You can walk with us," I called out. "I would like that."

She made no sound, but she was there. How long would she follow? "His heart is strong," I said. "Can you hear it?"

I listened to that striking beat. Like ours, that night we first sensed each other, that night we saw the gun.

Which was always going to fire.

ONE DEAD PETAL

Ville Meriläinen

The flame blooms to life on my palm, kissing cold skin with warmth. It is a blessing, but heat feels profane to one so used to its absence. Only my thoughts are free of its touch. In them remains the chilling resolution that I am doing the right thing.

To Aimo, the sudden brilliance is terrifying. The boy watches my work with the curiosity he is wont to show towards witchcraft, swinging his feet off the edge of the small room's bed while intently chewing his lip. Now, when the flame stretches out and softly burns my glove, he scrambles into the corner with a squeak.

"There's nothing to fear," I tell him. The flame wraps itself on my wrist and snakes up my arm as I lift the rest of it out of the ritual circle. "It isn't fire as you've known. It wants to help, not hurt you."

The boy stays in the corner, shivering as I stand up, but stops his efforts of what looks like trying to blend with the shadows I've made flicker. He shuts his eyes and scrunches his nose when I bring the flame closer.

"It's okay. Look."

"I can't. It hurts."

I worried this would be his reaction. Aimo is the youngest of those I've sworn to keep, nine or ten by appearances. When it comes to him and my art, it's a gamble whether he'll be fearful or fascinated.

The flame responds to my thought and returns to the cradle of my palm. I close it under the cup of my right hand and ask, "Is this better?"

He squints at my hands lit up like cinders, blinks and brushes his face. "A little." He sniffles, but his focus remains on the hidden fire when I straighten myself and lead him out. "I don't see how it'll help us, though."

"You will. Come, now."

Aimo regains his common cheeriness when we leave the storm cellar of my old hovel outside the city. The wind has calmed and brought out the stars.

"Nadia," he says, when I've forgotten myself to peeking at my flame and fallen behind. "Do you think the others are all right?"

"The night's been kind to us. To them as well, I'm sure."

"I still don't see why we had to come so far for you to work." I catch the glint of his eyes when he glances my way. "Could you not have drawn out your flame at the house?"

"I thought it might be dangerous. The ritual is volatile."

There is distinct annoyance in his tone. "Why'd you let me come, then?"

"Young man, I explicitly told you not to follow. The wolves are out tonight. Were it up to me, you'd be asleep under Sorry's watchful eye—"

While I speak, a snarl sounds up close and makes us both gasp. I part my hands to let the fire shine. The sudden light sends Aimo running, but only for a few steps—the pack has surrounded us, twelve huge beasts, each the size of a bear and the same shade of black as the fur tossed over my shoulders. Aimo stumbles from his sudden change in direction, but the pack leader's approach is hesitant. Her fangs are bared, though not at the boy. She stares at my flame and I at her nose. There is a nick and a furless scar along the muzzle.

"Aimo," I say, straining to keep my voice even. "Come to me. I remember this one. She doesn't fear fire."

The boy scrambles up and runs to me. A swing of my hand sears a trail in the air and makes the beasts jump back, but the leader merely flinches.

"Is she the one?" the boy stammers. "The one who ate Alice?"

I nod. The girl was as prone as Aimo to ignoring orders—but she preferred seeking Sorry over me, and he's harder to find.

The flame answers my fear and fury, feeding strength into my muscles as the she-wolf lunges, and I drive it into the side of her jaw when she crashes against me. Borrowed strength cannot last long, and the wolf's weight knocks the air from my lungs. She rolls off, jerking and smelling of burnt flesh, but runs into the dark instead of trying again. The rest of the pack has scattered.

Aimo watches the flame dance around my arm as I gain my feet. There is a tear in the front of my coat, but Edie will gladly mend it.

"She's afraid," he says, reverently. "*She's* afraid of *you*."

"As she should be," I spit, with a vicious creak to my voice that surprises us both. I tried my best to scare her without harm, but even knowing the nature of a beast, I cannot bring myself to forgive this one.

"You should've broken her neck," Aimo says once the surprise wears off. "We wouldn't have to fear her anymore."

"Beasts do not kill for sport, Aimo, nor do we."

"Then you should've done it to avenge Alice."

"Avenge? There's nothing to avenge. She was eaten. They did not do it to hurt us, but because they were starving." Aimo faces away with a scowl, and I reach out for him. "Now come, before she remembers how hungry she is. There is someplace we must visit."

I reflect upon the pack as we delve deeper into the woods. A frightful encounter, but also a lesson in trust. Aimo lets me lead him by the hand now. Without a cover, our beacon illuminates a part of the woods left enshrouded since wolves ate the sun and the people fled.

There is a small marker in the clearing where Alice sleeps. I buried her alone; Sorry found her bones, but without nails for a casket, he could not bear to send off our little sunshine the way wolves left her. The memory stokes the fire until shadows are exiled from the gravesite.

From the mound grows a flower, not quite a rose, but one with similar petals. I've come to think of it as her gift to us, pushing out of the icy earth to bloom secluded in the dark, just as she did. It is a thing as profane as my fire, laughing in the face of the endless night, and I adore it for doing so. Her gift together with mine will keep us safe until dawn, no matter how far away it is.

I kneel to feed the fire to the flower, and Aimo steps beside me. He wipes his nose and says, "I miss her."

"We all do, and it's why I want you to listen when I tell you to wait for me at home. If the pack had found you before you found me, we'd miss you next."

"But they never do. My eyes are better than theirs."

I pause my work, dropping my hands to my lap. "And yet they managed to ambush us."

"That's not my fault," he grumbles. "I wasn't watching the trail. I thought I was safe with you."

"What do you think Alice said every time I caught her? *Don't worry, Nadia. I know which paths are safe.*"

My words cut more than I mean to, and it shows on him. "It's not the same—"

"It is," I say, kinder but firm. "You can't blindly trust me. There are so many beasts in the woods, more than you think there are. Only one needs its moment to make us miss you too, and that one might be quicker than me."

Aimo says nothing when he kneels next to me and watches me weave the flame in small wreaths around the petals. After a while, when the fire fades from my arms and the petals flare up, he asks, "Won't the flower burn?"

"Yes, but never away. It's a gentle flame. I told you, it wants to help."

"Then what *does* it burn away, if not flesh and flowers?"

I could answer honestly, but that would only frighten him. I'm certain it is *right* to offer the children to the flame, but I have no way of knowing whether it is also the most horrific curse I could place upon my wards.

And so, when the petals fall and melt the snow around them, I lie through a smile—not to deceive, but because I'm not certain what the truth is. "Fear. So long as the petals burn, you will have nothing to fear."

Aimo frowns, but does not prod me further. He sweeps a look over the little craters and his brow furls further. For a glimpse I see a reflection of Sorry as a child in him—and imagine Aimo as he might become, those furls carved into grooves by time and hardship after he stops relying on others and takes their safety as his responsibility instead. A future I might steal from him. "What about that one?" he asks, dispelling the daydream.

On the snow lies one dead petal, blackened and curled upon itself. I pick it up to feel it smouldering, then stash it in my pocket. "This one's for Alice." The corner of my mouth twitches, and I can feel my smile breaking. "She doesn't need it anymore."

Aimo sniffles again when I gather the petals my spell has caught onto and offer him one. "Here. Keep it near your heart."

He does as told, patting his breast pocket. "I don't feel any different."

"You will. The fire dwells inside the petals, but," I say sternly, placing a hand on his shoulder, "don't forget what I said. Some beasts aren't afraid of you, even with this."

"Well, I won't have to fear them either, will I?"

I cock my head at his cheeky tone. "If you were fearless, the spell would have nothing to feed on and it would die out."

Aimo's shoulders slump. "I suppose I'm a little scared."

Our house is at the outskirts of the city, one of the few wooden buildings still in a habitable shape—rundown, yes, but still a shelter and a home. Sorry's good with a hammer, but with materials running low, we abandoned the second floor after snow made the roof fall in some time ago.

Sorry is awake. The fire pit burns low, painting his contour by the open door. "Everything all right?" he asks, ruffling Aimo's hair when the boy runs over. "I heard the howling. I was about to come looking for you."

"The pack found us," Aimo says. It's too dark to see Sorry's face, but the quickness of his glance at me says enough. "Nadia drove them off. She was great."

"Are you hurt?" Sorry asks.

"Just a scratch, and more at cloth than me." I nudge Aimo to go on inside. "Off to sleep with you. Sorry, please come out for a minute."

The boy shuts the door behind us and the lock clicks. Edie will be up to let us in by the time we're back.

"I didn't notice him missing until I heard the hunt," Sorry

says. The howls are close, but they won't come for us. "I'll be more careful."

I give him a weary laugh. "You can try, but I think we've both learned he'll find me whether or not we try to stop him."

Sorry hesitates, looks away when he asks, "Did you visit the grave?"

"I told her hello for you."

I lead Sorry into the city, down the streets of houses we've robbed hollow towards the marketplace. We stop at the old fountain and sit on the edge. The bowl from where water used to spout is chipped and frozen.

"I suppose this is about your work," Sorry says. I draw out the petals to illuminate his features. He looks as sad as he sounds. My hand quivers as he takes one—I can smoothen skin, soften my voice, but not hide the way age makes my arms tremble. Sorry's been with me the longest, grown from a boy to a man, and is the sole one of my wards whose orphaning rests wholly on me. Upholding illusions is difficult when he looks at me, and yet, even when we are the last people left in this land, my vanity demands I look the part of a sweet young mother rather than the withered crone I am.

"These are the answer to your worries," I say. "With them, we'll be fine even if you can't hunt."

He inspects the petals, turns his around on his palm. "How?"

"Never mind how. I need your trust."

Sorry won't voice it, but I know he's come to doubt me. I cannot say I blame him. I spent half a century sculpting my face and a full one perfecting my eyes, until a sultry look never failed to win me wine and company, but he isn't as easy to fool as those to whom I was a moment's delight. Sorry sees both the crone and the beast behind my beauty. I love the children, but I do not keep them for the kindness of my heart. He has come to understand it, now that he bears his own share of guilt for failing to protect Alice.

"I trust you, Nadia," he says, and I choose to believe him. "But not your spells. I don't like the way the petal feels. Its warmth is . . . biting, and fire has a tendency to destroy what it touches."

Such an apt way to phrase it. "You mustn't fear it. It has saved me from the beasts twice over."

He sighs, but eventually places the petal in the breast pocket of his vest. "Fine. Go tend to the others. I'll stay out a little longer."

I leave him to his musing and head back to the house. We've seen neither for a while, but still speak of days and tomorrows. The passing of time is difficult to tell when the dark is permanent and stars have stopped moving, but we've come up with a system to measure it: When Edie and Aimo sleep, it is night. When the three of us are awake together, it's day. Sorry is exempt from the cycle. The hours he keeps are much too strange.

The wolves prowl the same promenades of collapsed bricks and crushed wood as I do. I won't let Edie and Aimo out of my sight tomorrow, but the beasts respect Sorry and I'm safe for the scent of my cloak. They don't dare come close to someone who wears the skin of their kindred, no matter how hungry they are.

Except for one.

Edie rises early, while Sorry's still away. She shivers in the bleak room, and I see her crawling to the fire pit in the starlight from the open window. Aimo doused the pit—that wasteful boy—before settling down. The blanket he brought her only does so much, particularly when I've let the cold in for some fresh air.

"Good morning," I say, when she comes to me and yawns. "Did you sleep well?"

"I had a nightmare."

"Oh, no. The one you've had before?"

She nods, wipes her nose on her sleeve. "Is Sorry out hunting?"

"I think so. Are you hungry?"

She nods. "I hope he finds a fawn today."

I smile at her. "I'm sure he will." Why cease the lies now I've started with them—come what may, they won't matter after today, and it gives her comfort. Sorry hasn't found quarry in weeks, but had the foresight to preserve his kills when he noticed prey dying out.

Wolves howl outside, making Edie flinch. "In my dream, there's no one left in the world but us and the wolves." She may well be right.

"I've got something to take your mind off things. Come upstairs."

We sit with our feet dangling over the broken wall of the

second floor, where we shovel snow out to keep the house from collapsing further. The view's nice here—when the sky is clear, as it now is, you can see the stars shining on the ice of the lake behind the house.

I take out the remaining petals and offer her the bright one. She frowns at the dead petal and asks, "Why's that one burned?"

"The flame rejected it, but never you mind. There's enough for all of us."

"Without Alice," she says sourly. Such a small remark, but sorrow blossoms easier than nature.

"She will be the one to save us." The words choke me and my true voice creaks through. "She was an elemental, like me. When the earth took back her bones, the power hiding in her bloomed into these petals. Now you can hold a part of her soul, and mine."

Edie frowns. "Yours too?"

"My kind has long lived among people, Edie, but we are not human. We are forces of nature." I stroke her hair, part it into tresses to braid. "As long as we remember that, we can become whatever we want."

The girl sits quietly while I work, unravelling my answer. I'm not sure whether she's an elemental. Sorry is the only one I'm certain is not—the others I found lost in the woods. I thought they might have been left behind by the last people fleeing the city, but now that I know Alice was born of earth, I've come to worry these two may not be human either.

If they're not, the flame will make them my slaves instead of saving them. It's a better fate than letting them starve, but the thought still makes me shudder. Once more I tell myself I am doing the right thing. Even as I do, I pray they are abandoned human children and not my kin.

"Nadia," she says, interrupting my brooding. "If you could be whatever you want, why don't you turn into a bird and fly away?"

I tilt my head at that. "Are you saying you don't want me here?"

"Oh! No, of course not! I'm only wondering why you'd rather stay in the dark with us than let the wind carry you somewhere there might still be sunlight."

With a hum, I let her braid fall against her back. "It's nowhere to be found anymore, Edie. That's why we need the petals. They'll burn away your bad dreams, and your hunger, and your cold.

We'll be safe until spring, even if it takes a lifetime to arrive."

She looks at the petal with open-mouthed surprise, and my heart aches at how dollish she looks. She belongs in the city that was, the one that glittered and gleamed and where every day was revelry. My kin has forgotten it, and so they howl their way into her dreams and turn them dark the way they've turned the world.

"That sounds lovely," she says with a yawn. "I think I'll sleep a little longer. Should I put the petal under my pillow?"

"Hold it near your heart."

Aimo has crawled halfway out from under his blankets in his sleep. His hands are aglow, clutching the petal against his chest. Edie smiles at him, then at me as she nestles in against his back.

"He must be having a nice dream already," she says. Her smile broadens, becomes blissful when she shuts her eyes. "The petal is so warm."

Her happiness springs tears into my eyes. I make sure she cannot see them. "Good night, Edie. I won't be long."

Sorry has left the city.

After some searching, I find his footprints in fresh snow leading up to the mountains. There is a set of paw prints beside his trail. As fearsome as the beasts can be, now and again one becomes separated from its pack and cleaves to him like a lost pup. Strange to think only he and I walk in the night alone, and only he is comfortable with it.

My unease grows when the prints don't diverge. The two have entered the cave together, and both still sit here beside a torch propped up between rocks. Sorry cuts the meat from his last kill— a deer almost stripped bare—and the wolf chews on a piece of its own. It jolts up upon noticing me, growls and backs away. Sorry glances at it, at me, and goes back to work.

The hair on my neck stands up. The beast with a scarred muzzle, now branded as well. Her eyes gleam wild in the weak light, and as I approach, she darts forward and bounds past me.

Sorry remains unfazed when I slump beside him. My legs tremble as terribly as my hands. I thought it was going to attack.

"To walk with them is one thing," I grumble, "but to feed them with the little you have is madness."

He sets down the knife, but won't face me. "I thought about what you said, how the fire saved you from the beasts. Is the skin on your back your own?"

I cringe at that, shake my head when he turns towards me at last.

"Then whose?"

"My daughter's."

He doesn't seem surprised. I've always wondered if he could see the other beasts for what they were, but he asks, "Are the wolves people?"

"Not people. Elementals."

"You know what I mean. Talk."

I let go of the vestiges of my power. The warmth that's seeped into my skin, eyes, voice, posture returns to the hollow whence I drew out the flame now residing in the petals. He watches my transformation impassively. When I've reverted, I speak in a voice that creaks with rust. "We are primordial, born of the woods and soil to protect them. We watched humanity from the outside, then from within, but humans were always different from us. Or . . . so we thought. You are base creatures, easily swayed by beauty and glamour. In time, we began to crave your adoration and altered our shapes to gain it. In doing so, we forgot who we are."

"And became beasts?" he quietly asks.

"This is the dark side of our obsession. We shaped our beauty to fit human desire, but the more we yearned for closeness, the more of ourselves we gave up, until we reached into mankind's most primal and powerful emotion and lost control. For as long as there's been light, mankind has feared the hunters lurking where it can't reach. We made that fear manifest and it consumed everything. Even the sun."

Sorry stares at the dead doe before him. "When the wolves came," he asks, faces me, "did you kill my parents?"

Heart plummeting, I nod.

"You were a friend. You shared their wine more often than I can remember."

I place my hand on his. He stiffens. "I wasn't myself. I lost myself to the beast within. I should have been stronger, but the bloodbath was as intoxicating as stoking vanity was to our former selves." I expect him to ask what stopped me from hurting him, but instead he asks something even more painful: "You say elementals are born of the earth. How did you birth a daughter?"

"We are not human," I say, pause to consider what to say, and breathe out a confession. "But, as told by our fall, we are not entirely different. Especially not in the depths of our hearts."

"You loved one," Sorry murmurs.

"I did," I admit. "Once all the people who did not flee were dead, we turned on those who smelled too much like them." I shudder with a sob I hadn't expected. "When my daughter's neck crunched between my teeth, I burned my mouth on the fire she had inherited from me. When I did, I remembered myself."

"So, which is it," he says, so deep his murmuring sounds like a growl. "Do you keep us as surrogates, or because of guilt for the deaths of our families?"

"Both, I suppose. I do not blame myself for the others' lonesomeness, but I could not bear to leave them to suffer it. Yours, I do. I've kept you safe and, with the petal, always will."

"I don't have it anymore." His stare is as hard as his voice. "I fed it to the wolf. It felt vile. Now I know why."

"What?" I bounce to my feet, my skin and flesh straining with sudden tightness as panic makes fire surge into my skin and reshapes my motherly form. "You fool! The flame yearns to unite! The petal draws her to the house!"

Sorry blanches. "Are Edie and Aimo—"

"Sleeping! We must hurry!"

I dash off, ignoring Sorry yelling after me. If I could, I would lift myself on wings now, but I don't have enough of my essence left. What little I can lend goes into my legs to let me keep my balance running down the slopes, then the streets, until I see the house.

The door is open.

I creep nearer, terrified of finding nothing but the bones of the children, but they sit by the fire pit, petals in hand.

They do not lift their eyes off the petals when I come to them. The quickness of this happening speaks of their faith in me. They are safe now, but knowing I will never hear them laugh or see their smiles is crushing.

Crunching snow makes me wheel when Sorry's friend pads over. Her gait is no longer threatening, but strangely sluggish. When she stops and lays down at the threshold, I hear heavier steps closing in.

"What have you done with them?" Sorry demands before I see him. The petals draw his silhouette when he brushes past me to kneel by the children.

"The petals let my fire take root around their souls and burned them away, turning them into . . . extensions of myself," I say, reaching for him. He swipes my hand off his shoulder. "As long as they hold the flame, they will want for nothing, and cannot die. They will endure the night, no matter how long it lasts."

"Can it ever end?"

"I thought that given time, if enough of my kin remember who they are, we might restore the order we let slip into chaos. I meant to buy you that time with the petals, but now . . . "

He runs a hand along Edie's cheek. She stares dully at the petal. "Is there anything you can do to hasten it? Anything I could do?"

"Nothing," I whisper.

Sorry turns to Aimo, but finds no more lucidity in his empty eyes. "No. Revive them. This is not right."

"It's the only way they could survive. You have nothing to eat. Even the crows have died."

He looks at the children with fright and disgust, then unsheathes his knife. "Revive them, Nadia, or I'll put you down like the beast you are."

The way he says it makes me step away, and I hate myself for it. "There's nothing to revive. They are one with the flame—my flame. I can't rebuild a log from ashes."

"Then how can you say you're saving them?" he shouts.

A thud from the doorway disrupts his outburst. We turn to the wolf and my heart freezes. There are fingers between its fangs.

Sorry's shock breaks quicker than mine and he runs to the wolf, rips its jaw wide with a crunch. Inside is a slender arm in place of the tongue. The petal rests on the palm.

I cannot restrain a cry when Sorry reaches for the arm laced in saliva and pulls Alice out of the wolf's throat.

Her body is limp, but when she is entirely out, she crawls down from Sorry's arms, holding the petal and staring at it.

"How? Whose bones—"

"A girl's who was lost in the woods," Sorry interrupts, his face so white the petals' glow seems to reflect off it. "The night Alice didn't come back, I went looking for her and found a wolf chewing on the bones I gave you. I thought it had killed her and was about to attack it, but then I . . . *saw* her. The way I see you for who you really are. I thought it would be more merciful to let you think she was dead than know what she'd turned into, and that she had killed someone lost like her."

We gaze at the three children, oblivious of us, and Sorry asks, "They're all elementals? Like you?"

I nod, swallow away the dryness in my throat. "I know this seems awful to you," I tell him, "but they are not gone. To us, yes, but not altogether. They will continue to age, and the fire will grow with them. I can't lift the dark alone, but with them incubating the flame for me . . ."

"Then what?" he prompts after I trail off. "Make another sun?"

"I don't know yet. It's been long since I've used my talents properly." I pause for a second, sombrely continue, "But whatever I do will consume them."

Sorry nods slowly. "So, by giving her the petal, I condemned Alice."

"This is not your fault."

"Without me, she would have lived on, even if as a beast."

"Without you, she would've been as dead to us as if it *had* been her I buried." I reach for him again, and though he flinches, he lets my hand rest on his shoulder. "I know it seems cruel, but you must try to understand. I hoped this would not happen, but accepted that it might because . . . because the only way to begin returning what was lost is to remember my kin are not human. We were never meant to think, to feel, to develop a sense of self."

"But they did," he grinds, "and you took it from them."

He cuts wider the wound I opened myself. How deeply human of him. "It was necessary."

"It's a betrayal, towards me as much as them." The way he speaks chills me to the core. I know him too well not to notice the fury restrained behind an even tone and clenched fists.

He stands up. "One of the petals was dead. Give it to me."

"Would you not take the bright one? It would give you succour."

Sorry holds out a hand. "Give it to me."

Gingerly, I fish the blackened petal from my pocket and hand it to him. It stains his fingertips black as he grinds it to dust.

"What're you doing?" I stammer when he brushes past me to scoop up Alice.

"Leaving," he says and walks away with the girl in his arms.

"To where, I don't yet know."

"Why are you taking—"

"Did you think I wouldn't? That I'd leave them with you?" Again, his voice comes so close to a growl I clutch my shawl by instinct. "You've been my closest friend for so long I can't bring myself to hurt you, even now, but make no mistake—once I secure a place to shelter her, I'll return for the others. If I find you here, I'll kill you."

"How can you be this selfish?" I say, so stunned the words are almost nothing but a thought, but Sorry has a predator's senses and scoffs. "This is the only way forward. How do you not see the value in their sacrifice?"

"My eye was always sharper than yours." He stops to glance at the remains of Alice's beastly shell. "I find it strange you spent so much time trying to understand mankind, but never realised everyone saw through your disguise. People didn't flock to you because of your appearance, but because what the human heart wants most is to be seen and admired. It wants so dearly to belong with someone it'll fall in love with a flame and befriend a feral beast if they keep it warm for a while."

He half-turns to face me, too far from the light to read his expression. His tone is as murky, thick with something between anger barely kept in check and sorrow bursting at the seams. "If you can grasp that, maybe you'll understand why I'll sooner give up the world than let you use my little sisters and brother as fuel for your schemes."

After he's gone, I draw out the last petal with a shaking hand and sit with the children. Wind through the door left ajar blows the dregs of Sorry's petal to me, and I pick up the rolled-up pellet. I never considered the flower could have bloomed from a stranger. Maybe the dead petal *did* belong to Alice—after all, it was ultimately she who set me down this path. She was a vessel to my flame long before today.

Or maybe it was mine, burnt from the start because I am neither human nor born of the earth like the children. I am a wildfire, now reduced to a flicker, but soon to grow great and all-consuming. Children of the wood are my prey, and always have been. It is only right they burn when they willingly reach for the flame.

Reminding myself of that does not ease my conscience

tonight, but in time, perhaps the curse of flesh and feeling will fade and I will burn bright and carefree again—though hope itself is a human quality, and I dread to think it may be a sign I've already given up too much to recover. Either way, Sorry's threat will change nothing. Whether he accepts what must be done or rebels and hides the kindling, they will continue to feed me until I reclaim what was lost or we all fade into the night.

Drawing warmth from the pale crucibles around me, I close my eyes and dream of a newborn sun.

MIDNIGHT

Seize the Night

MIDNIGHT RELIEF

Jonathan Chibuike Ukah

To set my heart at rest
there is no more you can do;
you have raised my right hand to your eyes
and left your spittle on its crannies,
filling the veins with wetness,
and since that summer evening,
your saliva is the only breath
raging in my palms.

This spittle you said would alleviate my pain,
you do not trust on time; you do not care,
to heal me, to replace torn tissues
and make me young again;
time is the salt that opens up old wounds,
freshening them up, awakening them;
time steals my relief away,
leaving me with worries and worthless thoughts.

Midnight is a lonely and frightening time,
the fear that comes and goes like a flicker,
when ghosts of darlings old and past
play roulette with my mind and heart,
and throttle me out of the peace of the body;
it arrives with little disasters, eerie moments of fear,
tiny pots of horrors amplified, whipping off the rain,
dangerous silence bringing me relief.

OWL HOOTS FOUR TIMES

TOMMY CHEIS

An hour shy of midnight, Owl hoots four times. *You have no chance,* he says in our Chiricahua language. *All your people will get killed in this order: Eddie, Chuck, Vic. You're no leader.*

Chuck's not on the battlefield. You're a fraud. Show yourself, Owl.

Dudah. I will not.

And you left Phil out. Why?

He'll find a way to survive. He always has.

Will I survive? No. Don't answer.

Tooahyaysay, you cannot be killed in battle.

You dodged my question.

Before Owl answers, everything goes black . . .

. . . then Eddie's between me, the stars, and the moon. His voice fades in.

"—sign someone's going to die. He's a feathered *chinde.* What else did you hear?"

"Who cares? He was a hallucination beating into the past down the canyons of my mind."

"You fucking obscurantist. What did he say?"

"Who's going to die, and in what order."

"Well, there it is. The four hoots you heard are a dire warning. Did Owl speak your name?"

I shrug.

He helps me to my feet and holds me by my shoulders, bracing me until the dizziness and fear passes. "Owl carries the ghost of a person bad during life and worse after death," he says. "Often, it's a dead relative. But I've seen a case where the enemies a man killed in battle haunted him. He lost his mind and killed himself."

"By the medium of a machinating bird? Those I slayed deserved it. I give them no thought."

"Nevertheless, I'll perform an Owl Ceremony as a spiritual inoculation."

"Will it hurt?"

"Shut the fuck up. Normally, you'd give me a black silk handkerchief, a cross, and a flint knife. But since you have none of these in your rucksack, I waive payment. In exchange, I put on pollen and pray to the directions, asking Owl for your sake and his to leave you the fuck alone."

"On the ground that if he doesn't, I'll pluck and roast his feathered ass for breakfast?"

"Shh. He's listening. Then I throw a flaming stick at him while singing Owl Songs."

"Problem is, if you build a fire, you'll give away our position to the enemy."

"I'll use my Bic and a twig. Happy now?"

"Lay on, McEddie."

"Someday you'll believe." He heads to his horse to retrieve ceremonial supplies.

I relieve Vic from the watch and gather the guys to re-paint our faces. Camo base and a horizontal line based on band. Eddie and I, as Chokonen, use white clay; Vic, a Chihenne, red beryllium; Phil, a Bidanku, black ash from walnut wood. "Need all four Chiricahua bands present," Vic says, then applies the Ndendai mark in crushed turquoise across Henny's broad cheekbones and nose.

"*Ixexe*," she says, smiling as if it's a game.

Eddie emerges from the darkness, kneels, and hands us protective amulets on buck hide. Eagle talons. Chunks of turquoise, abalone shell, coral. Hummingbird feathers. "Wear them. They work. Four fucking tours and not a scratch. Just jungle rot, toes to crotch, and shit like that."

I check my watch. In thirty minutes, it's America's Independence Day. We're bringing ours closer. I nod to our *diyin*. "You're up."

Eddie pinches his cigarette. "Groovy. We'll perform the Gun Ceremony, which we have not done since Geronimo did it in 1886, so this is a bigger fucking deal than Nixon's resignation. Grab your rifle and line up facing east." He draws his boot through pine needles in a spot where stars and moon are visible through tree breaks. When we assemble, he faces us and sings secret lyrics.

When the last haunting word echoes, he turns to Phil. "Open your left palm." He spits in Phil's hand, then uses the saliva to make a cross atop Phil's left boot, thigh, forearm, and cheek. With each cross, Eddie calls upon the Four Thunders—Black, Blue, Yellow, White.

He tilts his head to the sky. "Black flint is overhead. Take the enemy's Black Weapon to the centre of the sky. Let our enemy's Black Weapon disappear from the earth."

He makes a quarter turn and repeats the incantation for each successive colour and direction. Blue Weapon to the south. Yellow Weapon to the west. White Weapon to the north.

Then he rubs his right index finger along Phil's lips four times.

Then he repeats the sequence for Vic, me, and himself. "Now guns port arms facing east."

We do as directed.

Eddie sings and prays. "Now shoulder arms facing north."

We comply.

He recapitulates. "Now pass your guns behind your back as you face west."

We obey.

He repeats. "Finally, parade arms facing south."

We do as we're told; he does his thing.

"OK, that's it. Your weapons are blessed. The enemy's weapons are cursed. Be brave, kill all the bad guys, and let no bullet hit you in the back."

23:40. Twenty minutes until go time.

After we're rucked up and taped for silence, Eddie puts pollen shields on us. Invisible spheres of life and purity against which enemy weapons are powerless. I put one on him at 23:50.

Until now, I've harboured a smidgen of hope we still might talk our way out of this. No more. "Guys, I wrote no motivational speech. I'm not Chris Fucking Farley and shit like that."

They muffle laughter in fists. Tension abates, then magnifies.

"You've been here before but you're plagued by worry and doubt. In every battle we find out who we are. That goes hand-in-hand with melancholy and spiritual distress. Eddie relieved you of some of the burden in his way. Let me relieve you of more in mine."

I pause and check the time. 23:55. Getting close now.

"We don't go to battle with joy in our hearts, but we shouldn't go with sadness, anger, or regret. We did everything to avoid this. We appealed to reason, morality, negotiation, and law. The enemy forced this war upon us. We're fighting for a sacred purpose. Our ancestors are watching. To see if we measure up, yes, but when we're fighting for them, they'll be fighting for us."

Vic's tearing up. Eddie too. "Willie Boy, maybe you're getting it in the eleventh hour."

One minute to midnight. "Phase One. Teams ready?"

My troops speak as one. *Oah.*

"Last chance to back out, Ms. Young."

"Fuck that and the horse you rode in on, sir."

"Not so loud. Smoke can hear you. She's an ornery horse."

"I'm a Buffalo Soldier descendant. I'm ornery. And my ancestors are watching, too."

"Glad they're on our side this time."

The clock hits 00:00.

I shiver. "Let's go to war."

Owl hoots four times into the black night sky.

NOTHING BUT WHAT YOU BRING WITH YOU

DAVID JÓN FULLER

 Terry had always loved nights in the Canadian Shield—even before he became a werewolf. *Nothing bad can happen to you out here.*

Before, as a teen, he'd gaze at the Milky Way running like a vast river through the deep darkness above, something he never saw in the fluorescent-bright suburbs of Winnipeg. He loved the quiet, punctuated by the hoot of an owl or the lap of waves softly bumping boats against the dock. Perfect.

After, as a wolf, it was even better. A geography of scents and sounds brought everything to life. Bats squeaking after mosquitoes over the glassy, dark water. The trill of a loon two lakes away, that a human would barely notice. And of course, the howl of his fellow wolves, calling.

That nocturnal comfort was gone now, ripped away.

His head banged against something and he surfaced from a smothering dream. He couldn't move. This wasn't the joint stiffness of turning fifty last year. He was literally tied up, crammed into the back seat of a jostling vehicle. What the hell? Who could do that to him? And why?

Everything was dark. He smelled melting, muddy slush. A rancid Tim Hortons cup somewhere in the front seat. And someone's familiar B.O.

He tried to speak, but all that came out was a groan. Then everything faded back into a surreal, sickening confusion.

Terry's twenty-six now, tromping through the boreal forest after dark near Mom and Dad's cabin. He's alone. He used to come out here with his friend Mike when they were teens, inviting him out to the family cabin; but after putting in a good word for Mike at one of the local fishing lodges, Mike's always working, and Terry's busy in university. They're drifting apart, and Terry feels his absence now on night hikes like these.

A gunshot cracks across the uninhabited lake he's hiking past. He dives to the ground, scared shitless. The echo bounces off the rocky shore across the still water.

Target practice? Not after sunset, in late September. But Dad says there's no night hunting in Manitoba.

Another shot, *crack*, and booming echo. *Where's the shooter? Are they aiming at me?*

Can't be; as usual, his flashlight's off. He loves the half-moonlight and doesn't like to spook animals. "That's illegal!" he yells, his echo mocking him seconds later.

No one knows he's out here.

That is, except for the huge furry shape that limps through the trees and across his path. *A bear?* It pauses. Terry's insides start to go loose. *Stupid, stupid, use the light—*

He fumbles to flick the flashlight on. Staring back at him is a massive wolf, more than a metre high at the shoulder. *Are they supposed to be that big?* A dark, wet patch on its haunch glistens red. It's wounded.

Despite his fear, he's fascinated. "Easy, big fella." He raises his hands. "I'm unarmed."

The wolf's tongue lolls as if it's laughing at him. It dips its snout, then limps away through the trees, footfalls fading in the damp leaves.

Terry stands, trembling. *That's the coolest thing I've ever seen out here.*

Well, so *far.*

The next day, Terry's chopping wood by the shed while Dad's

out fishing and Mom's napping on the porch. Autumn air cool enough he doesn't break a sweat. Until he sees the guy limping past the biffy, into the yard unannounced.

The stranger's about Terry's age, wearing a faded denim jacket, jeans, brown hiking boots and a black baseball cap. Long blond hair. Looks at Terry. "Hi."

Terry pauses, nods. "Hey."

"I, ah, wanted to thank you," says the guy.

Terry has no idea what he's talking about.

"The other night? Those hunters?"

Now Terry understands. (He *thinks*.) "Yeah, you shouldn't be doing that. You could shoot someone."

The stranger grins, lopsided. It looks familiar. "I don't hunt . . . with a rifle."

This is the part where Terry should get it. He always wishes he had. "So, what are you thanking me for then?"

The guy squints away. "For not being one of those assholes." Before Terry can put it together, he goes on: "You do a lot of hiking out here, eh? Looking for animals?"

Terry relaxes, in spite of how weird this is. "Yeah. Love it. Deer, owl, fox—"

"Wolf?"

"Not till the other night."

He gives him a measuring look. "What'd you think?"

"Coolest damn thing ever."

The guy chuckles and extends his hand. "I'm Richard."

Terry shakes it. "Terry."

"Nice to meet you. Look, I gotta get back to my place on Mildred." Terry knows that lake, on the other side of the train tracks. "But you wanna see a wolf again, let me know."

"You some kinda guide?"

Richard laughs. "Easier done than said."

Terry really should have gotten it by now. "How about tonight?"

Richard gives that same, lopsided grin. "See you up back." Then he leaves.

Weirdo, thinks Terry.

But that night, the cold September rain chilling the air, wind whipping leaves off the poplar and birch, Terry wonders if he's going crazy. Because up the back path, no one else around, he sees the wolf again. He shines his flashlight right at the wolf's face. Its yellow eyes blink, as if annoyed. Then the fur and fangs and paws melt into a naked guy with long blond hair.

Holy shit.

Richard squints, putting up a hand to block the light. "Mind pointing that elsewhere?"

That was how it started. Terry hiking with Richard-as-wolf, weekends they were both down at the cabins, through the next spring, summer, fall. Terry learned to step softly, even in boots, and how to wait, barely breathing, for prey to cross their path. They didn't kill anything. But he saw a whole new world.

So when Richard asks, after a year of this, "What do you think?" Terry knows what he means. Like an office intern at the end of his term, Terry's getting the job.

"How does it work?"

"We did all the important stuff. You getting comfortable with the concept. Seeing things like a wolf."

"That's it? I can wolf out now?" His heart races like it's Christmas morning.

Richard laughs. "Nah, I'm still gonna have to bite you. Maybe chase you first, get your adrenaline going so it sticks. You okay with that?"

"I . . . guess."

Richard leans back and folds his arms. "All in or all out. No maybes or guesses. I don't do this unless you want."

A flutter in Terry's stomach. "All in."

Richard's chuckle distorts into a low *whurff*; his words growl out as his snout grows: "Start runnin', Ter."

Terry runs, Richard-the-wolf bites him, and it changes Terry's life. But the next part is different this time. When Terry feels the wolf's teeth on his leg and falls in the murk of fir and spruce, Richard doesn't change back to human and say, "Welcome to the club," like he did when Terry was twenty-seven.

This time he stays a wolf, glaring through the shadows, and says, "Wake up, dude! Your friend's tryin' to kill you!"

But that's crazy. Wolves can't talk.

The truck was too hot, like the heat had been left blasting. The dusty smell mixed with the other cluttered odours in the cab. Terry started to sweat. He struggled to get up, but couldn't. *How did I get here? What's happening?*

Rope bit into his wrists and ankles. He tried to kick and a metal door handle poked the soles of his bare feet. *The fuck?* The vehicle jostled side to side, gears grinding. It was night. Snow went scatter-splat against the windows. He heard the whining *squib-squonk* of windshield wipers. *What day is it? What year?*

Driving his confusion, he felt the primal terror of being caught in a trap. That woke something else in him. But what? His throat burned and his head throbbed. His thoughts tumbled like puzzle pieces out of a box, disappearing into darkness.

Terry's thirty. He and Charlene are on the cusp of getting engaged, but he has to tell her. How did Richard do it, he wonders? Can't ask—Richard had to leave last year. "Dad's selling the cabin, and I, uh, have some stuff to take care of out west. Keep an eye on the Whiteshell for me, eh?" That lopsided grin, wolfish whatever shape Richard wore. "And remember . . . if you want to add to our little club, be careful who you trust with the gift. It matters."

Terry snorts. "Beware a wolf in sheep's clothing?"

Richard's expression clouds. "Poacher in a wolf's, more like. See you around."

So, Terry arranged for a romantic spring getaway, here at the lake, where he brings anyone important to him. To see the beauty of the boreal forest, full of ferns, birch, and poplar, just a thin veneer of soil over oft-exposed pre-Cambrian bedrock. Blueberries, raspberries, and saskatoons in the summer. Terrifying thunderstorms. Beautiful blizzards. It's glorious. *Nothing bad can happen out here*, he always says. He hopes that phrase sticks when he shows her, out under the moonlight.

"It's gonna sound crazy," he says.

She wears hiking boots, flannel, and fleece for the damp spring air. The night feels new, with the scent of fresh fir and spruce everywhere. "Crazier than that get-up?" she says, her brown braids sweeping over her shoulders as she turns to look him up and down, eyeing his slippers and bathrobe. "You got a hotel suite stashed out here somewhere?"

He gulps. He could lose her if he does this. But he'll *definitely* lose her if he doesn't and it comes out later. "You know how we never hear any wolves out here?"

She shrugs. "It's too bad, but . . . ?"

"It's because . . . I ask them for space."

"Yep, that *does* sound crazy."

He's trembling now, more nervous and excited than the first time they made love. "Keep the light on me, and just . . . watch."

Her skepticism is palpable, so before she can say anything, he doffs the robe and slippers. He crouches low. Then he pulls up that power he needs from the earth, letting it flow through him, remaking his body a wolf. Ancient, prehistoric, primal.

She screams. He doesn't twitch. Just regards her, staying calm. Even ducks his head, like a dog. *I'm no threat. It's me.*

Hand clasped over her mouth, she aims the flashlight at him like it'll wash away the sight. The beam trembles. He can hear her frantic, shallow breaths. Smell the fear in her sweat. But she doesn't run. She's not frozen, like a rabbit. She's taking it all in.

The moment of truth. *Did I guess right?*

The beam steadies as she squares her shoulders. "Sh-show me."

He wags his wolf-tail. *Right enough.*

And it's perfect, for a while.

Terry and Char spend night after night in the Whiteshell together. The "Nature Lovers," Terry's parents call them with a smile. Through the spring, summer, fall, and winter, Char sees all sides of him. And when she's ready, he shares that gift with her.

It's even better than before.

They get to know the wild grey wolves on whose territory the lake-dotting cottages squat. Terry finds himself echoing what Richard once told him: *Remember, we're on their territory, not the other way around.*

Terry adds something more: *We have to keep the wolves safe from the people. Run interference.*

"Why?" asks Char one sticky July evening, as they scramble back into their clothes with the mosquitoes swarming them. "They managed on their own for millions of years, didn't they?"

Terry tries to shut out the whine of jet-skis on the big lake to the north, a perennial summer sound thanks to the new road. "Because there's more people here now."

She looks at him, those deep brown eyes so serious. "There's going to be more of *us* soon, too."

His heart leaps. They've been trying for months. This is how she breaks the news.

But no, wait. That was years later, after they were married. Something's wrong.

Charlene's face sprouts that white, downy fur like it always does when she transforms. But she doesn't change shape, yet. "Those wolves can help *us* sometimes, too, Terry."

A sudden impact bangs against Terry's face, knocking him to the side. He throws a warding hand up, but there's nothing there, but there also is. Time slows, freezes, stops. Then grinds back into motion again. Now he smells wet fur and . . . blood.

His head aches. "What?"

"The wolves," Charlene urges, the sky going dark and the air falling into a deep chill. *"The wolves can help you.* Terry! TERRY!"

He groaned, pulling at his bound hands and feet, his neck cranked uncomfortably and his knees bent up. He was lying across the bench seat of a truck. It bounced over a snowy road in the dark forest.

"Shut up!" snapped the driver. He knew that voice. And yes . . . his smell.

Mike.

The truck growled. He couldn't think straight. The odour of oiled metal—a chainsaw? No, wrong lubricant. The clinking rattle of something small—like rifle rounds.

A gun. Shit! How did I get here? He retched. *Is Mike taking me to the hospital?* Rope chafed his bare ankles. *Where're my boots?*

He wanted to ask what was going on, tell Mike he was awake now. He couldn't form the words. He needed to get *free*, but then everything slipped away again. Why did his head hurt so much?

Nothing bad happens out here . . .

. . . unless you bring it with you, Terry thinks, as breath plumes from his snout over crisp December snow. He's forty-eight now. Dad sold him the cabin last year. Even though most properties inside the provincial park can only be leased, Terry's name on the papers gives him a sense of official ownership. The road that opened up development also makes it easier for him to get out

here in the winter. For a weekend, here and there.

Charlene stays in Winnipeg with Connor and Meghan, tweens now and a handful. They don't know yet. Terry wants to tell them. Charlene says they deserve a "normal" childhood. So when Terry wants to come out here and "run interference", it's just him and endless kilometres of snow-laden spruce, bare poplar, and birch scraping the sky, and other animals.

The new generation of wolves is cagey, at first.

For years, they've been content to give him space. He scent-marks around the cabins and resorts; the pack stays away. Black-Ear sometimes pushes it, but he's young; he reminds Terry of Meghan, especially when she hit grade five. Deer-Crazy sticks to the deeper woods; her tracks are always far from people's. Old Silver-Face, Terry remembers from when he was little Iron-Face, a cub. Long-Legs reminds him of Connor, gangly but fast. The cubs, Terry doesn't know yet.

But they need a large territory and people don't pay attention to lupine boundaries. Maybe, thinks Terry-as-wolf, it's a sense of ownership.

The wolves know he's different. Not just that he sometimes walks and smells like them, and other times like a man. But his wolf-shape is different too. Larger, stockier, a long-extinct variation. Dire wolf, Richard called it. Sounded like a heavy-metal band. But these days, Terry feels the "dire" more than the "wolf"—lonely out here where he should feel at home; Charlene and the kids in the city, unable to all share this together.

Well, how did I expect this to go? Terry thinks, wolfish instincts overpowering human regrets. *Maybe being a wolf is a full-time job. And every wolf needs a pack.*

What else did Richard use to say? As if to save Terry from mistakes he wanted to undo?

Don't try and do everything yourself.

So, Terry's out here, in midwinter, the early sunset burning orange in the west and the white snow darkening to baby-blue in the changing light. Waiting.

There are no other wolves around; their scents are old. But there's deer. And someone he knows.

Terry-the-wolf crouches low, downhill behind some juniper bushes, peering through the needles.

There! A buck charges past, heedless of him. It has more

urgent concerns. So, Terry waits.

He hears the shuffle-crunch of snowshoes racing over the snow before he sees the deer's pursuer. Dressed in a parka, ski pants, and balaclava, gloved hands clutching a rifle—and that scent, familiar after all these years.

Mike.

His old friend, all through junior high and high school. Sharing inside jokes, long talks under the stars out here, making big plans for the future. Before they drifted apart, and Terry took on his new life as a wolf. But he didn't forget his old friend.

And here he is.

Terry-the-wolf watches Mike huff by, breath steaming from his nostrils in the frigid air. He listens. Waits for Mike to shoot his quarry.

Many heartbeats pass. Nothing.

Terry shakes the snow from his fur and stalks after them both. Is Mike running down the deer? That doesn't make sense. He's not fast enough.

Shots ring out through the trees. Terry crouches, alert. Then, whoops of victory, different men's voices—none are Mike's. A hunting party.

In the twilight, when he can hear they're all gone, he tracks Mike and the deer to where the hunters shot it. Even in the darkness, the metallic scent of Mike's snow-shoed prints tells a story. They drive the buck's hoofprints toward the other men, whose smells of fireplace smoke, coffee and tobacco waft through the deep aromas of pine and birch. Mike wasn't trying to kill the animal, he was driving it towards the others.

Like a wolf.

Terry feels a new warmth in his chest. He doesn't have to be alone out here. He'll keep an eye on Mike, make sure he's right about him and his habits. Like Richard, Terry will reveal himself to Mike. And maybe . . . they'll be pack-mates, like old times.

But that's in the future.

And then it all goes screwy the next time, when Terry's secretly driving deer towards Mike and his latest band of weekend-warrior hunters. Overcast sky and wind, maybe that's why Terry loses track of where Mike is.

Blam! Mike tags him right after Terry catches up with a deer. The bullet rips through his right foreleg, near the shoulder, a sharp punch that knocks him forward. *Shit, that wasn't supposed to happen!*

Terry shifts back to human instinctively, despite the February chill. The change will help him heal, but now he's naked, vulnerable in the bloody snow. He can't escape like this before the hunters close in.

Snowshoes crunch on the snow just outside the clearing. Damn it! He hurries to change back into wolf, then turns to look. It's Mike—and he saw everything. But he doesn't fire again.

Hope this goes like it did when Richard showed me, thinks Terry. Then he limps between the birch and spruce as fast as he can, seeking cover.

Terry doesn't know all this right now.

That comes months later. Here he is, as a wolf, alone. That stings. He wants to howl, let the other pack know he's here. It feels important. Why?

Richard-as-wolf trots by, eyes glinting green in the twilight. *You gotta change, man.*

He can't be here now. He wasn't here when Terry got shot. Richard's out west these days.

"What?" barks Terry, even though wolves can't talk.

The Richard-wolf, golden-hued in the dim forest, yips back to another dire wolf. *Tell him, he doesn't get it.*

The white-and-grey Charlene-wolf answers with a concerned growl. *Something's wrong. He's forgetting something.*

Richard growls, a deep warning. *It's too much, he can't.*

Charlene howls, her call piercing deep into Terry's skull. Memories of their time in university, the things she said women had to look out for, that men never did. "Always pour your own drinks," she'd said.

"Why?" he'd asked.

That look from her that said *you really don't get it, do you?* "Because you never know what someone will put in them."

The forest is pitch-black now, and the odours change. He catches the stink of coffee gone bad, and dusty heat. How?

Richard's maw is right at Terry's snout. *Listen to her. Change.*

Charlene growls. *He can't, not yet.*

Shit, barks Richard, even the sound of his voice fading. *Use the change, Terry. Clean that shit out of your body!*

Terry thrashes, panicking. *How?*

Charlene grabs his ear in her teeth, like she always does, but harder. *Be yourself.*

Terry twists madly, trying to right himself. Something unseen bangs into him, like he's being tossed around.

Something's clouding my thoughts. Can't wake up. I'm in danger—

The primal need for safety grips him again. A bolt of realization. *I need to shift to burn this crap out of my body.*

Instinct takes over. He changes.

Terry-as-wolf was crammed into the back seat of a truck that stank of human-food-crumbs, coffee, and fear. He smelled blood—a scent he knew! And a human's, too. He growled in recognition.

But first: get free. He couldn't roll onto all fours, no space, and his forepaws and hind paws were bound in pairs. He tore with his teeth at the ties around his forepaws. *Damned nylon rope!*

A human voice screamed from the front seat and the truck lurched suddenly.

He changed back.

Terry-as-human shook his head. The fraying ropes still bit into his wrists and ankles, but his head was clearer.

Terry was *himself* again, skin tingling like it always did after he changed. He felt exhausted, but clean. *What happened? Where's he taking me?*

Shit.

Mike was the danger.

He sprang up to yell in Mike's ear, "What'd you do to me, you fuck?!"

"Christ!" screamed Mike, and the truck jumped forward, too fast. Terry hit the seat and felt ready to vomit. It wasn't just the acceleration or whatever Mike had given him—the vehicle was veering off the road bed and tilting—shit, too fast, too far, too *fuck!*—and then a terrifying weightlessness as the vehicle *rolled*, crackle-thump-*crunch.*

The truck came to rest on its cab. Terry now lay on the roof and had more room to shift his weight. Mike dangled from the driver's seat, dazed.

"Mike!" The facts pelted him like late November snow, each stinging. He'd trusted Mike enough to show him, and his old friend had done *this*. The dread certainty of it chilled Terry. *I'm such a fucking fool.*

Mike fumbled for something in his pocket, then sawed at his seatbelt. He came free and thumped to the roof like Terry.

Mike grabbed a rifle. "You fucking ruin *everything*." He shoved his door open and crawled out.

Terry managed to pull a hand free. *Yes!*

Bone-chilling wind blew frigid flakes into the cab. Still dizzy, he tried to focus on something he knew. *What time is it?* Usually, his sense of night was rock-solid. It was terrifying to be adrift like this, in a murky mess of snow and wind. *Can't go out Mike's door, he's armed.* Terry wriggled to the opposite side and pulled the handle. The door released, but was stuck in the bent frame. He kicked it with both feet.

Through the stench of oil and gas from the truck, Terry breathed deep the familiar scents of spruce and dead leaves. Who had he smelled before, as a wolf? One of his pack, wounded. Human nose no good for that. *Have to get outside.* He kicked again.

He was alone out here.

He wept in frustration and rage. *Not like this. Not like this.*

Then, his incompetent human nose caught the scent: wet fur, mixed with blood.

If there's even one other wolf out here . . .

He took a deep breath and howled. *I need help.*

From outside, through the wind, Mike hollered at him to shut up.

Terry heard an answering howl. Then others. *We're here/we're coming.*

He wriggled like mad, kicking as hard as the ropes allowed. *Fuck, fuck fuck, just open, you piece of shit!* His heels took a sharp shock of pain with each impact and the air outside was freezing. On the fourth try, the door bent open with a *scronch* of stressed metal. Frantically, he wormed out.

The fresh air was exhilarating, even though the clouds blocked the stars like a heavy blanket. Huge snowflakes swirled around him as he lay naked in the snow. The large, familiar shapes of wolves bounded through the trees toward him, lit eerily in the glow of the overturned truck's headlights. Black-Ear and Deer-Crazy, and a younger one he didn't know. Where was Silver-Face?

A grinding, mechanical sound churned from the other side of the truck. Mike had hooked something to it. *Can't worry about that now.*

The wolves surrounded him and he gestured them closer to pull at the ropes binding his ankles. A *wurrff*, a few yips. They understood.

With a crunch and a groan, the vehicle started tilting back upright. "Hurry!" he cried.

The truck crashed back onto its wheels. The wolves tore at his bonds with their teeth, wrenching his legs this way and that until the frayed ropes fell away. "Good, good!"

A gunshot rang out. Long-Legs yelped and they all scattered. Terry's head was killing him. He sat upright, disoriented.

Mike brought the rifle to bear on him. His mouth was set in a cold grimace. "Sorry . . . *pal.*"

Terry rolled as Mike fired. He wasn't hit. Then Mike screamed as Deer-Crazy latched onto his leg, pulling. She released him as he spun back, wielding the rifle butt like a club, and she bounded off.

Terry took cover behind a tree. The wolves circled, letting out barks and yips to signal to each other and keep Mike disoriented.

It worked. Mike hobbled frantically for the vehicle door, his left leg trailing blood.

Terry leapt up, making his head swim. He seized the rifle by its stock and tore it from Mike's grip. "Stop! Whatever this is, stop it!"

Mike sneered and swiped clumsily for the weapon.

Terry flung it as far as he could into the bush. "We're not done yet," he growled, then hauled Mike out and threw him to the ground. That leg didn't look good: deep, dark punctures gushed blood, soaking the shredded denim. Mike crawled away through the snow, babbling.

Angry tears burned at the corners of Terry's eyes. "Speak up. *Why?*"

Mike shuddered. "Fuck you! Not everyone has everything just *handed* to them. I'm just doing what I have to!"

Terry thought of Richard. Charlene. The wolves. *Never should have trusted him.*

He still smelled blood on the air—not just Mike's. The depth of his betrayal, and what it might mean, stunned him. *Where's Silver-Face?*

Then Terry caught sight of a lupine body in the snow. It had clearly fallen from the truck bed when the vehicle flipped. Old and wise, an elder of the pack, now crushed and bloody in the snow. And the scent of viscera and fur was nearer—the grill of the truck.

Silver Face was dead.

Terry swooned, his breath choking in his throat. *Can't be can't be can't be—*

"Woulda been worth it," spat Mike, still crawling away from the truck, struggling through the snow towards the rifle.

Terry tore his gaze away from Silver-Face's crushed shoulders and broken back, bloodied tufts of fur that would no longer ripple as the old wolf shook himself dry or fluff out as he wrestled with his grandpups. Terry's gut churned. *I was supposed to be protecting this pack. Instead, I'm destroying it.*

He charged after Mike, ignoring the rough ground and snow. Mike's injuries and the cold were slowing him, but he was getting too near the rifle.

Terry closed the gap. "You fucking asshole. What were you going to do? *Sell* me? Like goddamn livestock? To who?"

Mike spat at him.

Terry grabbed the bloody part of his calf. Deer-Crazy had bitten deep. Terry dug his thumb into Mike's ripped muscle, drawing a ragged scream from him. "You were worth more than you know, pal!"

Terry bared his teeth. *Is that what this is about? Fucking money? My friend is dead!*

He dragged Mike away from where the gun lay beneath the snow.

He'd wanted to offer Mike the chance to become a wolf, like him. Instead . . . . *This.*

Standing over his shivering, bleeding friend, Terry's hot tears spilled down his cheeks, the night wind mixing them with a spatter of frigid flakes. *Be careful who you trust*, Richard said. *It matters.*

The other wolves surrounded them.

Snow beneath his bare feet burned his skin and the chill wind grabbed through his flesh to seize his bones. He shuddered. It was time to change, before he went hypothermic, like this idiot.

He looked down at Mike, who shivered uncontrollably, his

breathing shallow. Whether he knew it or not, he didn't have long.

The power surged up from the earth as Terry called to it, flooding his body and giving him the energy to change. Now, it felt right. He grew into his wolf-self, awareness expanding with scents and sounds all around him.

There was nowhere for Mike to go. No way to reach his rifle. And no one but wounded wolves to show mercy.

To you, we were nothing. To us, you are worse than that.

When it was finished, Terry loped back to the truck, wolf-memories blending with human. Whatever Mike had given him was still messing with him, even if the change had cleared most of it. Terry's heart ached, not just for him and Mike, but for Long-Legs, injured, and Silver-Face, dead. He howled a lament.

There was still more to do, before morning.

Terry knew this area: it was an old logging road, only used sometimes by snowmobilers, and at the far end was a clearing that had once been an airfield. The snow had slowed and now, on the wind, his keen ears picked up the threatening mechanical patter of a helicopter, blades clapping savagely through the air. Right on time to pick up a drugged wolf.

The airfield wasn't far, as the wolf runs.

If they knew Mike had drugged Terry, the rendezvous crew wouldn't be expecting trouble. He yowled out a low request to the wolves still able to run. *Follow me.*

The black clouds overhead might hide the Milky Way, but Terry still sensed the pull of the moon. The cold wind couldn't penetrate his thick fur. He revelled in the storm's primal fury and bared his teeth.

Nothing bad happens out here—not unless you bring it with you.

GRAMPIRE

DAVID J. FORTIER

 Edward rubbed his neck and stared in the mirror, astonished and not ready to believe what he suspected: he'd been bitten by a vampire. Above his blood-stained collar near his jugular were two nearly invisible puncture marks where he'd been bitten. Truly remarkable that he'd healed so quickly. Last week, he'd cut his finger on a walker and spent half an hour with Nurse Becky to stop the bleeding. The cut took six days to heal, with typical scabbing, and a small scar. The vampire bite had healed overnight.

If he had been turned into a creature of the night, the lack of reflection myth proved wrong. The metal and glass returning his image didn't know he'd changed. He certainly knew; he felt different. More alive than he had in years, though quite possibly the opposite. A bit dreamlike in that it shouldn't be possible, but the memory of what happened remained crystal clear.

"Seize the night, young man," the pale stranger had said, right before his teeth plunged into Edward's neck. It had been half a lifetime since anyone had called Edward young man. His attention was torn from the words as sharp pain burst from his neck, followed by a growing sense of weakness flooding through his body. He hadn't wanted to die; he wanted to see his grandkids again. He wanted to get to know them better and see them grow up. Perhaps it had been Ed's defiant stare that had moved the vampire, or maybe it had a twisted sense of humour to grant Edward, an eighty-year-old man, the chance at an extended life.

Edward didn't feel old any longer. He did a few jumping jacks. His right knee that typically radiated pain under any impact, was fine. His back didn't hurt and he stood straighter, taller, than he had in decades. His mind felt crisp and alert, the ever-present brain fog vanished. But his reflection remained weathered and wrinkled, the sunspots on his forehead and cheeks still there. Why hadn't they gone away? Maybe his appearance wouldn't change, and he was stuck with however he looked like at the time of turning. Just his luck, vampires existed and he'd been granted extended life while a bloody old man. Why not at thirty so he could have eternally good looks and all his friends to wonder and gawp over the years, or at forty-five when the salt and pepper had kicked in and he had more income to enjoy life? He opened his mouth and removed his dentures, chest rising and falling with excitement, the habit of breathing. Did turning come with new teeth? He hoped so!

Surely all vampires had fangs. He made the classic vampire face and tried to will fangs to grow. This must be some kind of sick joke. He flexed his jaw again, hissing and straining. Nothing. He tried again, pulling his lower jaw back extending in an overbite like Gerry Davis in middle school. Still no fangs. How embarrassing. Maybe fangs only descended with someone to bite. Then what? A mouth full of blood, and he had to drink it? He didn't even enjoy salty foods, partly from decades of high blood pressure and a low sodium diet. He shivered. This didn't sound appealing at all. Movies and books made vampires out to be evil creatures doing terrible things to unfortunate people. He didn't feel evil. Maybe he could get by with raw meat and rats. Eating rats, provided he could catch them, wouldn't make him repulsive.

Or would it? What would his grandchildren think? To them, he had already become a befuddled old man who couldn't keep up with them at the park or remember what grade they were in. Except . . . Charlie was in grade four, and Andrea grade one. The answers were there, as quick as he thought the question. Charlie liked robots and dinosaurs, but talked about video games more each visit. Andrea had tea parties with invisible friends and wanted to watch cartoons on his tablet. He smiled, still toothless, but wider than he had in a long time. Remembering felt good.

He always thought his bathroom was similar to those cheap chain hotels with no flourishes, beige walls, white tiles, and stainless-steel racks. Living in a care home, everything was dreadfully plain. He exited into his one-room hovel to change into something else. Assisted living called them suites, but who were they kidding, there was nothing *sweet* about them. His bedroom didn't even have a proper TV.

Edward changed into a clean sky-blue shirt. While considering what to do with the bloody one, he realized the right side of his face had started to itch, but rubbing the skin didn't help. He scanned the room, and there hung the most likely culprit: a crucifix. Jesus on the cross hadn't meant much to Ed since childhood, but now it made him physically uncomfortable. Not the exaggerated burning he'd seen in films, just an aggravation. Perhaps lack of previous belief reduced irritation. Would it affect an atheist vampire the same? Or maybe the mass-produced plastic crosses affected their authenticity and power. Would a hand-carved wooden one, anointed by a priest, cause actual harm?

He took a step closer and it barely registered stronger. He reached out to take it off the wall but couldn't quite bring himself to touch it with bare skin. Wrapping his hand in the bloodied shirt, he removed the cross from the wall hook and wrapped it in the sunny polo, sliding it under the bed. Immediately the discomfort disappeared. But could he sleep with it under his bed? He was thinking about moving it into the dresser, when somebody knocked at the door.

"Mr. Norris, may I come in?" Nurse Jenny, delivering medicine. Her voice sounded clearer than ever before. He panicked, she knew his health better than anybody, even more than his family but he couldn't strand her in the hallway.

He popped his dentures back into his mouth to speak clearly. "Come in, Jenny." His alarm was no longer accompanied by a racing heart and tightness in his chest—the reaction was all cerebral now.

The door opened, and hallway light burst into his small room. The bedroom sat in near darkness with the blind fully covering the only window.

She strode into the room with purpose, with a smile that reminded him of his late wife Angelina. Not that they looked similar, but they both wanted to help people—make the world a better place. Nurse Jenny wore grey scrubs with cartoon characters on them, though Edward didn't know the names, he knew his grandkids liked them. She carried an iPad in one hand, a cup of pills in the other, and around her neck, a stethoscope.

Ed's senses were on fire. For the first time, he heard another's heartbeat across the room, and he could smell rose petals. Her perfume. Now that he was paying attention, he could smell other scents on her, deodorant, and lunchtime orange peels on her fingertips.

"How are you this morning, Edward?" She placed the pills and tablet down next to a picture of his grandkids, heading for the window.

"Okay, but a bit of a headache. Can we keep the blinds down?" Too late. Indirect sunlight burst into the room. Edward hissed at her like an angry cat. But still no fangs.

Jenny held her breath, closing the blind. "Sorry, Mr. Norris. Didn't know about the headache." By all outward appearances she was calm, but to someone who could hear her heart racing and see the vein in her neck working overtime, he knew it was a front: he'd rattled her.

Hell, if he was being honest, he'd rattled himself. What was that? Edward blinked, taking a few deep breaths of his own. Did he just hiss at Nurse Jenny? No, it was the sunlight, he hissed at the sun. He was shocked and appalled but had to chalk it up to survival mode.

"Sorry, Jenny. Not sure what's gotten into me." More truth than he'd intended.

"No need to apologize," she lied. He could taste it in the air. "If you're not sure, maybe we should check you out." Jenny removed the stethoscope from around her neck, and secured the earpieces. Eternal damnation. He almost asked for that. If his heart could beat faster, this would be one of those times. Was he dead, undead? Jenny checked her watch and pressed the head of the stethoscope on his chest, looking puzzled. Edward tried to appear bored—just a vampire getting an unscheduled checkup.

"Fit as a fiddle," he said, clearing his throat, hoping to end the examination. He put his arms out and above his head like a gymnast at the end of an event. She moved the stethoscope around, confused. "Problem?" he asked.

"You have no heartbeat, Mr. Norris." He was about to suggest a broken stethoscope, but she tried it on herself and then pressed it back to him. "It works on me, but not you." Edward tensed, uncertain of what to do.

"I'm not sure what that means. Clearly, I'm alive and well." He wiggled his body to prove it. Jenny smiled, her shoulders visibly relaxing.

"Maybe it's just a Monday kind of Thursday," she said, handing him the cup of pills. "Your medication." He took the pills while she glanced around. Her eyes lingered on the bare hook on the wall where the crucifix normally hung.

Don't go there, he thought, willing her to just let this be. Maybe vampire mind control—

Her gaze darted to window, then looked at Edward's chest, and they locked eyes. She took a hesitant step backward, her brow furrowing.

"Jenny, everything okay?" He slowly put his hands up, as if dealing with a scared child.

"What's going on, Edward? No sunlight, no crucifix, no heartbeat. This can't be real." She reached for her back pocket and pulled out her phone.

"Jenny, it's me, Edward. Sweetest grampa to Charlie and Andrea. Nicholas' friend, bad at checkers. What's the matter?" He stayed still. This was all happening too fast and he had no plan of how to deal with any of it.

"I think I need to call this in." She started dialing. "This can't be real, but I need to call it in."

"You're in no danger, Jenny. Honestly." He had to do something, but he couldn't hurt her. Her phone. Before her thumb slid over the dial button, he smacked her phone into the corner of the room, and she recoiled, shocked. He grabbed her by the shoulders with the firm grip of a younger man and walked her backwards, into the bathroom. "Thank you, Jenny. For everything."

"Mr. Norris? Edward?"

He pulled the door shut and torqued the handle sideways. Metal bent under his grip as easily as folding a garden hose to move the lawn sprinkler. He hoped that'd keep it shut for a while. But Jenny rattled the handle and started yelling. It wouldn't be long until someone arrived to investigate. He had to go but didn't know where. Edward grabbed his navy outdoor coat and left his room.

"Bye, Jenny," he whispered as he locked and closed the door. He couldn't go around breaking door handles. Casually, he strode down the hall to get out of the residence wing.

The door next to his creaked open and Margaret Finch peeked out, radiating curiosity. She wore a flowered blouse of red and beige, her white hair curly and unruly. A lovely human and gentle soul. He wished he'd told her those things before today.

"Edward? What's with all the yelling?" she asked.

He reached out and kissed her hand. "Farewell, dearest Margaret," he said, and then walked away, while she smiled, clutching her hand to her chest. Other doors opened and he nodded to residents as he passed, regretting not having time to say goodbye to his friends. Down the hall and around a corner. Earl always joked about escaping, saying he only needed a swipe card to access an emergency exit: front door, the roof, the kitchens, maintenance, or the loading dock. But those places led outside. Despite other myths being wrong, he didn't want to test daylight. It could end really painfully. Free or otherwise, he needed to stay in the dark.

It had been three days, sleeping under the city, in the dusty basement of an abandoned building downtown, and two freedom-filled nights, exploring a side of the world he'd never dreamed of. Bars in his era were full of rich woods and gents in suits. Most men of the current day didn't put the same effort into getting dressed up. A few wore a coat, but no fedoras or hats of quality. The young women dressed up, with a confidence that was less appreciated back in the day. The place he felt most comfortable was a pub with lots of wood furnishings, but even there they played loud sports on oversized TVs, and nobody talked to anybody outside their table. And there were other businesses that stayed open and even thrived late.

He hadn't realized the amount of activity that existed at night.

Delivery trucks docking at grocery stores, late-night couriers, criminal elements trying to avoid ever-present authorities. But mostly the people. People walking the streets, or mingling after hours in restaurants with the doors locked to the public The occasional lone light still shining in a dark office. He imagined burned-out corporate employees laundering money to escape the daily grind. Couples clinging to each other after leaving a nightclub, smelling of sweat and alcohol, laughing while they wandered home to explore the night together. Other people scratching out an existence in garbage enclosures or near the warm air exhaust of buildings. Far more humanity than he suspected. An entire world thriving in the night.

All the while, Edward could feel a hunger building that he soon wouldn't be able to control. He'd considered trying to feast on stray animals, but refused to give in yet. He couldn't bring himself to hurt anything or anyone. He'd scrounged some raw meat from behind a butcher's shop, but his dentures weren't held in place anymore, making it challenging to eat. It'd taken the edge off the hunger, the *thirst*, but not nearly what he knew he needed. He recalled the words of the stranger, telling him to seize the night, and Edward found himself tarrying between worlds.

On the third night, Ed was huddled in an alley a few blocks from the butcher shop. Being near the bin where they tossed the meat didn't help, as the lingering smell of blood was intoxicating. He'd learned to go in, take what he could, then dash away from the overpowering scent.

Down the street was a place called This Bar, and he wondered how many times it caused an Abbott and Costello conversation between people who had no idea who those guys were. The bright pink signs gleamed, clear from a distance, with no astigmatism halo.

A couple of young women left the bar, laughing and looking at a phone, the light illuminating their faces. As they got closer, Edward slipped further into the darkness, inhaling deep. They smelled of spiced meats, olives, and cheese. Definitely some red wine. He shook his head. No. Smelling like food and *becoming* food were not the same thing. He pushed his open palms into the cold brick behind him, but even this wasn't helping as it had past nights.

What if he fed on somebody despicable? Somebody vile?

Would he be helping the world? Surely, he would be doing some good? He wondered how he could tell if a person was evil? Would he have to catch somebody in a malicious act? Even performing an evil act didn't give him access to their motivations. He could drain somebody with a good heart by mistake. Everybody was somebody. Lives were sacred, or so he'd been taught.

Did even thinking about this make *him* evil? He wanted to visit his family, see his grandkids. There was no way in the world he could visit when he was unfed. He wanted to see them so badly, especially now that he could remember things and could enjoy talking to them about what they loved.

But to do that, he'd have to keep surviving. He went for a walk to get some fresh air, navy coat still smelling a little of the sewer he'd used to escape the care home. He'd washed in stagnant rainwater, but had no access to cleaning products. So many things taken for granted in life when you have nothing.

If he was going to catch a predator, he'd have to look like prey. It shouldn't be hard, since he was eighty. Except, he was walking upright, chin up and shoulders back, striding confidently like somebody half his age. He tried to remember how he used to walk, when he felt the age in his bones. His lower back had always hurt and couldn't straighten properly, so he hunched a little bit now, trying to replicate his former self. His right knee would hurt, so he always walked with the ever-slightest limp. How quickly his body forgot the decades of aches. This was more difficult than he thought. As he walked past This Bar, he had to focus so much on looking old, he barely paid attention to the people. If he was right, the wrong element would find him.

He'd tried interacting with a few groups of people.

"Shouldn't you be in a home, old timer?" a young guy with short, cropped hair teased. Well, he wasn't wrong.

Later that night, Edward was sitting on the steps of an old brick building, finally tempted to go find some rats to drink, when a rough-looking group approached. The fella at the front was animated, pointing at Ed and saying something about a broken old man to make the others laugh. Ed could hear their heartbeats, obnoxiously loud. It was almost all he could hear as they approached, drowning out the other sounds in the night. They reeked of beer and whiskey. Most of them looked vaguely uninterested, two seemed piteous, but the one in front had a slight snarl to his face, the kind who made his own trouble in the night. He wore a worn-out hoodie, with the pouch falling torn away at one end, with the word *KNUCKLES* emblazoned on the chest.

Edward got up and crossed the street before they came too close. The heartbeats drifted off, except one followed, and Ed guessed it belonged to the fellow with the fight-hungry eyes. Knuckles. This was all theoretical *hunting*, what was he supposed to do now?

"Hey, speedy, where you goin' so fast? Goin' to have a heart attack if you're not careful," he laughed. "You run away from the dementia ward or somethin'?"

Edward tried to outpace him without running, but it wasn't working. He slipped into an alley and tried to hide behind a garbage bin. He'd preferred the game of pretending to be prey a lot more than actually feeling like it.

"Aw, don't be scared, gramps. I ain't gonna hurt you," Knuckles said, slurring a little. "Unless you make this harder than it needs to be. Maybe you can give me that nice jacket of yours. And I'll go."

His jacket? It had been a Christmas gift from the kids a few years back. He'd forgotten about that, but the memories were clear now. They'd been so proud watching him fumbling it out of the gift wrapping, and Andrea had hugged him when he'd tried it on. There was no way he'd give it up. With a low growl, he shoved the garbage bin away from the wall and into the alley, wheels grinding over pebbles as it skidded across concrete like a grocery cart with a bad wheel. It thudded into something hard, clipping Knuckles as he dodged out of the way. His eyes widened for a moment, but they quickly squinted and his angry snarl returned.

Knuckles stalked towards Edward, fists clenched. "That was rude, gramps. You too senile for some fuckin' manners?"

"Bugger off," Edward said, "I don't want to kill you." He swatted at Knuckles, an open-handed smack to the head that send the younger man spinning. He'd never been a fighter even in his military days.

"Tough old guy, huh?" He ran at Edward, throwing a few jabs that hit Ed in the chest and swinging a right hook for a knockout. But Edward dodged backwards, then pushed him into the wall.

There was a scent in the air, more than his whiskey-stained

breath, something Edward had noticed in the room with Jenny. Fear.

"I'm going to end you, old fucker. Your family can kiss your wrinkly ass goodbye."

Edward felt a surge of fury that he couldn't hold back. Like the heady bloodrush he sensed in Knuckles, only stronger. Too strong. It took him like a riptide. He rushed forward, gripping Knuckles by the arms and hoisted him off his feet as if he were a child.

"No. Not anymore."

Ed threw him into the wall, hearing something crack when his skull hit the brick. Ed slashed out with a claw-like finger, tearing through Knuckles' throat. Blood sprayed from the wound, Knuckles' racing heart pushing his life's blood from his body.

Edward's entire world rushed at once. Willpower evaporated and all he could think of was satisfying his hunger. He closed his mouth over the pulsing gout of crimson, swallowing the salty fluid greedily as if it would be his first and last time. He wasn't in control anymore and couldn't push away, or even slow down.

As his body felt even more powerful than he had since the turning and there were things he could sense but didn't know how to describe. Shadows deepened and moved in the edge of his vision, like a rubber band being pulled and relaxed.

As his body absorbed the blood he felt a strange jolt of pain ripple through his skull, making his nose numb, and two long narrow protrusions stabbed through his gums and pushing his top dentures out of place. He spit his dentures out and snarled.

Ed had fangs.

The next day, Edward felt stronger and quicker than he ever remembered feeling. Guilt weighed on him for taking a life. The memory of drinking the man's blood hovered somewhere between haunting and pleasurable. Edward hadn't quite sorted it out yet, but he would in time. Now, at least he had more time. And he could see his family once again, especially with the thirst gone.

Edward wondered what Charlie and Andrea would think of their grandpa now. Would they think him a monster? He couldn't tell them what he'd done, but he also needed to let them know he would be all right. It had been nearly a week since he escaped the care home. He rehearsed over and over a list of things he wanted them to know. Things he remembered. How he felt.

When he got to the house, he picked out the grandkids' room from the outside and leapt into the backyard tree with branches nearby. The second-floor window was cracked open to let in the warm summer evening. He tested his weight on the roof and then lifted the window open. Ed tried to step into the room, but his shoulder pushed up against an invisible barrier. He couldn't go in. Some unseen force kept him from entering. Some myths, it seemed, weren't so farfetched.

"Grampa?" Charlie sat in bed rubbing his eyes. In the last few years, he'd only seen Edward in the home and a few times at a nearby park.

"Hey, Charlie. How have you been? I've missed you!" He struggled with the words; locating his dentures had been the last thing on his mind when fleeing the scene.

"What are you doin'? Mom and Dad said we can't visit you right now but they say your name on the phone all the time."

"Well, I came to visit you. It's been too long. Can I come in?"

"Yeah, sure," Charlie said, still seeming confused or sleepy.

The invisible barrier relented and Ed barely had time to swing one leg inside and straddle the windowsill to keep from falling inside.

"Gramps!" Andrea cried, running to him. He could hear their hearts beating fast, fast even for kids their age, and heard another pair beating steadily in the next room. He shushed the children and hugged them.

"How did you get to the window?" Charlie asked, brow furrowed and nose scrunched. He tried to look past Edward to the yard outside.

"I flew, like a bat," Edward said, joking. "I wanted to see you and thought I'd visit before . . ."

"Before what, Gramps?"

"I'm . . ." He struggled with what to say. "I'm going on an adventure. I might not see you two for some time, but I'll check in when I can." That felt good. A wholesome truth, though what lay ahead still remained unclear.

"Where's your teeth?" Andrea asked, poking in his mouth.

"I have new teeth, pointy ones, but I'm still your gramps," Ed said, not having the heart to lie to his little ones. "I'll always be your gramps." He forced the fangs to push through his gums, all bone. Thankfully he'd been practicing and the gums didn't bleed anymore.

"Whoa, that's cool!" Charlie said, a little too loud. "Like a vampire or werewolf? I killed one in a game the other day, and then I levelled up."

Edward chuckled, but heard one of the older heartbeats in the other room stirring. It was the one that beat like his own used to, and he didn't know if he loved or hated that he could tell the rhythm of his son's heart. "Off to bed. Your dad's coming." He kissed them both on the forehead, and while they turned to go back to bed, he jumped back into the tree. Ed hid on a branch behind the tree trunk and listened as Max entered the room. "What are you two doing out of bed?"

"Grampa was here, he visited us!" Charlie tried to explain.

"He's a Grampire now!" Andrea offered, trying to help with his story.

And Ed laughed to himself as he made his way out of the tree and back to the inner city. He liked that. He could be a Grampire.

HELD IN THE SHADOWS

Joseph Halden

 Clouds hung frozen in the winter sky. I jammed shaking hands deeper into my coat pockets, fumbling for the four pills of oxy that would make everything bearable. Melt away the ache in my hips and back. Stop my trembling. Make the lights not so damned bright. Make me feel like I was riding in a car with my friends, singing along to cheesy music.

Half of me fought the compulsion to take the pills though, fuelled by rage and stubbornness. I'd been clean a month; I couldn't let that go.

But I didn't know if I could stand not to.

I padded away from the vehicles rattling and buzzing in the snow-covered city streets, heading out of the downtown core toward the shadier areas with only the odd streetlamp. One month clean had felt like a year. I'd pushed through, driven by the same lie fed to me throughout my life: get through the pain and it'll be worth it.

It hadn't been worth it.

Instead, someone at the shelter had planted oxy in my locker, and I'd been thrown out. The oxy and—more importantly, my methadone—had been confiscated no matter how much I'd argued. You'd think they'd leave me my methadone, right? Nah. Not if you catch them on a bad day, or when you point out the plant had to have been staff because an addict would never waste their drugs.

Fast-forward twenty-four hours. After arguments with patronizing pharmacists, ER nurses who hated me on sight, and the methadone clinic intake staff who—you guessed it—also hated me. Bridges long since burned in a blaze of fuckups. Now my withdrawal was back: the sweats, the shakes, the goosebumps, and the sense that every light in the universe had been dialed up to eleven.

One month of gruelling effort, and this was my reward.

But taking the pills (that I'd been able to score easier than a fucking prescription) would make all those pricks *right*, and I hated that enough to hold out.

The shakes were getting worse, though.

Fire barrels glowed in a wide, rubble-strewn back alley. Shapes milled seamlessly with the shadows. Darkness was the great equalizer. Maybe they, like me, had had enough of the damning judgment of the light.

These were my people. Flames flickered as I approached.

Years ago, my people had been Vic, Chelsea, and Aisha. In high school, I was the serious one, determined to study when all they wanted was to play board games and go drinking. It took convincing but sometimes I'd give in and we'd drive around singing cheesy songs.

That was Aisha's favourite and, well, mine too.

We didn't do anything life-changing, but that didn't mean it didn't matter.

I missed it.

Bright flashes often jolt me into memories of things too painful, or things that could never be again. So here I was, getting as far away from that awful light as I could.

In the dark alley with the fire barrels, I stepped alongside a man with outstretched hands in patchy gloves revealing dirty and calloused skin. I held out my own thin-gloved hands toward his fire in commiseration. Neither of us spoke, each in our own world united by the need for warmth. Both of us content to keep things that way.

He bent down and threw a piece of cardboard in, making the flames roar.

The accident was when oxy'd gotten its hooks in me. I'd worked too hard—a sixteen-hour shift—and fallen asleep at the wheel.

White high beams had jolted me before a giant fist slammed into the side of my truck. A punch of radiance fractured my pelvis and one of my vertebrae. That was the crossroad where I tumbled onto the path of oxy.

From a societally prescribed path of working too hard for a harvest that would never come, to a medically prescribed one of being doped enough to endure endless disappointment and pain.

The flames died down after devouring the cardboard, and my memories quieted. The injection of warmth was good, but why'd it have to be so eye-burningly bright?

I fingered the oxy in my pocket. I could take the pills. Maybe crush them? Swallowing the pills straight probably wouldn't give me much of a high.

But goddammit, then they'd win. The eye-rolling shelter workers who'd waved away my truth. The curl-lipped aristocrats barely containing disgust as I trod to a public restroom, unwelcome. The clinic staff shaking their heads as their gaze pierced through me, magicking me invisible.

Copper through my clenched teeth then and now, the aftertaste of rituals, power that maintained a boundary I could never cross, guarding the inner sanctum of self-righteous, privileged assholes.

Taking the oxy? They. Would. All. Be. *Right . . . about me.*

Flames slowed their weft inside the barrel, as though the depth of winter drained the life of combustion itself. The shuddering wind snaked up my coat and down my pants. I fought to keep my teeth from chattering and squeezed my eyes shut, wishing the terrible reality away.

The wind ignored me. Worse, it seemed to carry the voices of everyone who judged me, everyone I was trying to thwart.

"Mom? Dad?"

The words came from a dozen directions, a young girl's voice intermingled with the entwining wisps of wind. I stole a glance over my shoulder. Only a few silent, shadowy figures lurked next to dumpsters, rubble, and other fire barrels.

"Mom? Dad?"

A kid shouldn't be out here.

No, Malcolm. You don't have time for this.

I shut my eyes and focused on the fleeting bits of warmth prickling through my fingertips. Fighting my body was already hard enough. My hips were reminding me how long it had been since they'd had oxy to make the grinding, throbbing ache go away. The memorized pain pulsed with each step, never letting up, a constant tormentor eager to sour every experience. It woke before I did. Growled with the first murmurs of motion. Rose to a screeching chorus the more I moved. The tormentor joined my hips to my legs with electric gloves.

I should just crush the pills. In a few minutes I'd be savouring pleasant, pain-free emptiness.

"Mom? Dad?"

With each warble on the wind, the girl's voice grew a touch more desperate.

Shoulders raised and gazes darted around. Yet no one was willing to relinquish their spots of warmth. If anything, they grew more paranoid and protective, leaning closer to the barrels. I turned to find her. I had to. Or I was no better than those who'd ignored me.

"Mom? Dad?"

Stepping away from the fire blasted cold up my calves and thighs. A chill like my clothes had ripped away and I was bared to the winter. I shuddered, fighting the urge to go back to the fire.

This girl needed help.

I traced the voice to deep shadows next to a stack of garbage bags. Thankfully, the cold stifled the smell. The insects stupid enough to try for the food had long since died in a delirious hypothermic coma. I shivered and tried not to think about how little time it might take me to freeze like that.

The girl was dressed in all black, almost impossible to notice in the darkness. All I caught were the wet flickers of her eyes when she blinked.

"They're probably not out here," I said, trying to strike a balance between being gentle but not welcoming. "Shelter's that way." I pointed in the direction of where I'd been thrown out.

The girl shook her head and sank deeper into the shadows so

fluidly my throat chilled.

"I need my parents; they're not that way. If I don't find them tonight, I'll never find them again."

Her flat tone was so matter-of-fact it disconnected from what she was saying. There was no hysteria, just sincere belief. Her truth: that her parents would be gone or lost in a few hours.

It didn't mean she wasn't nuts, though.

I wondered if the other shadows in this forgotten neighbourhood had made the smarter decision to ignore her. It was too dark to read her face to see if she was putting on a practiced act or if she was just unnervingly calm.

What would I have preferred—a child in tears? I had nothing to be afraid of.

Famous last words, Malcolm.

"Any idea where they went?"

"West. They chase the night."

Maybe she had better drugs than mine. Her voice whistled with the wind, banishing the dry air and even the light surrounding me.

Maybe I was the one who was stoned. I reached into my pocket.

Nope. Oxy's still here, Malcolm.

"That's West." I inclined to my right.

"I know that!" She snapped her head quickly, the shadows beneath penetratingly dark. A cloud of dwindling grey floated where her hair had been. "But I don't know how they crossed the thousand-lamp street."

My skin prickled, and I shook my head as though my brain had glitched. I tried to focus on the normal parts of her speech, anything I could tether to reality. I'd seen a lot of weird, scary shit, and she was some special kind of weird, all right. But not dangerous. She was a weird that raised the hair on my neck not because of what she might do to me, but because of what I might find if I stayed around her long enough.

Then again, I was also a weirdo who needed help. Who wasn't?

"You mean . . . a main street? Which one, 109th?"

"Maybe. I don't know this place very well."

"Well, if that's all that's holding you back, I can help you cross it." The words disgorged as though the wind's phantom voices had forced them out of me.

She tilted her head, studying me. At this angle, I could make out terribly black eyes. Her gaze froze me in place and cold filled my stomach.

"Will it be dark?"

"There's light, the cars can see us, and—"

"No light. Light'll kill me. I have to travel in the black."

What the hell is she talking about? There were layers of meaning or bullshit here I couldn't make sense of. Why was I freezing my ass here with her?

Bewildered, I did what I'd done too often when confronted by something utterly beyond me: I wrapped my fingers around the oxy pills.

I squeezed my eyes shut and mulled what she'd said over in my mind. Despite my uncertainty, her riddles pulled me in. Maybe it was because darkness never judges. It provides shelter from a world that claims to see us for who we are, but never really does. How much of my own suffering had been caused by trying to doggedly tread the paths of light, those pre-approved life trajectories bearing the false promise of fulfillment?

I loosened my grip on the oxy. It was time to take a different path.

"What's your name?"

"Natalie."

"Cool. I'm Malcolm."

"So, do you know a way through darkness?"

At the very least, I knew some paths to avoid: streets the cops never trolled, and laneways most street urchins rarely looked at. The darkest, most forgotten nooks.

"I think I do. Come on." If Natalie was right about needing to find her parents tonight, then we only had a few hours to travel until dawn.

I stepped into the shadows beyond Natalie, beckoning her to follow. She retreated into the gloom of the garbage pile, then took a step to follow.

I led her through the umbrage of neglected streets. At every crossing, Natalie insisted we had to wait for the complete absence of cars, which made the going slow. I shuffled and rubbed my arms fiercely to try and fight the chill working its way into my bones. My fingers curled and flexed tucked inside my jacket, but they were losing feeling.

Our progress was so slow I worried we weren't going to reach her parents in time.

"How far West?"

"They chase the night."

A helpful answer that clarified nothing.

Eventually, Natalie followed closer behind me. Her disquieting aura of mystic devotion begged me to stay in the shadows, and I tried to focus on that instead of the relentless cold.

"You know the dark well," she said as we stepped around recycling bins in an alley. "You almost live in my world."

"What world's that?" My teeth chattered when I closed my mouth again.

"The one penned in by black."

Was I hallucinating? It was a strong possibility, but I had no idea what would happen if I broke the illusion so I kept playing along.

"That's why you chase the night?"

"Yes. Tomorrow the crows'll follow."

I imagined a murder of crows flying overhead before diving at something on the ground.

My corpse, a mirror in the ice, covered in frost.

My cheeks stabbed with pain as though the crows were here now, pecking my skin with carrion-hungry beaks. I batted them away, seeing every bit of fog and condensate as a threat, a harbinger of what could devour me. The city's pulsing breaths from sewer grates seemed to whisper raspy judgment and offer to end the suffering.

I groaned. Gripped the oxy.

I worked my mouth to spark motion in my cheeks, anything to remind my body it was still alive. Then my hips lit with renewed pain, and I wondered if the gutter's offer of death was a kindness. The cold, empty air in my stomach murmured agreement.

Please. Give me food. Warmth.

Hope.

I cried out, my voice cracking as I roared. Everything stacked against me, always. Conquer a demon and ten more came out, like the tiny icicles constantly reforming on my eyelashes no matter how many times I brushed them away.

I took a deep, shuddering breath and looked back at Natalie. She had fallen a pace behind, but kept her dark eyes fixed on me.

"Sorry. It's freezing, and I'm not getting any warmer. Having . . . a hard time with it all."

"Should I go on without you?"

I closed my eyes, shuddering from the icicles on my lashes and the hollow in my chest. "No. I told you we'd find the way, and we're running out of time before dawn."

She stopped, and if I didn't know she was there, I would have sworn she'd vanished.

The shadows shifted. I thought Natalie was abandoning me until her dark form was right front of me. My breath caught. She seemed a phantom behind curtained mist.

"Let's walk together, Malcolm."

Her words buoyed me against the maelstrom of cold, withdrawal, and hunger. I blew into my hands and rubbed my cheeks, then my aching hips. We went on.

Several blocks later, the alley spat us out between two skyscrapers, revealing a wide main street. The brilliant clap of streetlamps and passing cars risked breaching the division between clarity and obscurity.

We tucked into a shadow at the edge and made a plan to cross: I'd use my jacket to create a barrier between the streetlamp and her, my arms held out like I was shielding a movie star from the paparazzi. Thankfully, the trees in the central boulevard obscured the light from both sides, so we could catch our breaths halfway.

Natalie stood closer to me, the shadows on her face looking like they'd been etched in black ink. They sharpened her features and shaved off even more of her already small form. I wondered fleetingly if this was what happened when you resigned yourself to a life in darkness. The black seemed to have taken hold and wouldn't let go.

We waited on the shadowy corner. I wished I had a watch to know the time and how long until threatening dawn, but I guessed we didn't have more than an hour no matter how fast we "chased the night."

Cars streamed by, their lights burning meteors in the atmosphere. The stench of exhaust hung over the ground as though the earth had been charred and smoked from the headlights.

Finally, the street emptied, not a headlight in either direction.

"Now!"

I unzipped my jacket, letting the cold rush in, running along my ribs and deep into my chest. The temperature drop was so quick and violent my vision blurred and for a second, I couldn't breathe.

This is your window. Don't miss it.

I quaked from the bite of winter's teeth but focused with everything on Natalie and the dark alley we needed to reach across the street. We shuffled out, my arms spread like a dark guardian angel. My legs quivered from near-hypothermia, oxy withdrawal, or the poisonous blend of both. We moved slowly at first, both tracking the other to match careful steps. Headlights flashed in the distance like flames ready to torch a moth. I picked up speed and Natalie followed, our steps synchronizing as though we danced an increasingly frenetic and deadly tango.

We reached the central boulevard, our feet crunching the snowy ground, gasping momentary relief beneath the trees. Checking again, we shuffled forward to bridge the last half, and traded places.

A car sped out from a side road, its beams of light sweeping toward us like a scythe.

I recoiled, dropping my arms to shield my eyes. The truck was hitting me again, my hips snapping sideways as the metal shell crunched around me. Something went pop in my back. Glass shattered. My ears rang.

I staggered. Gasped, wrenched between two realities.

Natalie screamed as the light hammered her. She fell toward me and arched her back, ink bursting from her shoulders and neck.

She curled to the ground and I went with her, trying to shield her as much as I could with my jacket and body. Her pants tore and flecks of ink spattered the ground near her ankles. I wrapped myself around her like a cocoon to try and block all the light. I tasted cold ash and smoke.

The car slowed as it reached us and the driver laid on the horn. The lights burned my eyes, and I took gasping breaths to stay here and not fall into the agony of memory. It took an eternity for the car to move beyond us.

Then it was gone and Natalie and I were alone.

Moaning, I picked up the bundle of Natalie and my jacket. I ran with rust-clogged joints, fighting the phantom pain in my spine.

We made it the rest of the way and into a back alley, but didn't stop until I found a dark space between two dumpsters. I set Natalie down, then gently peeled back my jacket.

Through the tatters of her hoodie, her back and shoulders were bruised white and her exposed ankles were bleached and seeping ink from pores crushed by the light.

Oh god.

"Natalie? Say something!"

My stomach knotted itself around a baseball-sized lump.

"We need to get you to a hospital."

"No," she groaned. "No. That won't do anything." Her small voice quavered, but the message was firm. "My parents are close. There are traces of them." She got to her feet, trembling from what must've been a million bursts of pain on her back and ankles. The first few steps she winced as she moved along the shadows.

Realistically, I could've argued but I was too stunned and tired. Realizing how numb my whole body was, I put my jacket back on. Tucking my aching fingertips into my armpits warmed the cold flesh but the uneven chill spreading through my veins was excruciating.

The sky had turned a tone greyer—the first precursor to dawn. We were running out of time.

Natalie tugged on me, and I walked with her through the delirious pain. I would have sold my soul for a fire barrel and a bowl of soup. My thighs sparked pain where they rubbed my pants. My toes lost feeling and made me stumble.

I slurred directions and couldn't taste whether my mouth was dry or not, while sounds took on a sharp timbre as though my body was trying to amplify something useful with its last strength.

I couldn't believe Natalie was still going.

After seeing the damage from the headlights, I didn't want to think about what would happen to her if she got caught in the sunrise.

Hints of illumination stippled the sky and I gaped at Natalie. Maybe I could find a place to cover her the whole day . . . and if I got to see the sunrise before I died, it wouldn't be so bad.

I fell against a brick wall and wrapped my hands around my neck to try and warm the cold leeching down my throat.

Natalie stopped. We were in a back alley somewhere, hopefully still in the city if I hadn't lost my mind.

"There," she whispered, pointing.

A block away from us, the alley pitched into darkness between two tall buildings and a group of dumpsters. There was nothing odd or remarkable about it—it just seemed like another spot where light didn't shine.

Natalie grabbed my arm. "They'd be really unhappy if they saw you. They don't really trust your—people like you. And to be honest, before tonight, neither did I. Thank you, Malcolm. I wish more people were unashamed of the shadows."

"Th—thanks, Natalie," I managed. "Glad we found . . . them."

Natalie squeezed my arm and ran into the darkness, her form gradually dissolving and blending into the umbral shroud until she vanished.

Natalie was gone. We'd made it—or at least she did—before it was too late.

Life's small miracles. They needed help, sometimes a bone-chilling amount of help.

I fell to the ground, my whole body quivering in fits and starts, too cold to maintain its last shivers. My vision highlighted forms in white, and I wondered if this was what people meant when they said they saw light at death. My hips no longer hurt because I couldn't feel anything.

I listened to the hum of the city, the early-morning sounds of the streets coming alive.

The streetlights flickered off as the sun took over illumination.

"Malcolm?" A forgotten voice startled me. At the other side of the alley, a garbage bag in hand, stood Aisha.

I hadn't seen her in seven years. This must be life flashing before my eyes or something. I hoped I would see a good memory.

She seemed older, though, and I didn't recognize the rabbit-patterned pajamas nor her brown hair cut short and in curls. Yet she couldn't be here—I didn't think she still lived in the city.

Maybe this *was* real, and was life's final way of punishing me by showing an old friend how pathetic I was before I died.

Guilt and anxiety flooded through me. I jammed my hands in my coat pockets and searched for the oxy, the only thing I had left that might make this easier.

I found the wrinkled Ziploc bag, but the pills were gone.

"H—hi, Aisha," I stammered.

When had I taken it? Had the chill made me so delirious I couldn't remember? Had I hallucinated Natalie, or had the pills just fallen out at some point? Or worse, had Natalie found the pills in my jacket when I dropped it around her?

Aisha's expression flickered as dozens of thoughts must have passed through her mind upon finding me. Questions she didn't want to ask and I didn't want to answer. "Are you all right?"

I bit the inside of my cheek until I tasted blood, fighting to stop the tremors and to hide the hollow I didn't want her to see.

But the pain everywhere wore away the last of my pride. "No. I'm f—freezing."

"Jesus, Malcolm! Let's get you inside. Vic! Vic, come help!"

She dropped her bag of garbage and ran back along the narrow path beside what must have been her place. She called out louder for Vic, and a moment later he emerged, looking like he'd gained some weight and grown a neatly-trimmed beard. His eyes went wide and he stopped, stunned, before Aisha ushered him over.

"You're okay, you're good now, we'll get you warmed up," Aisha said, grabbing me under the arm. She and Vic helped me inside.

I was too cold and delirious to remember much of what happened then. My tenuous grip on reality released as soon as I had safety in sight.

I think they covered me with blankets. I remember being in tingling pain as my temperature crawled its way back to normal. Vic clasped my shoulder and said, "We've got you, bud. You're good." Said something about leaving for work, and coming back after lunch.

At some point, I sat up and was on the couch, with Aisha sitting on the coffee table nearby. Concern on her face.

"Warm water." Aisha offered a mug.

I took it gratefully and sipped.

Her expression wavered between concern, incredulity and flickers of wariness. She pursed her lips and furrowed her brow, trying not to stare too much as I drank. She must have been going through a whirlwind; I could relate.

"It's been a while, man. Can I get you anything? Water, coffee, tea? Toast?"

"All—all of the above, please?"

Aisha laughed quietly, and it felt great to see her expression ease. "Sure thing, buddy."

"Just coffee and toast, Aisha, thanks." I looked around at her brightly-coloured but very much adult decor. "I had no idea you were still in the city."

"I had no idea *where* you were, Malcolm. Nobody did. I'm sorry you—that you're having a rough time."

I wanted to make a joke, to be fun with her again, but I couldn't. "Me too. Sorry we had to meet again like this."

"Don't apologize. I'm glad I can help. After you eat, you can shower if you want, and I can run your clothes through the wash."

"That'd be amazing. Thank you so much." I felt like I couldn't say it enough.

Before stepping into the shower, the bathroom mirror showed me how I looked: it seemed like I'd been rolled in ashes. As I washed, I found black marks on my body, which could've either been from all the places where Natalie had pressed against me, or maybe where I'd deliriously hugged the barrel fire.

The marks were thick and dark as ink. I scrubbed my skin raw but those shadows remained.

I had no idea what to believe anymore.

Sitting down on the couch, relatively clean and clutching another cup of coffee, my hands didn't tremble as much.

Aisha sat with me at the opposite end of the couch with her own cup of coffee.

"All right, awkward question time, Mal. Was last night a one-off or do you need a place to stay?"

I guess my defeated silence was answer enough.

"You can stay here for a while if you need, but I'll have to start work in my office at around nine." She pointed down the hall. "I won't be far, though."

"Thanks again, Aisha."

We settled into conversation, the wheels a bit rusty but eventually stirring from a friendship I thought I'd long lost.

As it approached nine o'clock, through the front window I caught sight of a flock of crows flying west.

"Maybe they have to go to work, too," Aisha said.

I thought again of Natalie, and wondered whether the crows really did follow her. Had I helped her find her path, or had she helped me find mine? Aisha tapped her phone a few times and a familiar cheesy song sounded from the TV speakers. "We've only got a few minutes, but . . . remember this?"

A cloud slid over the sun and in the pale light, Aisha and I sang.

MIDNIGHT MAN VERSUS THE LONG NIGHT

CHADWICK GINTHER

It was going to be a long night.

The longest night.

Winter solstice had rolled up on Mort Cheval, a little city on the vast prairie where monsters were too comfortable for their own good. Normally, I appreciated the growing dark. Darkness gave me more time to work. But tonight, the Long Night had come to town. Tonight, of all nights, I couldn't fail. Not again.

Fortunately for Mort Cheval, the Midnight Man knows a little something about working nights.

The nested double *M*s on my uniform jacket's shoulders and chest weren't just a logo I used for my calling card. They were also luminescent. I lit them up, the glow they cast—bright enough to give a vampire pause—forging eerie shadows. I was inside Mort Cheval's art gallery. The Long Night had a flair for the dramatic. We had that much in common, at least.

The art gallery's front door was bricked over, as if it never existed. Windows, too. I hate mind games. Stairs led up into darkness; a door on my left opened to the gift shop and main gallery. Jewelry, pottery, and knick-knacks took on weird angles in the shadows. Somewhere in here, the Long Night lurked.

I was clearly expected, but I love to make an entrance, and always appreciate an audience, so I refused to worry. My Hades cap emblazoned with a Jolly Roger, looking like something a World War II aviator might wear, made me invisible unless I wanted to be seen. My red-tinted Grave Sight goggles revealed everything the shadows wanted to hide. A black leather jacket and shitkicker boots completed the look. The look matters. "The look" keeps me on the right side of the grave. Nobody—especially necromancers, who take themselves *way* too seriously—expects a superhero to thwart their plans.

Your move, villain.

I drew one of my twin Colt model 1911s loaded with tombstone bullets from my left shoulder holster. I wanted one hand free. I didn't know if my weapons would affect the Long Night, but I'm always willing to improvise. Necromancers and other beasties typically bring their *undoing* along for the ride. The trick is keeping yourself alive long enough to snatch and use it.

Don't try it at home though, kids. I'm a professional. Most nights.

I listened for the telltale creaking of floorboards, trying to pinpoint the Long Night within the darkness. A whispered lullaby found my ears instead.

"Sleep will be no refuge for you
No one coming who can save you
Long Night, longest night. Long Night, longest night . . ."

He had a song. Of course he had a fucking song. It wanted to earworm me. I hummed Queen's "Another One Bites the Dust" in defiance and banished the singsong voice. I ascended the stairs, my steps in time with Roger Taylor's drumbeat.

The clock in the art gallery's tower chimed.

It shouldn't chime. That clock hadn't worked since the Fight took my parents from me. Remembering them, I lost my song. The chime cast me backward in time, while my feet dragged me forward, matching the lullaby's cadence. I tried to remember the last time I'd heard that chime. My parents were alive, I was sure, but life only had one destination: death. Momentum kept me traveling that same road, terminating on a night I didn't want to remember.

". . . Starts to kill when light starts dying
Kills again while you are crying
Long Night, longest night. Long Night, longest night . . ."

Black edged my vision. From further in the gallery, a second, deeper voice said, "Welcome back, Midnight Man."

Back?

". . . In the midnight hours he's creeping
Souls and meat are his for keeping
Long Night, longest night. Long Night, longest night . . ."

The verse surrounded me, clutched me tight, and dragged me into the black.

It was going to be a long night.

The drive into my parents' funeral home hadn't been plowed. Strange. My folks knew better than anyone that death could knock anytime, anywhere, and they needed to be ready to lend hands to help, shoulders to cry on, and more importantly, their hearse to take the dead away.

My little shitbox car didn't make it past the first bend to the parking lot. At the top of the hill overlooking Mort Cheval, nothing stopped the snow from drifting. Down the hill, holiday decorations twinkled in multi-coloured splendour. Closer to the funeral home stood a ring of shelterbelt trees, and the family house tucked behind it. I'd have to hoof it through the snow and wind, dragging my bags and Christmas presents.

The lights weren't on in either building. No porch lights, no twinkling icicles. Dad was getting too old to decorate the eaves. I abandoned my car for the breath-stealing cold that hit me like a slap in the face, sucking air from my lungs like a vampire gorging blood.

It was going to be a long night.

Barely past the black awning and Tyndall stone and concrete steps marking the art gallery entrance. Not even a foot on the stairs and I already felt . . . sifted. Broken into my component parts and loosely tossed back together. I knew—somehow—the Long Night was dragging me along old roads best left untravelled. I was used to foes I could shoot or punch. The Fight was supposed to be *a fight.*

I'd been warned the Long Night was coming to Mort Cheval this year. My suspicions had been confirmed by the tell-tale disappearances. The Long Night's yearly spree always culminated in his own "work of art"; a human abattoir displayed on the solstice. Coming in like a whisper and leaving like a scream.

You'd think he'd have run out of ways to kill people by now.

You'd be wrong.

Inside the gallery, death flooded my Grave Sight goggles' red-tinged vision. I've seen the worst necromancers and monsters could show me, and yet, I wasn't prepared for the Tetris wall of meat that used to be people I knew. What remained of their mouths rasped the Long Night's lullaby.

". . . *Walk among them, he will be you*
Try to fight him, he will be you
Long Night, longest night. Long Night, longest night . . ."

My lips begged to sing along. I reached for a different song, any song to keep the sing-song lullaby away. Nothing. I clamped my jaw tight. I wouldn't give the Long Night that power. Not tonight. Sing about sleep, and I'll damn well drag you into the sun. I popped a caffeine pill. No sleep tonight. Sleep belonged to someone else. Sleep belonged to people ignorant of the Fight.

Sleep belonged to someone I used to be.

Three people, unrecognizable *as* people unless you were a *Hellraiser* fan, framed the doorway to an office in a grisly arch. They were all dead, and yet, not silent, jaws clacking.

". . . *Hear his song and it is too late*
Sing along and seal your own fate
Long Night, longest night. Long Night, longest night . . ."

Three left hands pointed upstairs.

Stairs it is.

My thick-soled boots, still wet from the snow, squeaked with every step. At the top, in the centre of a secondary exhibition room near the access hatch to the bell tower, the Long Night waited on a simple wooden chair. Hands folded in his lap, waiting for me, with a dim smile that didn't touch his eyes. My glare narrowed on him. He was unremarkable in every way: a pale man, medium build, receding hairline, crow's feet peeking past drugstore reading glasses.

"You've been looking for me. Well, here I am." He rose—not

stood—as if his body was being jerked aloft by hooks in his flesh. A final wrenching awkward motion and his eyes met mine. Shit. He could see me. He wasn't following the sound of my boots, or the trail of water they left behind. I was wearing my Hades cap, and he could *see* me. But something was off, his soul didn't match his body . . . vessel. "Show me your real face, monster."

He chuckled. "I'll show you mine, if you show me yours."

Darkness swelled around him. I drew and fired before it took me.

My shaking hand couldn't turn the key to the mudroom door fast enough. It took effort to push the door shut against the wind, and the snow hounded my heels inside. I reached out for the light switch, and muscle memory found it quickly. The Felix the Cat clock on the wall ticked and tocked, eyes scanning the room. No note on the kitchen table. The furnace turned to a chilly 62 degrees, but still running.

"Mom? Dad? I'm home!" No answer. "Where are you?"

With every step, every creak and groan, every tap of skeletal branches on windows, a grue crept up my spine. Spoiled food filled the fridge, and I choked back vomit as I slammed it closed. Mom's puzzle, the same one she'd started when I'd left for university, rested unfinished on the dining room table. Dad's summer read, a World War I history book, set face down on his recliner, marking the page. Tears broke, burning my cheeks. I bounded across the yard, sprinting and stumbling through the snow to the funeral home without putting on my jacket.

No. Stop. *No.*

I'm not going to see this now. I won't see this again.

It was going to be a long night.

I often helped my parents clean after a funeral, but I'd never had to clean up a murder so the space could be ready for a funeral. Blood—and worse—was everywhere.

Dust sprinkled the air, moonlight lances streaming from the stained-glass windows amid the gore. Lights had burned out and the service room's edges were hinged in shadow. My parents would've been appalled. Not only the cruor. I ran a finger through the dust on a pew, carefully avoiding the dried blood. No one had cleaned in ages before tonight. Until the estate was settled, I couldn't afford to hire anyone. I'd barely had gas money to drive home for the holidays.

Behind me, a woman coughed. "You look lost."

It was Hannah Klassen, the cleaning lady at my parents'—now my—funeral home. I wouldn't call Hannah family, but when I'd been a kid, she'd always shown me more kindness and understanding than she'd ever needed to, or than I'd likely deserved.

"I know where I am."

"Do you?"

I stood in the middle of everything. Still as the dead. "They sent me away before . . . I think they knew this would happen."

Hannah raised the supply bucket in her hand. Her voice changed and deepened as she spoke again, becoming familiar and strange all at once. "Let *me* help you."

It was going to be a long night.

I didn't remember gearing up or driving into town. I didn't remember kicking in the art gallery door. But I *was* here. I *was* geared for action. Ready for the Long Night.

Or was I? This wasn't the first time a villain had played with my perceptions, so I did an inventory check. I was down two ball-and-chain bombs, and three Tombstone bullets in one pistol, two in the other. Still enough to do the job. Not what I'd left with.

The shattered door slammed shut. Bricks filled the frame in an eyeblink.

The gallery's main hall had been transformed into a funhouse of mirrors—no, not mirrors. Bones. Bones polished mirror-bright, distorting my reflection, twisting me into a broken thing. Beyond the clattering curtain, the Long Night's victims clad the walls like grisly exhibits. My eyes were visible through my red-tinted lenses, reflected in the bones. A vision of what I could be. A warning of what I mustn't be. My reflections, broken across the many bones, led the song, while the Long Night's victims rasped the chorus.

". . . *Comes like a whisper, leaves like a scream*
Leaves behind their blood and this dream
Long Night, longest night. Long Night, longest night . . ."

The Long Night lurked behind those mirrors. A void. An abyss

I needed to stare into, trying to make me sing along. I've stared into the void before. My reflection bared its teeth. I drew a pistol. Always outnumbered, never outgunned, that's my motto. I hurled a ball-and-chain bomb. Then another. I fired. Again and again, emptying the clip. The bombs locked spirits into their bodies, and the bullets killed the bodies. Tombstone bullets, carved from dead murderers' broken grave markers, didn't believe in "flesh wounds" and they worked on things without flesh.

The Long Night laughed in my ear. I reloaded, firing again until not a single polished bone hung from the ceiling.

Red lines in my Grave Sight bound me to my reflection and to the Long Night. Those same lines stretched beyond both into unfathomable shadow—to the night I wouldn't think about. I stepped back. My reflections stepped out of the shattered bones and merged, seams not meeting neatly, following me. Gravity keeping us in time. I shifted, and it matched me, Jupiter dragging a comet to its demise. Each time I moved, the shadowy me grew closer.

"... *But winter's night lives within you*
Sun starts dying, he is now you
Long Night, longest night. Long Night, longest night ..."

An inch, a foot at a time, my reflection undulated forward. It whispered, sharp as its broken edges, "I'm you. I'm you. I'm you."

All it will take is a little push ...

A leather aviator's cap, Jolly Roger emblazoned on the forehead, rested on a mannequin head. I *hoped* it was a mannequin head, the cap was hard to focus on. I grabbed it without thinking and put it on. It made me look like a pulp-era vigilante. In the mirror, I saw it hadn't been a mannequin head the cap had rested on, but I didn't see myself.

I should've been home when my parents died, but I wasn't.

I wasn't home because they knew *what* was coming. Maybe they didn't know when their axe would fall or who would wield it. I'd learned a few things, creeping through the house, trying to piece together what'd happened to them. There was no world in which we were a "normal" family, although my parents did their damnedest to make me believe the lie. Normal is relative, but most people don't sell grave goods, dispose bodies for money, or truck with the supernatural.

Had they sent me away to protect me from their world, or to protect their world from me? Did they assume I'd betray them? That I'd join the Fight before I knew it existed? How did I know there was a "Fight" and why did I instinctively capitalize that simple word? They'd died before I could ask.

A voice—sounding like a playback of my own—intruded. "You keep saying, 'They died.' Very tidy. *How* did they die? *Who* killed them?"

Let's try again.

It was going to be a long night.

Only 4:29 p.m. The sun had already died and the Long Night had started killing. Mort Cheval has more streetlamps than any city its size should. To brighten a too-dark city, but bright lights always cast long shadows. I could see the death like a red dun glow shrouding the city. I roared into the city, my black Lincoln Continental Mark III's engine drowning out Queen on the radio.

The clock tower of the old red brick post office dominated Mort Cheval's downtown. People in Mort Cheval loved giving directions by where places used to be, or what they used to be. It gave the citizens a means to sort out who didn't belong. The post office-then-library-now-art gallery was among the tallest buildings in a city that had spread out, not up, gobbling farmland instead of reaching at the stars.

Lines of death stretched from all over the city to the gallery. To where the Long Night waited. Waited for me.

Waited for Midnight.

Down the hill and in the city, the streetlamps came on one by one.

It was going to be a long night.

. . . going to be a long night . . .

. . . a long night . . .

. . . long night . . .

Long Night.

The lullaby repeated as a round, after every rhyme completed, a chorus of *Long Night, longest night* from the lips of fresh victims here and unseen, dead hundreds, stretching before I was born. My lips moved, but soundlessly.

A voice teased from the darkness, "*Almost there . . .*"
The funeral home became more nightmarish as I stepped deeper in. Bodies, everywhere. Some I recognized from funerals before I'd gone to university, bodies I'd helped inter dug out of their rest, others I didn't know at all. My parents would know them. They knew everybody.
Eventually.
An impact from behind drove me to a knee. I tried to scream, releasing a wheezing grunt, as if I'd been stabbed in the back. Something thick and wet dribbled down my back. I *had* been stabbed. I reached for the knife to pull it out and slapped the handle with my flailing hand. Pain exploded from the knife into my body. Then, fear. Adrenaline. Strength. The knife came free as I pulled away to see who'd attacked me.
My parents were alive.

It was going to be a long night.
I was in the art gallery entrance. Bricked in. I'd gotten complacent, betting I could stride right in, perky as piss, ball-and-chain bomb to lock him in, Tombstone bullets and he'd drop. Like all my enemies. But the Long Night kept dragging me through his illusory abattoir. It felt as if he'd spent days making me relive the same moments. My Grave Sight had led me to the gallery but the bodies inside shimmered and faded with my touch.
I yelled at the shadows, "Where are they?"
"Who?" He cackled like a cartoon supervillain. "My 'victims'? They don't matter. Not yet. I've been waiting for *you*. And you walked. Right. In."
"*. . . Walk among them, he will be you*
Try to fight him, he will be you
Long Night, longest night. Long Night, longest night . . ."
The Long Night's song bored into my brain. I ground another caffeine pill between my teeth. How many had I taken? I needed

to be focused. Sharp. I needed sleep, but I couldn't sleep. The overwhelming bitter taste would help keep me alert until the drug actually hit my system. Couldn't let the Long Night keep luring me into the past. If he did, fates worse than death in the Graveside world are cheaper than chewing gum.

The Long Night oozed out of a crack in the hardwoods, a bloody shape wearing a Ministry t-shirt and torn jeans that could've been ripped right out of my university closet, and wafting a stink like an outhouse in July. I blinked and he sat in a simple wooden chair, surrounded by shapes half-hidden in shadow, the bodies fixed upon the walls.

"Welcome back, *Midnight Man*. Almost there." The words came out amid a grim chuckle. The scorn he'd heaped on my name was a casual backhand. One I was well-used to. He'd said: "Welcome back." I've heard him say that before . . . How many times had he said it? How many times had I failed to stop him?

"I've heard of you, Protector," he continued. "And your '*Fight.*' While you wait to die, I want you to know: *you* are the reason I'm *here*. *You* are the reason *these* people will die. So that I continue to live, and to kill."

I love a good monologue. Usually, I was the one delivering them, invisible, from the shadows. But I'd heard this one before and I had no time for it. "You kill because you want to kill."

"And why do *you* kill?"

I didn't answer.

The Long Night's chuckle cascaded through his flaunted puppets, one by one. "After I kill you, I'll *be* you. I only go where someone worthy might try and stop me. Next solstice, *your* hands will make *my* art. All your fault. If only you could have stopped me."

"If you're gonna do something, just do it already."

The Long Night glided closer to whisper in my ear, his voice an apple peeler slicing through my will's thin veneer. "Did you know you can die from sleep deprivation? Something gets lost when dreams and nightmares become reality, when you can't tell the three apart. There are things hungering beyond sleep's veil. Things that will core you out, fill you up, and walk you around. Things. Like. Me."

I wondered how long we'd been doing this dance. It felt like forever. Maybe he was right. Maybe I *was* dying. My folks, conjured from my nightmares, watched dead-eyed and singing from above. The hardest thing about seeing them again was seeing them as I remembered them, the only way I *can* remember them, an image I'd tried to bury with them. I laughed through the pain. *Nothing* stays buried in Mort Cheval for long.

My parents weren't alive.

But they *were* moving.

Their killer had made no effort to preserve them. Had let them rot and bloat and stink. They'd filled with fetid gasses and insect colonies while being used as marionettes. A button popped off my dad's jacket as he expanded further. Flesh sloughed off. Fluids sluiced and oozed from their pant legs, squelching under discoloured feet. Decedents never looked the same. Never looked alive, despite embalmers' best efforts. They couldn't. Because the people you loved were alive, and you were viewing the dead. Tonight, I wasn't looking at anyone's "best effort".

I still knew their silhouettes before they stepped from the shadows. I kept the Hades cap on, not to be safe. If anything of my parents remained in their shells, I didn't want them to see what I was going to do. We didn't keep guns in the house. My father didn't hunt. He'd seen too much of what weapons could do to a body.

I crept back to the kitchen for a knife . . .

". . . *But winter's night lives within you*
Sun starts dying, he is now you
Long Night, longest night. Long Night, longest night . . ."

"What do they matter to you, these strangers?" The Long Night whispered with my voice, through my parents' lips. "Who are they to you?"

I told myself the Fight was justified. That I could make a difference. It didn't seem like the Long Night had access to my *real* nightmares or dreams, but he could shove me in that direction. Dreams or nightmares, for me they're flip sides of the same coin. In my dreams I'm somebody else. Someone who never needed to be me. In my nightmares, Midnight Man never found his way to me, never became *me*. I'd remained powerless, small. Locked in a life without Midnight Man. Trapped in a life where I couldn't fight back.

The shapes hidden by the shadows stepped into the light. Hannah was there. Will, my middle school bully. Carollers I'd passed on the street.

"Just kill them and I won't make you see it again. You'll never have to relive *that* killing again."

It wasn't enough for him to murder innocents every year. He wanted *me* to do it for him. Did he think this revelation would break me? As if I'd never sweat through the night unsure if I was awake or dreaming. He might believe I'd never faced anything worse than him. He might believe I'd never worried I'd become the thing I fought against.

I needed to ground myself in something real. The Hades cap. The thing that'd kept me alive the first time. The first piece of my uniform. The beginning of my look. My identity. I focused in on my uniform, on the look, rebuilding it piece by piece in my mind, feeling its reality.

He'd made a mistake showing me my parents. He'd made a mistake letting me keep the look. The Long Night had reminded me that *he* wasn't why I did this. There would *always* be another monster. I breathed in the leather stink of my Hades cap, soaked in years of sweat, though still supple, and remembered labours past . . . What I'd done. *Why* I did it. Why I fought.

So others didn't have to.

I'd never been in a real fight before that night. Only dust-ups at country drinking parties. Nothing where my life was on the line.

Only it wasn't a fight.

Not really.

I could see them and they couldn't see me.

My parents' bodies shambled around the funeral home, pawing and sniffing the air, trying to pinpoint the intruder. Looking for me. I could still escape. Run and never come back. But eventually, someone would come to check on my parents. And that person would die. And that death would be my fault.

So, I slipped behind them. I cut tendons to make them fall. Whatever animated them still needed their bodies to function. But they wouldn't stop coming for me. Crawling. Gnashing. Groaning and croaking. They wouldn't stop until they were stopped. Completely. I stopped them. Limb by limb, joint by joint, humming as I worked to drown out the kitchen knife sawing, I made sure they couldn't hurt anyone else.

They could still hurt me plenty.

The song. The bloody fucking unending song.

"... *Hear his song and it is too late*
Sing along and seal your own fate
Long Night, longest night. Long Night, longest night . . ."

"You failed. Failed to save your parents. Failed to avenge them. Failed even to honour their remains. There's so little *you* left. Fight if you want, but you're just a hollow costume."

Costume. I ground my teeth at the insult.

It would be easy to give in. Lay up the guns. Take off the uniform. Let the Fight belong to someone—anyone—else. All I had to do is sing his song and mean it.

I used to think my parents were weak. If they'd been strong, they would've gotten out, or they would've fought. That was a mistake, grief and rage speaking. They must've fought. They died to give me a warning. A chance to get out.

I hadn't gotten out, only deeper in.

By the time I came home on the Solstice, my parents were dead. By Christmas I'd killed them (again). Or I put them at peace, if you preferred a more positive industry euphemism. At peace, but not avenged. The clock struck twelve on New Year's Eve: Midnight Man was born.

I was finally *me*.

I focused on that sound. On midnight, a liminal space between the days, but still *night*. Still *now*.

"Don't pretend you're special. You'll be another vessel. There were many before you. There will be many after you. This. Will. Not. End. *I* will not end."

"No, I don't think I'll be your vessel. Every night has an end, even you." I drew my pistol; from the weight, it felt empty. I had to hope he didn't know. He'd studied me, but I'd studied him too. I bet he thought I wanted to use it on myself. Protect my honour. Go out on my own terms. The gun was a distraction. He fell for it. He rushed me. I broke my last ball-and-chain bomb against my jacket and smiled as its silver dust enveloped me. Whether he'd been lying about coring me out or not, my spirit was now stuck in *this* body, and *he* wasn't getting in.

His illusions dropped, my parents' leering corpses faded with them. There were no bodies displayed. The gallery returned to normal, except standing, unmoving, were the people the Long Night had wanted me to kill. The once-and-future victims sang the Long Night's song but I scarcely heard it. The Long Night's "true" form—his nightmare self—cracked out of his host, revealing a starry night beneath the skin. Arctic cold radiated from every seam.

When I'd crushed the ball-and-chain bomb, it hadn't just coated *my* body. The Long Night walked right into that same silvery cloud. I could only hope it would lock the Long Night inside his current vessel.

Palms stretched skin and flesh to the limit, seeking escape, but it crumbled like a dry cookie. Tears trickled from each eye. His rasping laugh now alternated shrieking and weeping while eyes bled until only inky blackness remained.

The clock on the wall ticked over to midnight. The dead bodies may have faded from sight but they hadn't faded from memory: Hannah, Will, the nameless carollers. They ran. Had they heard everything that he'd said? Seen what I'd seen? Did they know what I'd done? Who I was? Were they afraid of him, or me? It didn't matter.

Outside, the holiday lights flickered and blinked. The streetlamps were lit. Another memory flashed in my mind, a true memory, not some singalong nightmare courtesy of The Long Night. Words meant to be comforting at my parents' funeral. "The sun always waits. Even at the end of the longest night." People might sleep soundly knowing night had to end. Not me. There were always other monsters waiting in the dark. I laughed.

The night wasn't over yet.

LIMBO OF SUN
AND SHADOW

LAURA VANARENDONK BAUGH

 It is the first day of falling back from Daylight Saving Time to standard, so I can go out an hour earlier.

Of course, it's not truly an hour earlier; neither the sun nor my body heeds the wanton change of digital clocks. I am old, and I still think of noon as the moment when the sun is highest.

Yet greater even than mankind's hubris at ordering the cosmos according to an arbitrary notion of when rush hour should start is the hubris of denying night altogether, as has been done on the Strip. It is a glorious, ghastly rendering of—not neon, not for years now, but LEDs and other lights, glowing and flashing and beaming into space. It is bright on the crowded sidewalks, approaching twilight only when the large screens briefly switch from bright to dark colours, and a heartbeat later the dark is banished once more.

This is when I can go out.

I start along the street, matching the pace of the crowd that drifts in apathetic languor. We pass shops and kiosks which offer vapes and drinks, snacks and drinks, desserts and drinks, and drinks and drinks. We pass beneath advertisements for circus shows, magic shows, strip shows. We pass vending machines selling flat shoes for women whose feet can no longer bear the expected high heels.

I tip back my head, closing my eyes against the thirty-foot tall images of singers distorted by plastic surgery and Photoshop, and I inhale. The air reeks of cigarette smoke and exhaust, and yet it is fresher than the air inside, which is far denser with smoke and additionally laden with perfume, sweat, musk, pretense, desperation.

I have lived in Las Vegas for six years, although it feels like much longer. This Strip is the one place on earth where night both least exists and is constant. By day, tourists are lured into windowless buildings where light is carefully managed, curating an ever-night to blur the passing of time, to delay meals, to lose inhibitions, to loosen wallets. The flashing lights from slot machines and advertising screens are the only sun, worshipped by obedient adherents who believe that if they watch more closely, serve more dearly, spend more freely, they will be blessed with happiness, however ephemeral.

By night, the streets are lit in a blaze of consumerism, celebrating the religious rituals of commerce. Over $485 million dollars are spent each year to light the Strip into its blazing glory. It is a refuge from both the accountability of day and the intimacy of night.

And I loathe it. I miss the night sky, which I have not seen in years. I miss grass and trees—things which exist in this place only as incomplete and hungry ghosts. Palm trees tower over the walkways, growing up from concrete basins, their roots never touching a sister plant. Flowers grow at some of the nicer resorts, but no pollinators drink from their sterilized petals. Everything here is dead to the world around it, carefully staged in scenes meant to help visitors forget they are dying.

I stop at the Venetian, because I am a masochist. I cross the wide water features (ridiculous in a desert, but no less so than many competitors' aesthetics) and climb to the porch. Here, if I rest my hands on the railing and close my eyes to mere slits and ignore the canned pop music, I can almost remember other times. I can almost remember parties, arguments, laughter, feasts. I ache for those memories.

The Venetian is a cruelty. It was in Venice that I left my mortality behind, one night at a party lit by small flames reflecting in a hundred tiny pieces of glass. It was in Venice that I had my last glimpse of family and frailty and my first taste of predatory power.

I did not stay in Venice; it was awkward to be in the same place but in a different position. But Venice's ports led to all the world, and I had new longings for travel, and for other things.

Now I am trapped here, pinned not only in place but in time, and I chafe.

I go into the Venetian and walk along the shopping mall modelled upon a canal. Above me, the painted sky is perpetually blue and mildly sunny, enough to give an impression of day but not enough to disturb the careful manipulation of light. A saleswoman pushes a sample packet of skin cream at me as her partner insists he can clear my wrinkles. His accent . . . He is from Heidelberg originally, I think. His inaccurate accusation of wrinkles does not offend me. He is only doing his job, quickly flashing a warning of age and death and then as quickly offering a reprieve for a price.

It is ironic that I, for practical purposes immortal, must come to this city of defying death to put off my own.

I listen to the gentle splashing of the gondolas rocking with rowdy tourists, and I find a place on a bridge to stand and pretend. It is not stone under my hand, and the buildings around me are painted facades full of sequined plastic from sweatshops. The sky is only fresco. But it is the nearest thing to day that I have known in a long time, and the nearest to home, and what is the Strip if not the promise of something almost, but not quite, what we long for?

There are so few of us that even in a place like this I am the only one. That is good—we can be territorial predators, and I'm not sure I could bear to watch another walk in the dark without my restrictions—but at the same time, the Strip is a lonely place for those whose needs run beyond the hedonic.

At last, I leave the canal shops and go back to the street. Outside, the sky is real, if invisible. There is a single shoe abandoned on the sidewalk, undamaged. A man is lying against a concrete barrier, propped against it like a side sleeper without a pillow. It looks like one of the more uncomfortable positions against it, but it may be how he landed, unmoved since. He is waving a cigarette and reviewing aloud all the ways he has been wronged.

Two women dressed in fishnets and pasties rub and grope on the sidewalk, breasts sliding over each other, hoping the watching men will tip them or pay for pictures. Another set, these dressed as showgirls, stump up the sidewalk in their difficult boots, trolling for tourist photos. They pause and exchange greetings with the fishnets set, all of them falling out of character briefly. Then they are on their way again, each set admonishing the other to "Be safe!" It's a wish worth a discarded sequin in a place where women are a commodity, routinely bought and sold.

I wonder what the priest would have thought of his curse trapping me in such a place, binding me as my despair slowly grows to a tipping point.

You might think a creature like myself could not be further cursed, but that would be short-sighted. Nature is often a collection of compromises; the horse gained greater speed to elude predators in exchange for more fragile legs. I am a fearsome predator, but I cannot bear the sun. This should make the Las Vegas Strip a most hospitable place, with nights calculated to bring as many potential victims into milling chaotic circulation as possible, a city where predation is sold as just another experience.

But that priest cursed me further. I do not know what variety of holy man he was—Anglican, or Eastern Orthodox, or Catholic, or something else. I was bored enough to choose more dangerous prey, but not bored enough to note the details. And I paid for that folly.

I saw in his face the moment when he realized I was no casual mugger, when he recognized me for what I was. "Wait!" he protested. "I can help you!"

I bared my teeth. I did not want to be helped. I was not the one who needed help.

He said something else, but I was not listening. I killed him in the usual way. And as he bled through my hands and upon the sidewalk, he whispered and gurgled his curse. "The night will consume you," he choked. "I pray . . . You will be consumed by the sun's shadow, and your evil will die . . ."

Consumed by the sun's shadow. I did not understand at first. But the next evening when I went out to hunt, I stepped out my door and into the dark, and I felt the assault. Night reached for me. Darkness crept upon my skin, giving me goosebumps and a sensation of something first crawling and then *clawing*. I had to flee back into a cave of artificial light, afraid for the first time of my natural domain.

His dying curse of a prayer set the night to hunt me, as I've hunted others, and now I cannot bear the sun, which seeks to burn me to ash, and I cannot bear the dark, which seeks something more.

Each segment of sidewalk is blasting different classic pop mainstays, so that I hear roughly two lines of each different song as I make my way through the crowd. The songs compete with the buskers—a woman playing violin versions of the current Top 40, a man playing classical guitar.

I walk south. An aging singer towers over me like a kaiju, face contorted mid-note until the image rotates, glowing with commercial nostalgia. A middle-aged woman stands crying on the sidewalk, while a man beside her asks rather pointlessly if she is all right.

I wonder what kind of meal I will find tonight.

There is an enormous hollow *crack*! like a snapping tree trunk, and every light goes dark. All the Strip, at once, like the falling of a hammer. People shriek first in surprise, and then mock horror, and then indignation as some take advantage of the dark.

I feel it. There is something on my skin, something touching me through the dark, through the air, through my clothing. It is grasping me. Claws slide over me, rose canes tearing my flesh, scraping but not quite holding—not while I am beside a group of tourists raising their phone screens to light one another and me.

I wrap my arms about myself in useless defence and edge nearer the group.

There is a woman with them, and her long black gown does not match their short sparkling minidresses. They do not speak to her as they laugh and curse their phones' flashlights, which fall into her matte dress like a void. She is looking at me. She *sees* me. Her eyes are deep and unblinking, and the irises glitter like dark moissanite, and she stands among the sequined women who do not see her and she looks only at me.

Night has come. I turn and I run.

It is foolish, for how can one outrun the night? And where can I hope to go? Already the blackout chaos is spreading. It is not entirely dark; the headlights on the boulevard make a river of light, and phone screens and cheap LED souvenirs are everywhere. But the Strip has fallen to ordinary night, and that is enough to make a difference for me. There is no shroud of artificial light between me and the dark of night.

Horns are blaring, with the traffic lights gone. I dash through the intersection, slapping hoods and fenders to change course as I weave through. I rush toward Caesar's Palace, hoping to hide among the false ruins.

But she is waiting for me on the far sidewalk. She stands beside a fountain, cheap to build and expensive to fill, and she watches me slow as I approach her. I consider running again, but I return to that inevitable truth: one cannot outrun the night.

Generators kick on inside some of the buildings, offering glimpses of hesitant light through the doorways. But the massive screens and displays on the street will be the last to be restored. Her black gown clings to her and yet drapes smoothly, rippling in an endless black that gives back almost no reflection. When she trails the fingers of one hand through the fountain, I can see a glitter of scattered silver within her hanging sleeve. She looks like an Art Deco rendering of an ancient goddess.

"I will fight you," I warn, though I do not know how I intend to wrestle an entity who can snuff out the Strip like a candle and leap six lanes of angry traffic.

She smiles, the patient smile of someone who has waited for years and is prepared to wait through one final, useless tantrum. Then she lifts the hand in the fountain and turns up her palm, and water droplets fall like stars. "You have tried."

I have tried. For so many years, I have tried. And I am so tired of trying to fight, of trying to flee, of trying to survive in this place that is meant to be something other than a place to live. I am so tired of living in a perpetual twilight and watching the worst of society prey on each other, an unsatisfied ouroboros. I am wearied and despairing.

When she looks at me, her expression carries neither smug victory nor despising disgust. She speaks again, and she offers sympathy. "We could talk first."

I did not expect this. I am weakened with futility and unexpected kindness. I stare at her, the fight drained from me. I have nothing to say.

"It is hard to resist the inevitable." Her voice is somehow soft even through the honking traffic.

I am still bitter. "He cursed me. He cursed me to die."

Her expression softens. "Is that what you think?" She gestures, encompassing the dark city and the greater world. "Are you not already dead? What have you been doing, hiding here for so long, if not dying?"

I want to argue, but I have nothing left. She has pursued me to exhaustion. I am ready to end—end the hunt, the curse, existence.

She extends a hand to me, showing little sparkles again within her sleeve. "Will you come, now, at last?"

I briefly consider running again, but I know I have nowhere to go. I bow my head and step into the inevitable.

She raises her arms, black fabric cascading endlessly. She envelopes me in an embrace, wrapping me in velvet darkness. Star-pricks gleam through the dark—not enough light to see by, but a promise of hope in the infinite black. I close my eyes and let myself fall into the abyss.

Death is far more terrifying in the abstract than in the moment.

I wait for a long time, suspended in the dark. I should no longer be thinking. I should no longer be thinking about the fact that I am thinking. I am still here—somehow, in whatever meaning *here* has now for me.

I open my eyes, to learn if I have eyes. I do. She is still beside me. Stars dangle from her ears and her expansive cloak waves over both of us in indigo, purple, midnight. We are sitting together, shoulder to shoulder.

She feels warm.

I test my voice and learn I can speak. "What happened?"

Consumed by the sun's shadow . . .

But I am still here. Or, part of me is. I can see. I can speak. I can feel her against my arm.

She turns her head and kisses my temple. When I look at her, starlight shimmers in her hair. And then she tugs her dark mantle down and it settles like mist on my face, and I cannot see in the darkness.

I raise my hand to rub my eyes clear. I blink, and I see the faint silhouettes of signboards and empty streetlights. I sit up on the edge of the fountain, and the three men walking by ignore me in a studied way. To them, I am only another overindulging tourist.

But what am I to myself?

I look down at my hands, and they seem no different. I run my tongue along my teeth; they are ordinary teeth, but they usually are except when feeding.

I stand and look around. The blackout is still in effect, but for the occasional windows of rooms served by generators. The voids where advertising should be are almost disturbing; the street has become a new kind of liminal space.

You will be consumed by the sun's shadow, and your evil will die.

I don't understand. I am not dead. I . . .

I pinch the back of my hand savagely, tearing the skin. I watch. Blood seeps from my injured flesh, just as it might on any hand. Just as it has not since that candlelit night in Venice.

Your evil will die.

His curse did not doom me. His curse doomed my curse.

—Oh, God.

I stare at the pavement between my feet, struggling against nausea. I did not want to be saved. I did not know I could be saved. I did not know I killed my saviour.

The natural horror all things feel at undeath has returned to me, newly purged as I am of my inoculating immortality. I want to retch, I want to flee, I want to plunge again into the abyss and find a deeper void where I would not feel or remember. I have been something horrific.

For a long time, I sit, afraid to move. I imagine myself vomiting up old blood, and I squeeze my eyes against the image even though I had not yet fed tonight. I don't know how to think; I am too newly flung into human emotion once more.

At last, I feel less nauseated. I dip my hand in the fountain and pass it over my face. Perhaps the sickness was also due to whatever had just happened to my anatomy; the first change was unpleasant, too. But I know the horror will return, like a second wave of grief.

I rise on weak legs and walk up the stairs to a pedestrian overpass, unwilling to risk the snarl of honking cars competing through the intersection without traffic signals. The crowd is not as thick; some must have given up on waiting for the lights and returned to their dark hotel rooms. I pause at the middle of the overpass and look down the street.

There are stars. They are barely visible in the haze of headlights, but they are returning.

"They cannot keep me out forever."

A woman stands a few paces from me, leaning upon the overpass rail and looking at the sky. She wears ordinary black jeans and a silk blouse, and her hair does not shimmer with pinpricks of light, but I know her.

"All nights must come to an end, they say. And they are right. But all nights do come." She smiles, content in her power.

I should feel something specific about her, but I am exhausted with feeling, and I have only vague awe left. But I am not afraid; if she meant to hurt me, it would be done already.

I lick my lips and offer a pale scrap of apology. "I thought I would be consumed."

Her expression sobers. "True darkness is an absence of light," she says softly. "But shadow, even one so great as the sun's shadow, is born of light." She looks down at the railing. "He meant to find someone like you. You found him before we were ready."

My throat closes, and I sway slightly against the railing, overcome again. Then she is beside me, her arm around me, her hair falling over me. "The intensity will pass," she whispers. "Not the reckoning, but the intensity."

I nod and draw back reluctantly. "What now? What am I now?"

"Now, you have a choice." She gestures to encompass the dim city. "You can return to an ordinary life, pretending you have only mortal memories, or you can share with others the help you've received." Her face was grave. "It will not be easy to offer a cure. You considered yourself evolved rather than diseased."

I swallow against my tight throat. "How did he know it would work?"

She gazes across the dead buildings. "It worked for him." She raises a hand and points between buildings. "Look."

The sky is grey and pink, the opening of dawn. I automatically tense, and then I realize I no longer need fear the light. I stare as the sky brightens, brilliant gold over the dull, unlit Sphere.

Beside me, she sighs, part resignation and part satisfaction. She does something—I see nothing, but I *feel* her act—and lights flicker along the street, dancing into sparkling billboards and flashing marquees. A hundred different speakers come to life and compete with different songs. Night is lifted off the Strip.

I can go. I can leave this place and go anywhere. I can dine in rooms of happy conversing people, eat real food with a thousand flavours. I can see the sun each day, and the stars by night, and I may even bring the sun to someone else.

Gold spreads in the sky, and the first low streaks break through the towers and touch my face. I close my eyes and breathe in the light.

MORMOLYKIA

Thomas C. Mavroudis

 I drive to keep from killing. I'll say that much.

Before I go out, I wash the car. Nothing fancy—it's a wreck in daylight. I vacuum the bits of trash, the undefinable remnants of people: skin, hair, other dead cells.

I vacuum black salt scattered beneath the driver's seat like a nebula of dead stars. The salt doesn't start out black. It's not some trendy culinary extravagance from Whole Foods. It's generic kosher salt. I turn it black. The presence inside me turns it black.

So long as I shake fresh salt under my seat before the sun sets, everything is okay.

I drive without frills, no gum or mints, no spare phone chargers. I get thirsty, so I bring an extra bottle of water. Sometimes I have to give it up. If necessary, or if I am in dire need of gasoline, and if it's not too late, I'll get another bottle in the convenience store.

I play music, mostly jazz and blues. If it's the holiday season, I'll play Christmas music. When it's Stock Show time, I play old country tunes. If a passenger asks, I'll let them jack into my cord (no Bluetooth) and play their own. I get more compliments than complaints, yet I still can't get one fucking badge for awesome tunes.

Excuse me.

Overall, my rating is consistently in the high-fours and that's fine, especially if I'm outside downtown and pretty much the only ride after 2:30 a.m.

As far as other badges, I do have eleven for great service and eight for going over the top. For some reason I have one for "cool car"—it's a grey Corolla.

I keep the salt in the glovebox with the insurance and registration. Two boxes of it. When one is completely empty, not a single grain rattling in the cardboard, I replace it.

Tonight, after a few snappy jaunts in a rough two-mile orbit, I pick up Sage from an apartment complex that's reported to have been built on top of an old Catholic hospital's graveyard. The second she says *hi*, I feel my personal commuter twitch. It trickles from my pores, through the fabric of my clothes and the seat, through the foam and plastic, collecting in a thumbprint of salt, filling each grain with darkness like smoke in a bubble.

Sage gets on her phone immediately. I don't mind. I never mind. Her destination is across downtown. It's early enough in the evening that it'll take a little more than twenty minutes. I hear but don't really listen:

". . . so exhausted. Yeah, the snow was great. No. It's beautiful in town . . ."

In this city, people have forgotten how traffic signals work, especially the red light. I don't think they've ever seen a green left arrow before. Or green right arrow, for that matter. It's a balance, appeasing the laws of traffic, appeasing the impatient, the impractical of humanity. Imbalance is dangerous.

". . . meeting Mike. Yeah, he's working, but his shift's over at nine, so I'll just hang out at the bar. All right, call you tomorrow."

The light turns green and we finally cross into the southeast corridor of downtown. Without surprise, a horn blasts from behind at the driver in the lane next to me scrolling their phone. The street's busy, but traffic flows. Not more than ten blocks from where we started, I hear a rhythmic buzz in the back and can see in the rearview mirror that Sage has dozed off. Makes sense, that unending stop and go drive down the mountain. A little powernap won't hurt her. I won't hurt her. My feet burn, turning the calluses to ash—the entity struggling to resist the pull of the salt. Her comfort is my grief. At another stoplight, I roll the balls of my feet, crack my toes, grind my heels to the floorboard.

With about eight minutes left in the trip, I start coughing, clearing my throat. Howlin' Wolf comes on, talking about a spoonful. I turn the volume up.

I take a turn a little rougher than normal, faster, intending to jar Sage awake. We come to a straightaway with sparse traffic. Sage's phone rings, a klaxon. She groans and declines the call, otherwise undisturbed. I crank the volume and roll all the windows down a sliver, late winter air seeps in.

I relent. "Hey, Sage."

A thousand feet to destination and the windows are all the way down. It's not cold enough for a freeze out. "Linus and Lucy" hits the speakers next, the volume at max, Vince Guaraldi's piano coming down like hail and lightning on a tin awning. I pull to the curb.

"We're here, Sage," I yell.

Nothing.

Calling the number the app uses to disguise Sage's real number, her phone rings, the sonic blast clashing with the music. Then my phone blares, intoning I have a new passenger to pick up. I decline it. Another pings. And another. And another. I have to switch off the app so I stop missing opportunities. I consider prodding Sage's knee. I don't, but I want to. The thing inside wants to. It wants to grab Sage's knee, claw away her kneecap and taste it, but the more it wants, the more it drips into the salt.

Turning off the car, I look around outside to see if someone is obviously waiting for her, but there is nobody.

"Hey, Sage! Come on . . ."

Sighing, I open my door. The dome lights come aflame like a fake dawn. Sage snores, unwittingly covering her face with her hair.

I don't like to get out of the car unless I'm alone. It's risky. And if I do, it's not for very long. Seven, eight minutes tops. I don't want to get out of the car, but I can't just sit here all night and do fucking nothing.

I'm sorry.

Driving is how I focus, how I stay grounded. The daylight

hours I spend alone, physically and mentally drained in bed, night after night driving from sundown to sunup. No vacation, no recreation, stranger after stranger, and this thing inside me, this ravenous thing that is more than hunger, a desire we are unarmed to experience. Pleasure and reckoning. Satiation and fury. Can you imagine that wonder, if you could embrace those feelings unyielding?

"Okay, Sage, we've got to get you going now."

I get out of the car and peer into the back window to see if she stirred at all with the beeping and the clunking of the machinery. Nothing. I slam my door shut so the car actually shimmies. Still sleeping. The presence is fixated on Sage, it doesn't notice we are away from the salt. Until I enter the tavern and it rushes to the ends of my fingertips.

I select one of two bartenders, the younger, Ken Doll-like one, and say, "Does anyone here know a woman named Sage?"

He closes his eyes and takes a deep breath. "Shit. Is she asleep?"

"Yes," I respond. "So, this is something that happens?"

He nods. "I'll get her."

He is gentle, kind, loving. The thing inside me floods my system with detestable sensations. My hands burn and itch. My teeth pulse. I can feel the beginning of a hard on.

When Sage finally awakens, she is frightened. I bite the inside of my cheek to stay focused, to prevent the thing from screeching, or whistling, or growling—from making the sound that is all three. Her eyes roll, trying to recognize this bartender's face. Her eyes are empty and I feel how sweet it would be to occupy that space, to plunge her nails into his chest and bite through his lips, blood and lipstick mingling in a lascivious jelly.

"Thanks again," he says, helping her to her feet and away inside.

I quickly get back behind the steering wheel. There is a moment before I do, a release of tension like when a nagging headache disappears. The relief is temporary, looking at the driver's side door. There is pressure in my eyes, buzzing in my ears, my bowels cramp. It will all go away if I just stay out of the car. Dusty oil drip-drip-drips from me, splashing the shards of kosher salt. I can hear each splash, and the crystals drinking the aberrant influence inside, like one universe absorbing another into itself.

I roll my neck, the bones crack. The popping feels good, better than the poison leeched from my skin.

I start the car, turn down the music, and turn the app back on. An immediate ping. Santiago is at a restaurant only three blocks away.

When I arrive, Santiago nods at me, getting in. He has earbuds in.

Home, I think, looking at his destination east of downtown. This sort of passenger, even more focused than I am, is the kind I like best because the entity finds it so unappetizing. Actually, it finds him bland, and the thing inside me is actually bored. I can feel its uneasy apathy. These respites are nice, but I know if every ride was like this, both the entity and I would descend into desperate unpredictability. My frustration, my irritation with other drivers, it's just chips and doughnuts for the shade inside. I do my best not to let one-star passengers get to me.

I accept another ride halfway through the drive. This is perfect. Keep busy.

It's the long drives back to civilization that are difficult. The payouts are worth it, but on those stretches of road on the lonely, dark plains, all by myself (mainly by myself), my mind wanders, my focus evaporates like water on a nightstand. I try not to take too many rides out into the country where I know the chances of return fares are slim. But I can't snub them either. It's balance. Balance is the key to survival. Not just my own.

I drop off and I pick up. It's that time of night, and I'm in a section of suburbs where folks are going home or going to work, shifts over and shifts beginning. I'm not even halfway through my work.

A group of guys in sunglasses, smelling of four conflicting colognes, compliment my "old timey" music and get me back downtown. Then it's an underage group of girls complaining how the bouncers took their fake IDs *and* their vapes. Couples, out-of-towners, more people going to work or going home.

The constant stimulation is enough to placate my traveller. It is enticed and the black salt keeps it from becoming ravenous.

Balance.

And then over half of the night is gone. Every night, when the car is clean and full of gas, when I turn on the app, it feels like I've just taken my first step into a type of purgatory, an infinity of neither rest nor torment, simply unending. The first thirty minutes drag into an hour, the first two hours crawl into a viscous evening. But the faces and voices shuffle, tips and bonuses collect, music plays, and I arrive at the way station of night. There is less of it at this point. And these last few hours are usually the most strenuous.

It's difficult to get more than one ride at last call. Sometimes I can snag two. It seems though that many of those revellers dedicated to seeing the house lights turn on in the club often live far away, making the most of their time out. This is how I typically end up on the fringes in the quiet, lonely dark. Just me and the thing inside: the thing begging for company.

I get off the highway on an arterial street with a three mile stretch of hotels. It's plastic hope; if I were going to get a ride, I would have been pinged on the highway.

At this point, dawn a few hours away, with the entity well-subdued once again, its power and influence absorbed and neutralized in so much salt, the primary obstacle is staying awake. Naturally, I am also drained, but that is what the presence hopes for. A predator snared in a trap, weakened and starved, lies in wait.

The request from Niko startles me like a fish biting a line. The dose of adrenaline is good and pure. I am renewed, and inside me, the thing settles, defeated, too tired to care about the prospect of sustenance. There is always tomorrow, I think it might believe.

Nightclubs, restaurants, hotels, music venues, even many bars will show on the app by name. But not strip clubs.

Hidden behind office parks, dispensaries, and a Target, I was surprised Razzle Dazzle was still open. This little pocket district was under major redevelopment, just like most of the city, not to mention that it seemed like it changed hands (and names) at least once a year. The last time I drove past, maybe a summer ago, it was called Platinum Gold.

Closed for at least an hour, I'm not sure who I'm expecting to pick up.

Out on the sidewalk is a man in a dark sport coat with long wavy hair and sunglasses. What is it with these guys and sunglasses? I drive a few yards past and pull a U-turn. He waves at me panicked, as if I'll desert him.

He opens the door, asks my name. When I confirm I am who he's waiting for, he steps back into shadow and leads out an almost too thin woman with a duffle bag, helping her into the car. She is young, pretty. Her head rolls around, her shoulders weave, her eyes are half closed. She wants what's in the bag, fumbling with the zipper and he tells her to wait. Then he gets in after, almost on top of her. "Move," he says in a sing-song way.

"Thanks for the pick-up," Niko says, as though I do this out of the goodness of my heart. He reeks of bitter cigarettes.

The destination is in the hills, as I predicted. A good fare for the time of night, but they both make me uneasy, which interests my companion.

"No, Didi," he barks, like *she* was a dog. "Later."

I watch Didi in my rearview. I hope she will relax, or pass out, even though that will arouse the entity like with Sage. She flashes brief moments of awareness. Looks around the car agitated, glances at the night world rushing by outside the cold window. Then she disappears again, a body on autopilot. She keeps trying to open the bag and Niko keeps stopping her. His castigation does not escalate. He doesn't seem to be the sort of person to carry a lot of patience, but obviously, if he won't let her have whatever is in the bag, he won't smack her in front of me.

The freeway is nearly empty except for the usual cross-country semis. We move fast, but time slackens, or the distance extends. Behind me, I sense the rising glow of a new day, but that's just wishful thinking.

Didi starts humming. She is humming to the music, Count Basie's "April in Paris", coming to a little more. Her movements are less involuntary, more dance-like. I turn up the music a tiny bit for her.

Off the freeway, into a round-about, and along the edge of the hills, there are stop lights and reduced speed, with ten minutes still estimated for the trip. The adjacent town is dreaming.

"More," Didi says. At first, I think she means what is in her bag, but when Niko doesn't protest, I realize she means more music.

Let's say *I* change the music. The music changes regardless, the volume increased. Razor guitars, an electric march of drum beats, and soul-splitting bass rip from the shabby speakers. The music is accompanied by a hum that may or may not be outside my head.

I look back at Didi. Her eyes are closed but she is grooving. Niko has a big smile on his face. A revel has begun.

And in me, a key has slipped into a lock, and turned.

The salt works. Trust me. Nothing has gone wrong. I am in control.

And yet, I am filled to the ends with the being; it stretches the limits of my skin, it swells my tongue and bulges my eyes. Appropriately, I suppose, it is pressed against the glass of a peep show.

In the back, Didi has slipped off her fuzzy black hoodie. She draws her T-shirt up, teasing her ribs. Niko cheers and claps his hands. He's lit a cigarette without cracking the window.

The road winds up a low mesa engulfed with aspens. In just a thousand feet, we come to an estate overlooking the north side of town.

"Hold up," Niko says. He gets out, thinks for a second, and then punches a code on the keypad at the gate. The iron of the gate makes me tingle with the sort of electric shock that is not necessarily unpleasant.

Meanwhile, I notice Didi dip into her bag, put her hands to her face.

"Fuck, goddammit, Didi! Can't you just hold on for one god-dammed second? Jesus."

The gate trundles open and I drive through without waiting for Niko. His arms flailing adamantly, fast walks up the driveway to the car.

I don't know what Didi needed from her bag so badly, but I think she's finally gotten it. Her eyes are wide and bright. She continues dancing.

Niko is at my door, trying to wrench it open. "What the fuck?" He yanks his sunglasses off his face, like that will make a difference.

"Fuck you," he tells me. He gives me the finger. "One star!"

I shrug.

"Let's go, Didi. Hey, slow down!"

Didi clutches her bag, fidgets to open the door. I unlock it and put the car in park.

Niko grabs her arm and yanks her. I can see the bruise that will be there later. It pulses purple and yellow, hot, salty. I get out of the car.

This parasite, this inhabitant, is it in me, or is it *me*?

I feel like I'm floating. Then I say, "Are you ready to fucking party?"

When it emerges, I see it from outside myself. Its beak, its muzzle breaks from my mouth and I am suddenly detached, a vapor only watching the violence. Its claws are shadow, talons and nails ripping, filth tipped, disease inducing. Niko doesn't even have the chance to scream, his throat torn open somehow from inside: his scream, perhaps, trying to escape.

To our side, Didi gyrates to the noise. The music is off with the car.

We gorge what we can. This is a treat, a choice selection we are unable to deny. This delicacy may last a year: it may last six months. I drive to keep from killing. We are not always successful.

When we have had our fill (more than), we pull gore from Niko's body, tear it, shred it and feed it to Didi, our pup, our fledgling. She swallows, nurtured by the meat of Niko, and our collective appetite. Her eyes come alive, flaring with untethered flame.

We are terrible wolves. We breed. We infect.

We dress in the night, and we will never be deprived.

DAWN

Last Call

RED ON WHITE

Beth Cato

time stretches out in the winter night
as if dawn threatens to never come,
the world still as if all life has stopped,
and for some, this night, it will, but
the girl in the red cloak
she keeps moving
her breath forming hot clouds that flow back
against her numbed nose

she pauses, hearing the faintest crunch
of paws on powder, a warning that
the wolf-who-is-not-a-wolf is nearby
that he still hunts her
as she hunts him

as falling snow whispers threats
through bare-branched trees
the girl wishes it were not quite
so cold, not quite so dark
that the red in her cloak
was not so fresh
but even so, she'll keep going
because her grandmother
didn't raise her, train her, to give up.
She'll kill this thing that wears the skin
of a wolf, this thing that only hours ago

wore her grandmother's visage, and she'll
tack his hide on the wall, just as she has
common wolves, deer, and raccoons

but as she rounds a trunk, she sees
the flash of a dark tail, as a laugh
sparkles in the air like falling ice
the figure rises to stand
her own face staring back at her
grin sharp-toothed
flesh pale grey by the thin light

the wound he gave her—he already
committed her blood to dark magic—

horrified, quivering, she still
raises her rifle
and fires

the sound shatters the
cold dome of night
dawn, finally, pinks
the jagged horizon
as she stands over her own body
its flowing red resembles
her own cloak
fresh and bright
warm blood melting the snow
as it spreads
revealing
a hint of green
upon the soil beneath

THE TIYANAK

Teresa Aguinaldo

 From her hut perched on the peak of Palemlem Mountain, Flor watched the moon climb the speckled velvet sky. Spectral vapours churned the air. Waking movements stirred the jungle.

Her thick sable hair swept the moonshine as she turned her gaze to two-year-old Juana, her long limbs sprawled on a sleeping mat. Grown past her mother's hip, the child reigned over the mountain top. By day, she gambolled in her woodland playground; by dusk she lay blissfully asleep, shallow breaths and tiny nostril whistles filling the room.

Flor was grateful for the quiet. She drew a jagged breath, reached for the child's cheek, then withdrew her hand, brown against Juana's orchid-white skin and flaxen-streaked hair. Flor looked for traces of herself, maybe her mother's strong chin, but saw only the face of the priest.

"*It's time you go to the village . . . live a whole life,*" she remembered Mama telling her. Before Juana, it was just them, living behind the church at the tree line that separated the jungle from the village. Villagers both feared and shunned those dwelling at the edge of the darkness, sheltering in a hut but hunting in the jungle, something between human and beast. Mama saw how some shook a finger at her daughter, shoeless though dressed in a pineapple silk saya, like the church-going girls. From the trees, Mama had been watching the Spanish priest, who wore a large wooden cross around his neck to worship with his congregation, and thought him a compassionate man. *"Go now, the Father will take you in. Better to be among the people than between two worlds, always divided,"* she said.

"When will you come, Mama?"

"I will always be here, Flordeliza. You can see me whenever you'd like."

Now, at the window, a silk moth shimmering in the darkness became a shadow that mimicked Flor—facial contours tipped to the sky, black eyes bronzed by moonbeams.

"Mama?" The figure fell like ash through the bamboo-slatted floor. Flor sobbed, glaring at the empty space. "You said you would be here, but you're not! You're just a ghost."

Earlier that morning, Juana found a dead gecko by a tree.

"Wa happ'n to her?" the child asked. She laid down the handful of blue-green blossoms she picked for her hair and stroked the lizard's tail with a blade of grass.

Flor glanced away from her chores. How soulless the gecko seemed, stiff and wrinkled, dried bark littering the grass. She returned to hanging wet clothes on branches. The child's question persisted in her head, *What happened to her?*

"Aiiee, girl! Don't bother me now!" Flor waved her hand, avoiding her daughter's hazel eyes.

Juana cried until a yellow toad enticed her toward the garden.

The child now out of earshot, Flor finally breathed her reply, "She's dead . . . she's dead . . ."

Two years raising Juana alone in the mountains, Flor learned how to hunt like her mother. Palemlem's peak to where the waterfall emptied before the treeline marked their territory. She lurked in dark pockets of the moonlit jungle. Instinct and her mother's sense of smell, keen vision, and strength meant she could track, capture, and kill a small sambar or a young boar in an evening's work. They never went hungry. There was comfort in the wild.

With Juana deep in slumber, a pair of narra trees bowing overhead like doting nurses, Flor stepped outside to answer the beckoning night. Her nostrils filled with the musk of nearby game. Where the garden abutted the thicket, she heard rustling. Red eyes like prickly rambutan fruit stared out from the brush. *What's this—an easy meal?* Perhaps a young boar, uninclined to charge or run away. *A stray,* she thought.

Flor clicked her tongue and kissed the air, as if to coax it from hiding. Grunts and a high-pitched squeal sounded, as the animal fled into the jungle.

No time to prepare for the hunt. Flor swooped her hair up in a ribbon, then knotted the hem of her saya at the hip as she sped barefoot, weaving between trees and leaping over patches of thicket. She followed the squeals down the incline to where the air grew damp and the canopy blocked the moon, save for one cone of light showering an ancient balete tree.

Flor slid to a stop before the tangled bark of the old trunk—strangler figs entrapping their host tree like children entwined in a mother's embrace. A hundred times she'd traversed the mountainside but somehow overlooked this giant. Its straggling treetop pierced the clouds. Reptilian-like roots hung from branches. Similar ones slithered from below toward the centre of the trunk. There, like a tiny doorway, was a dark cavity, resident lizards and bats revealed by the intermittent light of fireflies, flickering as if sowing a message in the night.

Flor's eyes darted around, seeking any sign of the animal. Low to the ground, eyes gleamed back at her.

Flor crept toward the balete, grasping its dangling extensions one by one. She tripped on the crackling ground roots, nearly losing her balance, certain she'd scared away the little beast, but as she steadied herself, the red eyes appeared again. Flor bounced on her haunches. *This one likes to play hide and seek.*

Flor dove behind the fat tree, arms outstretched to grab her prey. She expected another round of grunts and squeals, but instead heard a child cry.

"Mama! Mama!"

Flor landed in a bundle on the soft, damp ground. The red eyes had disappeared, and a tiny being toddled from the shadow toward the edge of the light. A baby girl. *So small . . . and frail,* Flor thought, contrasting images of a rambunctious Juana in her head. Tied at the waist, a rice sack covered the baby's bottom, over which a melon-shaped belly hung. Tufts of fine black hair framed dirt-streaked cheeks. Tears glossed dark eyes.

"Who are you? What is your name?" Flor stood, her stomach fluttering at the sight of the babe in the middle of . . . where? She didn't really know. Water rushed in the distance but stillness pervaded; she had left the mountain behind.

The baby whimpered and extended her arms; tiny hands grabbed at the air.

Flor shuffled forward and noticed a wilted blue-green vine laced in the baby's hair and thought of the flowers Juana laid beside the gecko. Unlike hoisting her sturdy child, Flor lifted this babe like a basket of figs to rest just above the knot of her saya.

The showering moonbeam brightened, and Flor felt the balete's roots swell under her feet. The baby placed a gauzy hand upon Flor's cheek and the two locked eyes.

"Tsut, tsut," Flor soothed, tickling the girl's chin. She hummed her mother's song about a boy going to market, bouncing the baby on her hip the way she tried with Juana but could never get the rhythm right.

The baby gurgled, her hand still pasted to Flor's face.

Adrift in the sound of her own voice, Flor was slow to notice the change—red circling the baby's brown irises, then seeping through to the centres. Only when they sizzled like burning meat did Flor go quiet and stiffen, as the baby began to thrash. Flor gasped and let go, nearly dropping the child before catching her by the armpits, when she recalled the story of the "baby demon". *The tiyanak*, Mama called it.

"This lost spirit hides near the village and appears as a baby to passersby, until you pick it up and it reveals itself a demon. If you meet one, remember the tiyanak is but a child. Try calling it a sweet name . . . Babet or Cherry or Dulce. If you're lucky, this will please the aggrieved spirit. You see, it needs a proper name to enter the afterlife, or else it will be left to wander."

"Your name . . . Can I call you Babet?" Flor tipped her chin and tried adding a smile. "Hello, Ba—"

"Be quiet, girl!" A giant's voice boomed from the tiyanak's thin, quivering mouth. "I do not have a name!"

Flor winced, the sound so thunderous she pressed an ear to her shoulder for relief. In the air hung the smell of soured milk.

Tears sprayed from the corner of the tiyanak's eyes, petite arms flailing. Even wet, her pupils flamed and grew to the size of peseta coins. She wailed as her few front teeth stretched into daggers that glinted in the light. Claws grew from her tender fingers grasping Flor's upper arms. The tiyanak's sudden weight dug into Flor's hip.

Flor shuddered, attempting to thrust the baby from her side, but the tiyanak held tight, her claws pinching flesh, drawing blood.

Mama! Flor's thoughts screamed, unable to fight her own tears. *Help!* In the night, she wrestled beasts but never a baby demon. Flor wished only to flee, leave the hellish child to torment another.

In the periphery, Flor caught the still flashing light in the balete. She wiped her tears and pivoted toward it, the tiyanak still glued to her side.

The child will be fine, hidden in the tree, Flor told herself, and as they approached it, the tiyanak's cries abated and grip eased, as if she sensed its safety. But as they got closer, roots wriggled along the tree trunk and snaked across the opening. Flor sped forward, but the gap had sealed.

"No!" Flor cried.

The tiyanak jerked her head toward the darkened hole and the wailing returned.

Flor tried to soothe the child and her own growing panic, bouncing then humming in bursts. The baby's tears were abundant, pooling at Flor's feet, turning soil into mud. Flor lunged to dry ground, then tucked the thrashing demon under one arm like a slab of firewood. From her waist, she untied her apron and threw it over the baby's face to soak up the tears.

"Enough now!" She wiped and dabbed, when all at once the child lay quiet. "There, that's better," she sighed, moments passing as the tiyanak stayed still.

"Are you all right?" Flor pulled the apron from the tiyanak's face to see, and the baby flinched. Large and flickering, her deep red pupils stared up and her wide cheeks wrinkled. Then the tiyanak began to laugh—a titter, followed by a cackle deep in her throat.

Flor threw down her apron, steeling herself for more demonic transformation. Instead, the baby's eyes cooled, as she gurgled and pedalled her legs. When Flor was small, her mother would hold a towel between them at bath time, then yank it away to reveal her face—how astonished she was to see Mama vanish then appear. "Again! Again!" she would squeal.

Flor scurried to snatch the apron for another round of play, but the tiyanak's burning eyes returned.

"You wicked girl! Trying to trick me into forgetting I have no name!" the baby roared, snorting hot air. A dark grin bled across the demon's face as she aimed a needled finger between Flor's eyes. "Tell me your name and I will eat you and take it as my own!" The tiyanak stretched her jaws, sliding her tongue along the back of her teeth, leering.

Instead of cowering, Flor bent her brow and gritted her teeth, then raised her palm to swat the tiyanak's finger aside. With a humph, she plopped the baby in her self-made puddle.

"Shelter or no, I have a mind to leave you here by yourself!" Flor crossed her arms and turned her back to the baby. "You can't just take someone's name from them!" she shouted, jerking her head over her shoulder. "My mother gave me my name and it will always be mine!"

The tiyanak looked at Flor with round eyes. Her wails dwindled to a whimper. A deep frown tugged at her face.

"But I . . . I have no mother!" the baby screamed, tilting a trembling chin toward the treetops and pounding her fists in the slush.

Flor swung back around and stared at the child, its monstrous features quelled by a heartache that shook the drenched earth. Flor held out her hand, feeling her shoulders drop and knees buckle. In her thoughts, Juana's sleeping face appeared within reach.

"I . . . I understand," Flor cried, as her body crumbled in the puddle. She wrapped her arm around the baby to draw her in.

But the tiyanak pushed Flor away with a sideways sneer. She clutched the ties of her rice-sack diaper and glared.

Flor looked down at her mud-stained clothes, flicking grass from her lace-frilled cuffs and checking the ribbon that kept her hair intact. Her saya's pineapple fibres glimmered and the berry colour of her apron shone along the edges.

"What do you know of a demon's plight?" the tiyanak spat. "You villagers abandon your fears and drive them into the night, hoping they'll die there, but they don't! They become your monsters."

The tiyanak's words took Flor back to that night in the church. In the torrent of a typhoon, the priest led her into the safety of the stone church. There, on the altar under a life-size crucifix, he violated her. Mama swooped in, but not in time to save the priest. *"She's a witch! Demon Witch!"* the villagers shouted when they found him, his throat gouged by his own wooden cross, staring lifelessly into the dome of the church. The villagers—once Flor's neighbours, fellow congregants, friends—grabbed torches and bolo knives, pointing them at the treeline to where the savage mother and child had surely retreated.

"Flordeliza, I . . . this is my doing . . . I'm so . . ."

Flor remembered Mama choking back tears, her eyes on lookout.

"I see them! Leave—go to the mountain top, child! They won't get past me."

"No, Mama! They could kill you."

"They're afraid of me . . . of us."

"I know, that's why . . ."

"They'll try to force me deep into the jungle, but I will not abandon the tree line."

Flor felt the tiyanak's big eyes upon her and wondered why a baby would be so feared to be driven into the night. Had she been someone's mistake? A shame that threatened to shatter a wholesome village life?

Flor stared into the tiyanak's face like a mirror and breathed, "You're a . . . monster."

"Yes, and I will devour you and take what I want!" the demon growled, raising her claws and, once more, flashing her fangs.

Flor turned to the tiyanak and tilted her head, considering all the angles of the threat, then smiled. It wasn't a sweet name or even a mother's comfort the child desired. It was someone upon whom she could reflect her pain. A monster like her.

"Your claws are sharp and your teeth, they are big indeed," Flor praised, nodding her head. "But I'm certain they will not be enough to eat me."

"Why . . . how dare you! You're just a human . . . an easy meal for me . . ."

With that, Flor rose up, sleeking her back and bending her arms at her side. Under the moonbeam, she bowed once, then twice. After the third time, she gritted her teeth and made a fist in the air, wrenching her muscles as if pulling on an invisible vine. Flor sucked in her breath, holding her chin high as bone-framed sheets of leather, spanning twelve feet across, erupted from her shoulder blades. With each downstroke of her wings, she stretched her torso, causing her body to rip at the centre. Flor's face strained as she twisted her rib cage to snap the last bits of skin from her lower abdomen, releasing the pain in one mighty exhale as her entrails severed. Like a monsoon rain, blood showered the balete roots.

Flor fluttered her eyes as she ran her claws against her scalp, shaking loose the ribbon from thick ropes of hair that sprung and slithered about her face. She snapped a serpent's tongue then slid it across her serrated teeth. Bright yellow eyes rivalled the moon and exposed the jungle, including the tree line bordering the village. The winged-woman smiled, hovering above the baby demon.

The tiyanak gawked. Her teeth shrunk to kernel size and her pupils cooled against the gemstone brown of her irises. The toddling baby appeared once again, clapping the butt of her tiny hands with a babbling grin. Her joy grew so that she flung her head in a fit of giggles. Then, she stood on her tip toes and stretched out her arms.

"You are the creature who splits in half! A mana . . . a mananan . . . !" the baby screeched, dancing in her mud puddle.

Flor's thin, pointed tongue slipped in and out between her teeth as she spoke.

"A manananggal, yes! My name is Flordeliza. I am glad you found me this night."

Flor drifted down and extended a sinewy arm, scooping the baby from her diapered bottom. The two embraced and looked upon Flor's lower half. Released from the weight of its torso, it wobbled in the mud, until the balete roots grabbed the ankles, firmly grounding them.

Flor stared out, recognizing the row of trees outside the edge of her light, the patch of land where she and Mama had lived. Their hut had been destroyed, but the haze of village life lay just beyond it.

"Will you hunt there tonight? Is that why you've come near the tree line?" the tiyanak asked.

"No, I have all that I need from the mountain," the mana hissed. "I cannot return to the village."

"Return? But you're a mana."

"Yes, my mother too. We lived at the tree line until she sent me to live in the village, but then I had to flee."

"Flee . . . why?"

"It's as you said." Flor gazed down with a knowing smile. "I am their monster."

The tiyanak pursed her lips and nodded.

"Your mother, what happened to her?"

"What happened to her?" Flor whispered, a net of smooth balete branches and glossy leaves encircling her. She brushed the bone of her wings against it. "She's . . . she's here. I think she's always been."

The tiyanak scanned the circumference of the balete and asked, "So, what will you do now, Flordeliza?"

Flor stroked the baby's cheek, noticing the wilted vine that had decorated her hair had all but shook free. Only a few wrinkled petals clung to the crown of her head.

"Hold on to me," the mana cautioned. With a stroke of her wings, Flor breezed toward the sound of running water. There, near the pool of the waterfall, she picked a fresh cluster of jade vine—sea green and blue with purple stems—then set the child on a fallen palm leaf. "I shall call you Jade-Ann," Flor declared, lacing the vine atop the baby's head.

"Aah!" the tiyanak squealed, spurting spit bubbles that sparkled under the gleam of the mana's eyes, and reaching up to pat her new tiara.

Flor swept her wing, harnessing a few dozen fireflies to scoop into a cup-shaped flower before curving its long stem into a handle. Jade-Ann poked the cup, so it rocked back and forth. Dozens of tiny bulbs twinkled, and she squealed some more. Flor joined in with a breathy titter, as she slid the stem onto the baby's wrist to hang like a lantern.

"Now, you'll need this, so hold on to it," Flor instructed.

"What for?"

Flor glanced toward the light of the balete that shimmered through the trees. She hugged the tiyanak and flew back. As she drifted toward the centre of the trunk, the roots withdrew from the opening and a warm light shone.

"Ohh!" Jade-Ann gasped.

The mana set down the tiyanak in front of the small archway, then pinched her wings behind her back and tipped forward to poke her head inside. The inner tree was cavernous, expanding into darkness, no borders in sight. The resident woodland creatures were gone. In their place were glowing shapes of people—ones like her and the tiyanak and ones like the villagers. She saw families sharing a meal, children playing, others planting, reading, running or just sitting quietly—spirits occupying the afterlife the way she lived each day on the mountain.

Flor stretched her neck. The light faded farther out, but on the ground was a faintly lit path that meandered through the shadows.

"There!" Flor pointed, turning toward the tiyanak. "Follow that path, Jade-Ann, and hold your lantern high. Say your name to all you meet, and someone will find you."

"Come with me, Flordeliza." The tiyanak tugged her hand. "Maybe someone will find you too."

Flor floated down to kiss the baby's forehead.

"No, this path is yours, Jade-Ann. Mine is here."

The tiyanak embraced the mana's neck with the might of a baby's longing, tears pearling upon Flor's cheek.

Flor gave a gentle pat, and the baby toddled into the light. The mana waved, but the glowing figures circled Jade-Ann, bowing and smiling like guests at a cotillion every time she said her name. Children ran past their mothers to admire the firefly lantern and blue-green tiara, pointing the newcomer farther down the path. Flor watched the sparkling bob of Jade-Ann's light as she teetered into the darkness.

As Flor raised her head above the opening, she noticed more spirits merge into the balete itself, coming from beyond its cone of light, as if returning from a visit to the world of the living. From the rapid waterfall and the steep mountainside, from across the thicket and through the trees—they approached the tree from all directions, before disappearing into the entryway to the afterlife.

Flor witnessed the first ray of dawn pierce the haze at the tree line. A shadow stood in its midst. The mana unfurled her tongue between her lips and gazed in silence, tipping her chest and angling her wings toward it. Around her, she felt the warm light of the balete softening in the waning night, now emptied of its travellers . . . with the exception of the new figure before her.

A second and third beam steamed into the clearing, giving the ghostly figure shape. Flor pulled away from the rising sun until the figure's spectral wings spread beneath the trees, preserving the darkness. Flor advanced, recognizing the long hair rippling in the woodland breeze, strong forearms bent outward with taloned hands, sharp facial contours lit by golden eyes.

"Mama," Flor whispered, touching her pointed fingers to her quivering smile.

Like moths in the pale light, Flor and her mother floated, their shimmering wings sustaining them as they embraced the space between the living and spirit worlds.

A gust of air, humid with the morning dew, came through the trees, pushing Mama's ghost toward the balete. Her lips brushed her daughter's cheeks as she passed, her words echoing against the emerging dawn.

"I'll always be here, Flordeliza."

Mama nodded toward the mountain top, lit by sunbeams, and smiled before disappearing into the ancient tree.

Flor's eyes welled with joy and heartache for her mother's promise to guard passage at the tree line. Even in death, she'd kept them safe.

Flor watched the shape of the giant balete merge with the surrounding jungle, coming back to light. She looked up the woodland path and thought of her daughter's waking wonder and grumbling belly. With a sparkle in her yellow eyes, she glided back to her legs, waiting by the large trunk. There, the mana rejoined with her waist, shimmying into the comfort of her body. She plucked her feet from the wet earth and turned from the village to face the mountain. At last, she tightened the knot of her saya and swept her hair from her face, ready to speed her way home to Juana.

DIGGING FOR BEAR IN THE EVERNIGHT

TAIS TENG

*Above the rough-hewn statue, the winter stars stand unwavering, impossibly bright. Before it, a girl is kneeling, looking up at a face that only shows empty eye sockets. Or perhaps not quite empty: in one socket the starlight gleams, perhaps reflected by an icicle? She is holding a painted egg.*

The statue is carved out of lava, long since cooled, and perhaps it is just natural and only resembles a human. A red glow lights the face of the girl as she starts speaking.

I don't know if you understand my language or can even hear my words, you being stone and a statue. I'll explain why I'm now sitting at your feet and why I ran away on my very first foraging tour. There is nobody else who would want to listen to me and I can't tell my brothers the truth. Or my uncles. If I did, they would throw me in the burning lake or exile me for speaking heresy.

If you could speak, I imagine the first thing you would ask is why we are living here, on your mountain?

Well, after the Fenris Wolf ate the Sun and the Moon, only the northern lights were left, green curtains flapping above the iron mountains. You could hear the clash of sorcerous swords, my grandfather told me, flaming spears howling across the sky. It wasn't like an eruption or an earthquake at all: nothing rumbling and majestic, but a frantic din that shook the whole land.

"The cold will be moving in soon," Sigurd Single-eye declared. He was the jarl, half warrior and half gothi. Having only one eye formed no handicap: like Odin he had exchanged a mere eye for supernatural wisdom and guile. "Midgard is lost to the ice giants, all the summer-fields smothered by snow and avalanches."

"There will be a new world!" one of the villagers protested. "All the skalds and priests promised that!"

"Not in our time, and I think that is a fable, a tale to keep children from crying when the night looms, filled with whispers and wolf howls. No, there is only a single place where we may survive. A campfire that'll never go out." He smiled. "Trollhome."

That was long before my time, three generations back, and we now live on the inner slopes of a volcano. All our windows look out over Trollhome's magma lake, with only blind walls at the star-side. When they built the houses they put windows there, too, but they are all bricked up now. The villagers couldn't stand the sight of the stars staring back at them like spider eyes, mocking them.

It isn't a bad life here, inside the ring-wall. Flightless grebes bob on the hot pools, dining on watercress and pale shrimp. Just like us, only we eat the birds too.

Out in the Evernight, winter roses bloom. In their own season, they grow sweet berries. Cold-berries are as clear as a frozen dewdrop, perfectly round with three seeds always in the centre. The roses allow the foragers to pick that strange fruit, but you have to plant all three seeds at a new place. If you accidentally crack one between your teeth or spit the bitter seed in the lava lake, the juice will turn to poison and burn a sizzling hole in your stomach.

Long ago, in the sunlit times, our men went out in the wilderness to hunt. The Evernight with her searing cold put an end to that and there was nothing alive to hunt anyway. That left foraging, and women were better at that.

Without bear meat, we would only have grebe-flesh or rats and snakes roasting on the hot stones.

I'll explain. When the sun went out the bears understood deep in their bones that *the* winter had come. They dug holes in the snow and their hearts slowed until they went to sleep. They hibernated, waiting for a spring that would never come.

Us women, we were quite good at locating their burrows and carrying in the meat. The bears weren't sleeping, of course, but frozen stiff. Each bear formed a larder of perfectly preserved meat, big enough to feed a household for simply *weeks*.

Grandfather told me the men tried to forage in the beginning but too often they returned with no more than a frozen hare or a handful of songbirds. They never found even a single bear burrow so now only women venture out in the dark. We are better made for the cold, our faces round as the lost moon or winter berries.

When you turn sixteen you become a woman. A cousin takes you on your first hunt and when you return you are one of the Sisterhood, one of the providers.

If I am being honest, I don't like men much. Their faces are bearded, bestial, and furry like a bear's. I like smooth skin and long curly hair. Chapped lips that proved she has braved the cold. Like my cousin Gudrun. She wears her hair in a long braid and it is as yellow as the daisies on the gobelin in the gothi's den.

A gobelin is a hanging on the wall, from the old times. The stitching shows a green meadow with huge white rats and a shepherdess with a crooked staff. You see mountains in the distance with only their tops snowy. The sky is all blue, without a single star.

You get it, you say? You have seen that kind of sky? Well, you're probably older than my grandfather then.

Oh yes, I was talking about Gudrun, right. Well, when I stared at her, she looked back across the table and winked at me, and then I understood things would be different in the Sisterhood. Especially when we are out in the Evernight. Stars don't tell tales and they aren't interested in who kisses whom.

On my birthday we had bear meat of course, but I got a whole grebe of my own and they lit a candle. Candles are very special, made from the fat of our beloved dead.

When the candle had burned to a stub, Gudrun stood up and handed me a cold-berry.

"Save the seeds," she told me. "We'll plant them in the Evernight." She paused. "Together."

Then I knew she must love me, too.

There were three more girls in our hunting group, all older than me. Gudrun handed me a cape made of rat fur, with a big hood. I already wore triple-layered trousers and boots. I wondered for a moment: why such a complicated patchwork of rat fur? A bear must have a much better and warmer pelt, yet women only ever carried the meat to the village, never the carcass or bones.

"You wear the cape inside out," Gudrun instructed me. "And this felt mask, you only breathe through the mask. Open your mouth and your tongue freezes right away against your palate. Your lungs fill up with tinkling rime. It is *cold* outside."

"I understand," I said and forgot to ask about the rat fur.

"But we aren't outside yet." She took my face in her hand and kissed me right on the lips. The other girls giggled but it didn't sound cruel. More like approving.

We passed the statue that guards the winding road up to the Evernight. I greeted it as usual with a handwave.

It was huge: three times the height of a tall man. Grandfather claims it is a statue of Sigurd Single-eye, but if that is true, it isn't very well made. It could be just about anything standing on two legs and leaning on a staff or a sword. I made the obeisance, bending my knee and drawing the sun-circle in the ash.

I often played there with my older sister. Dagmar, yes, the one who didn't come back from her first hunt. Dagmar found a cracked egg at the foot of the statue. It was bigger than any grebe's egg and someone had painted a blue eye on it. It was the most beautiful eye we had ever seen and surely must have been the statue's. So, we knew the statue was something special.

We tried putting the egg back but the lava was too rough. It tore Dagmar's palms when she tried to climb up to the statue's face and we finally gave up.

Later, after Dagmar was gone, you listened to all the secrets I couldn't tell my sister anymore, and never sneered like my brothers.

Well, that is why I came back to you. You are the only one left who ever listened to me.

I walked beyond the statue for the very first time, to the top of the ring-wall, where we were told by our parents never to go. Every step felt like a dare and a joyous fear filled me when I finally could look out over the Evernight lands. A wind was blowing right in my sweating face and every third gust felt monstrously cold. Black, bear-freezing cold.

The lands stretched all the way to the mountains, a glacial plain made of broken ice shoals and snowfields. The mountains, though, seemed curiously jagged, with hoops and curves quite unlike any rock I had seen in our caldera.

"Those mountains, Gudrun?" I asked. "Why do they look so strange? No, not strange. They seem somehow familiar. I have seen them before, but . . ."

"It is their size," Gudrun said. "Remember grandfather's tales?"

And then the mountains snapped into focus. When I had finished a roasted water-snake to the very bone, the same intricate puzzle shape was left on my wooden platter.

"Jörmungandr," I gasped. "Those mountains are his ribs!"

"Yes, his skeleton surrounds the whole of Midgard and dips down in the frozen oceans. He was sly Loki's middle child and Thor killed him. Bashed his head in with his hammer and then he took nine steps before he fell face forward in the snow. The Midgard Serpent's poison kills even immortals."

"If we only could find his hammer . . ." I mused.

"Jörmungandr's head must lie somewhere behind the horizon," another girl said. "Too far to walk."

The three girls in front, Torun, Frigga, and Helle, carried a shield heaped with burning sulphur and glow-stones. That made a bubble of precious warmth when we went down the slope and stepped out on the ice. The fire smelled like a thermal spring, a reassuring and cozy scent.

The silence was enormous, and you could hear the northern lights flap in the sky, a sound like distant whips, followed by a stuttering buzz as if ghosts were talking. With every step the snow crunched beneath our thick soles: in that stillness, the sound must have carried for miles.

"How do we find the bears?" I asked. "Breathing holes in the snow? Grandfather said that they needed air when they slept."

"No holes," Torun said and laughed.

"No," Gudrun said, "we found a better way to locate bear meat."

"An easier way," Torun added.

My eyes slowly adjusted to the aurora glow and the landscape sharpened. Between us and the mountains lay a shape. It was as pale as the snow and it merged almost seamlessly in the landscape. I had been holding Gudrun's hand and I let go of it to point. "Any idea what that is?"

"We never could walk all the way," Torun said, "but my mother carved a spyglass out of clear ice and looked. It is a wolf's skull. The skull of *the* wolf, we think. It's at least a mile long."

I could discern the eye sockets now, the teeth which must be a dozen man-heights long.

"She also said there was a big hole in his skull."

"In grandfather's stories, Fenris the Wolf devours Odin," I said, and Gudrun snorted.

"Eaten by a wolf. It isn't very fatal if you are magic. I mean, the Red Imp's grandmother was eaten by a wolf and the woodsman came and cut him open. The grandmother climbed from the wolf's entrails, none the worse for wear."

"That's a stupid children's story!" I protested. "Like the swan who flew up to the moon or the table that walked back to the poor woodsman, bearing all King Hagar's feast food."

"It was smashed from the inside, my mother said. If he swallowed the Allfather without chewing . . ."

"We'll never know," Gudrun said. "Me, I haven't seen many gods walking around lately."

That shut both of us up. There was strangeness and wonder enough around us without revenant Aesir climbing from monster skulls.

A hill covered with winter roses was our first destination. The pale creepers stirred at our approach, lifted thorns as long as daggers. An angry buzz arose.

"We don't come to steal anything," Gudrun called, "or to pick your flowers." But they kept waving their thorns. "We planted a hundred seeds. Some in places *miles* from here."

The thorns withdrew and a path opened between the creepers. In the distance cold-berries sparkled.

Frigga took the basket from her back and we filled it with berries.

"Can I taste one?" I asked, "or is it so cold it'll glue my teeth together?"

"The roses would never harm a potential planter," Gudrun said. She bent down and plucked a berry, lifted my breathing cloth, and put it in my mouth. She followed with a kiss, withdrawing before our lips could freeze together. The taste was wonderfully tart and fresh, quite different from anything I had eaten before. It must be because they were just plucked, still infused with the star magic of the Evernight. Or perhaps because Gudrun gave it to me? My lips still tingled and it wasn't from the cold.

You ask if Gudrun is my lover, statue? I guess she was, then. I had only kissed her twice, but I knew there must be more. All the drinking songs are about men lying with women, giving quite explicit instructions. There must be other ways, girl-ways more tender and longer lasting than just rutting like the rats.

At the top of the hill, I looked back at our volcano. Trollhome was a truncated cone, surmounted by a red glow. In this wonderful new landscape, it seemed quite dull, devoid of any magic.

"Look at it," Gudrun said, waving her hand. "See the slope to the left? That darker patch is the famous footprint of a troll. It is the last one left. Once there were hundreds of footprints but the volcano is always trembling, raining ash and now most of them have been covered."

"You mean the trolls in Sigurd's saga were real?"

"They lived in this very volcano. Thousands of them. Why do you think we call it Trollhome? They were man-eating monsters. Cannibals."

I remembered the final stanza of Sigurd's saga.

Like an avalanche   they stormed down
And the fell creatures   would have devoured us all
Not even spitting out   the bones and our poor skulls
But single-eyed Sigurd   that most stalwart of men
He stepped in front   and raised his sword
And called down   the glorious sun
Turning all monsters   into pitted stone.

It has cost him his soul, the saga goes on to tell, all his magic, and he died in the act.

I stared at the footprint. It might indeed be three-toed as troll feet were rumoured to be. But you couldn't call it clear. The side of the mountain bore a hundred patches and in the shifting aurora light, you could see just about anything in them. Daylight would kill a troll, all tales agreed, turn him into stone, and Sigurd had become a sun, even if only for an eye-blink.

"Just pulling your leg," Gudrun said. "My mother pointed it out to me but I think it was just a tall tale."

Beyond the hill, the plain became ridged, huge ripples that went on and on.

Gudrun halted. "You still have the seeds?"

I nodded.

"Spit them out then. This is the right place to plant them."

We pushed them deep in the snow, all six seeds. Gudrun made the sun sign and the snow stirred. Pale shoots pushed up, opening flowers to the stars and the aurora.

Gudrun took my hand again. "Almost there. Just a short walk."

"Almost where?"

"Where we dig for, well, bear meat," she said with a strangely secretive smile.

We topped the ninth ridge and a snowed-in village sat at our feet. The steeple of a stave church rose, the sides hooked like a harpoon. The villagers must have been renegades who had turned their backs on the true gods and followed the accursed White Christos.

We slid down the icy side, entered the village through an ornate gate. You know the kind: angels and holy men who should have remained in their hot desert and not come north to bother us and the Aesir. Still, Ragnarok did take them and there would be no Gabriel blowing his own counterfeit Gjallarhorn.

The snow filled the street and only the roofs showed. We passed a stable, with a hole hacked in the roof of frozen sod and I understood that there would be no bear meat.

"That is clever," I said. "The cattle, they all huddled close together and froze in their stalls."

"No cows or goats," Gudrun said. "The stables were all mined out, to the last lamb and chicken. That was already the case when my mother was a new girl, setting out on her first meat hunt."

She swerved to the right and we climbed a new roof. It was one of the bigger ones: perhaps the house of their jarl or their priest? Standing on that roof, I noticed most of the other roofs had holes too. Gudrun raised her obsidian knife, cut into the sod. The others joined, and I had nothing to do, just a useless bystander. I decided that when I got home the first thing I had to do was get a long shard of volcano-glass and knap my own digging knife. "Stand back!" Frigga called and a part of the roof sagged with an alarming rumble. She threw Torun a rawhide rope and went down into the hole.

Time passed, so much time I saw a star wink out behind a rib of the Serpent. The sulphur on the shield had turned white and only the glow-stones still gave off heat.

"Got one!" Frigga's voice sounded quite close, only meters below us. Something pale and elongated emerged from the hole, and Gudrun took it, tugged it on the roof.

"My, my, that is a fat one. Lots of good eating in that."

"Their priest, I guess," Frigga said. "They never stint themselves none. Dining on partridges and strawberries, even in the middle of the winter."

I stared at the snow-white arm, the clenched fist.

"Have a good look," Gudrun said. "This is what we have been digging up all these years. *Bear meat.*" She laid her arm across my shoulder. "Now you know. Now you are one of us."

I pushed her away, sick with horror, and ran.

"Let her go, Gudrun," I heard Torun call. "They always return. She has nowhere to go."

I sprinted past the ornate gate, across the hill with winter roses.

All beauty was gone from the Evernight, all wonder. This was just a slaughterhouse, a frozen slaughterhouse, and we had been eating the most forbidden food of all. We were cannibals, bone-gnawing trolls. When the promised sun ignited in the sky, we would all turn into stone.

I ran and ran, climbed the outer slope of Trollhome, then stumbled down in a cloud of ash. I halted when I saw you. A dozen steps more and I would have looked out over our village.

I couldn't go there, of course. They would sneer at me, a failed provider, and I couldn't tell them the truth. The ones who knew would eye me and wonder if I would blurt out their gruesome secret.

So, I sat down at your feet and wept. And when no tears were left, I looked up and saw you gazing back at me with your single eye of ice.

You never asked why I had been weeping, but I felt your question hanging in the air, waiting. And I told you.

I realize now who you must be. The saga tells that Odin went down to the spring at the roots of the world-tree and bartered an eye for wisdom. Just like Odin, the saga says about our jarl. Only Sigurd Single-eye wasn't *like* Odin. You were the god himself all the time, the Allfather! Leading the last humans to safety after Asgard fell.

I can hear your voice so clearly now.

Not the Allfather, you say? I get it. I get it! Stop chuckling. Right, you went down to the spring, following in Odin's footprints, and paid your dues. An eye for a silver tongue, for the ability to tell perfect and beautiful lies. But why has . . . I mean the sagas only call Odin one-eyed?

Ah, you painted a blue eye on that large egg and put that in your empty socket. An eye that looked so innocent and clear that all mortals would trust you and tell you their guiltiest secrets.

Oh yes, stealing Sutr's flaming sword when he fell asleep after burning Asgard, that is quite in character. As is never using it to fight with the other gods. You could have turned the tide, stopped Ragnarok. But the monsters were your children, so why would you? You used the flaming sword only once, making it flare like the sun and using up all his magic.

A final jest, you say, making the last surviving humans into trolls, even if it cost you your own life.

Because you love us? Because we have entertained you for a hundred thousand years and the only way we could live in Trollhome is by becoming trolls? Yes, names are compelling magic. I understand how that works, Loki.

I see the other girls coming down the slope, clutching their long knives. They are wondering if they must kill me and add my meat to the priest's. It happens, a new girl falling in a crevasse on her first hunt. Like my sister.

They don't have to worry. When I look down at my hands they aren't clawed. I have no tail, but I'm still a troll. I understand now. I'll be a monster with my Gudrun. Two monsters in love, willing to do *anything* to survive the Evernight.

A HEALTHY, HAPPY HOLIDAY

DEREK DES ANGES

Dear Rafe,

Having a blinder at the seaside so far. Obviously there's the beach, there's a historic lighthouse, there's the view, there's "local colour", there's the possibility of actually seeing a constellation for the first time in years . . . all the stuff that a relaxing get-away is made of. You were dead right about needing to get away, detox, and put the out-of-office on *everything*—even the social medias; having no internet was like a weird itch at first but I'm happy to say that after getting settled in ~~(and compulsively checking my phone three or four times)~~ I can feel the benefit of being cut off from the rest of the world already.

Lorena and I went for a walk after dinner while the sun was setting. The houses are all levels of picturesque which would make Instagram vomit blood: exposed timbers, uneven roof tiles, quirky little windows that look like eyes when the lights go on. There's a sharp drop down to the beach at low tide and the narrow steps are slimy with red seaweed which smells like piss. So you know I'm not over-romanticising things—did I slip on the red seaweed and bruise my ass? Guess.

But it's really a nice village. Even the seagulls are relatively polite. Absolutely sod all in the way of night-life, even the pub closes at 8:00 p.m., before the last glimmer of light is out of the sky, but the cottage is cute. It has a good library and I *did* bring a draft of the proposal (don't hate me) so if I get really bored of listening to Lorena explain the plot of every single *X-Files* episode I can always work on that.

Very exciting to be writing letters longhand like some kind of Victorian or caveman, isn't it?

Much love,

Chris

[Image description: Postcard of a perfectly ordinary beach in the south of England]

Dear Rafe,

Can't be arsed to wait for reply. Was on my way back from sticking the last letter in the post box when I saw someone swimming by the footpath and red piss-weed, during high-tide! It was gone 10:30 p.m. and pitch-black apart from my phone light. Creepy.

I don't know what these people consider normal and I don't want to make myself look like even more of a tourist when we've only just got here, but should anyone be swimming at night? Is that sensible? This is going to bother me.

Enjoy the postcard. I picked up a box, I suspect you'll see the whole set. (I'm sort of worried I'm going to run out of stamps.)

Love,

Chris

*[Image description: postcard of a pleasant view from the top of
a cliff, out over an unrealistically blue sea]*

Dear Rafe,

Sorry for treating the postal service like WhatsApp but you
knew this would happen. Obviously Lorena was incommunicado
when I got back, and I'm going to have calves like a *RuGbY
pLaYeR* if I keep dashing down to the box every five minutes.
There's something truly satisfying about chucking an envelope
into the red-painted cast-iron maw of those old ones. So I didn't
get to tell her about the Beach Weirdo until breakfast.

She was predictably Italian about it: *clearly they're insane but
it's also not your business if someone is insane. Maybe we should
be swimming at midnight too.*

Rafe, you've seen me swim in broad daylight, haven't you? I
don't think I should be doing anything in the water after dark
except bobbing up and down like a buoy.

Today's main activity was walking to the headland point and
back: there's a disused lighthouse up there, the new replacement
being out at sea and remotely operated, etc. They put a plaque up to
some disaster or other and there's a viewpoint but very little in the
way of tourist infrastructure. Unfortunately the beach up that end
absolutely *reeks*. Rotten seaweed or dead fish or something gone off.
Presumably why they don't have a cafe or an ice cream van.

Writing this in the pub, where a local is giving a poetry reading
from his book. It's mostly unbearable "modern life is rubbish"
stuff, the kind you get into when your broadband is abysmal and
you try to make it a virtue, but it's honestly no worse than the
stuff you hear at a radical slam, something I'm sure both sides of
the comparison would hate to hear. He's switched over to some
more atmospheric and fanciful stuff about the moon and not
going out when the night is bright and white, terrible rhyming
scheme, and "the howling of dogs". Pretty gothic, but the locals
are all nodding along.

Lorena has failed to convince the kitchen vegan food is real
and is moodily picking at some chips; I've strayed from the path
of righteousness and have some sort of approximation of *moules
marinière* which tastes oddly oily. I don't mean olive oil, I mean
sump oil. ~~For all that, not bad. Cheap, too.~~

Asked at the bar about night swimming and the overbearing response was: for God's sake don't do that. Something incomprehensible about tides and currents, presumably, but they didn't want to be drawn on the topic. So much so they gave me a free pint.

I could get used to this, although I will say I miss being able to shitpost about it *and get an instant response*. So you'd better be writing an answer.

Much love,

Chris

[Image description: postcard of a quiet-looking churchyard, partly overgrown with weeds. An obelisk-shaped memorial stands in the centre, looking vigorously clean]

Rafe,

Okay please seriously hurry up and get down to the post office.

After dinner, dropped the last letter off at the post box, as you do, and stuck around with Lorena at the harbour wall/beach path to watch the last of the dying sunset because it was one of those gorgeous blood orange guys that says "it's going to absolutely shit rain tomorrow, real stair-rods weather".

Tides apparently shift around all over the place because they're not on a 12-hour cycle? There was a little chart of them at the cottage. Anyway, the water was lower than before. We were just about to leave, I turned around because Lorena had said something about glass buoys, and I saw this *thing*. Like a fish crawling up the side of one of the boats. *Huge.*

Obviously I freaked out and tried to point it out to Lorena but you know she can't see a damned thing after dark and she *will not* admit to it. So there I was desperately pointing at this thing and shouting *look, it's a bloody great fish, woman*, and Lorena was just irritably arguing *there's no such thing as a fishwoman stop making a scene you're embarrassing everyone will think you're nuts.*

So naturally I went to bed in a bad mood. Woke up around 2 a.m. to the sound of thunder and rain like someone was trying to tear a hole in the roof, and because I was half-asleep managed to convince myself that someone was *actually* trying to tear a hole in the roof.

I locked myself in the toilet which is on a kind of weird halfway landing in what probably should have just been a cupboard.

Now that it's light again and the clouds have boiled away and it's a roasting bright blue day and the sea pinks in the garden are bouncing in a light breeze, I feel like a fucking idiot, of course.

Can fish climb? I feel like you know this.

Much love,
Chris

[Image description: postcard of two cyclists on a clifftop path, reading a comically large map]

Dearest, dearest, non-replying Rafe,

I admit, the evenings are getting to me. This morning was fine: Lorena got up at a Mediterranean hour and made fun of me for half an hour over coffee: the phrase "if you're so attached to your phone that you start having a mental breakdown without it you don't need detox you need therapy" was used, in fact.

Nonetheless (what a great word that is, I feel like a Victorian explorer), we decided the day's walk would be inland because both of us were feeling a bit off about the lighthouse end of the beach, and if you go much further past the cottage in the other direction you run into fences, private property signs, and warnings about an unstable cliff. Past that, there's the remains of coastal fortifications, according to the OS map, but there's some fuss about leftover sea mines from WW2 so you can't go down there. The mention of WW2 probably just deVictorianed me, didn't it? One last "henceforth" for the road.

Our walk inland gave us the Historic Gardens, or rather garden, singular: it's deconsecrated churchyard (took me a while to remember the word, I kept wanting to say "decommissioned", as if the church was some sort of battery gun) and the bombed out remains of a church which has been turned into a rockery. The gravestones are all gone although some of the raised tombs were creatively turned into planters. They've kept what I thought initially was a war memorial, there's nothing to say what it's actually a memorial to, just a bunch of dead people's names on a rude pillar of rock in the middle of the path. Lorena says it's probably a shipwreck or a storm.

So far, so normal.

Writing in the pub again. We'll see how the evening goes this time. Lorena has valiantly promised me she'll figure out the cottage's TV so we can watch some godawful gameshow or something. Like in the stone age.

Please hurry and write back,

Chris

[Image description: postcard of a butterfly on a flower]

Rafe, dear Rafe,

Have you broken your writing wrist? Is someone holding you hostage? Answer your letters, *please*.

The evening went like this: we left at kicking-out time a little the better for a bottle of surprisingly good wine, and Lorena started talking about how rural places lose all of their brightest and most talented people to big cities and it drains the life out of them (she should know, that's what she did: left some little place in Calabria pay through the nose to rent a 2-bed in a massive city in a different country), and while she was going on about that, I was watching the moon, very big and almost full. There was this loud *splash* directly against the footpath wall. Not like a wave, but like someone slapping it with a hand.

The water was low, again, enough that I couldn't see the water line. I'd literally just complained that it was a quiet as a grave around here, so I thought I was on good footing when I asked her if she'd heard it, but no: she just looked me dead in the eye and said *no, and neither did you.*

And then she got right behind me like a sheepdog and just about herded me along to the cottage.

I could not get another word out of her on the subject all evening. She couldn't figure out the TV either but we spent two hours or so pushing different buttons and arguing until I'd almost forgotten about the splash.

Went to bed at *ten-thirty* like a *child*, and lay awake for about a million years until I absolutely *had to* get up and look out of the bedroom window. The other choice was lying in bed wide awake and driving myself insane, which in hindsight would have been the better idea.

At first it wasn't so bad. There were all those stars you can't see in the city, and the sound of the sea is everywhere in that village, and I thought I could hear a bell somewhere in the distance. And then I made the mistake of looking down.

There on the lawn that overlooks the sea there was something squirming under the moonlight. I don't know how to describe it exactly. It just looked like the dictionary definition of the word *squirm*. Like if you'd distilled *squirm* into a physical entity that would be it. *Squirm* was on the lawn, glistening and moving.

I hope you don't think I'm nuts or a coward but I closed the curtains very firmly and went to hide in the toilet again.

I miss sleeping.

Much *impatient* love,
Chris

[Image description: a postcard featuring a quaint-looking pub with a hand-painted sign. The sign shows something which could be a mermaid, if you squinted and had never seen one before]

Rafe, Rafe, dear God Rafe, answer me. Answer me because I need to know someone else is in receipt of this nonsense and I'm not just banging my head against a wall.

The tenor of this holiday has gone south somewhat; I tried explaining the squirming presence to Lorena but she just pointed out that the lawn was entirely devoid of eels and worms (examples I used to explain "squirm", a word she'd not come across before), that it was a pleasant day, and that I looked like shit.

Wisdom of Lorena: You just have to ignore animal things in the countryside. They happen, they're not for you to understand.

Further wisdom of Lorena: she came here to relax, she has a very stressful job, and if I am not going to let her relax, she is going to lock me out of the cottage and I can go back home. The word "relax" has been repeated several times, with increasing stridency. I don't think she's any better at it than I am.

Contrary to this advice, I searched the entire cottage for some kind of wildlife guide: climbing fish, squirming lawns? But there was nothing. A nice and pointed copy of the King James Bible in both bedrooms; Lorena pointed this out sniffily. Apparently, bibles that aren't in Latin don't count.

I'd worn out her patience with my bullshit by then, so we agreed to make up and go and do something suitably relaxing and holidayish, like we'd planned. We went back up to the lighthouse so Lorena could take some film photos. `I MEAN, PHOTOS ON FILM.` The view is fantastic, of course, but the *smell* is unhinged. Whatever is rotting is down from the promontory, towards the beach.

Lorena puttered around trying to find any further clues as to what the churchyard memorial was for, still convinced it was a shipwreck or storm; I sat down on a bench and unfortunately also a bramble, and while I was picking thorns out of my leg discovered that someone had chalked what looked like one of those hippy moon calendars on the side of the concrete viewpoint marker closer to the water.

In isolation I'd've said teenagers will be teenagers, but it was on the side of the stench so I pinched my nose and struggled down the side of the hill.

Once I got out of sight of the viewpoint marker, the air absolutely filled up with bluebottles. Loud, shiny, distracting, buzzing bastards all over the place with their little poop-walking feet, landing on my sweaty face and trying to drink my eyeballs. I flapped them off, took one step forward, and narrowly avoided standing in a poodle.

I mean *in*, too. It was very dead.

Despite her reticence to engage with the wildlife, it was Lorena, when I'd found her and burbled hysterically at her, who pointed out in a disappointed voice that the animal seemed to have been caught in a choke snare intended for a fox. Someone's pet, clearly, because it had the stained remains of a cute little pink bow bitten deep into the mess of its throat by wire, and what looked like one of those doggy GPS trackers, riddled with bite marks.

By then the tide had gone down enough to climb down onto the beach, which wasn't very easy; I slipped over a few times and ended up limping down onto the sand. None of what I'd call the *normal* beach debris around, no beer cans, no remains of beach fires, no dropped kids' toys. I wouldn't say it was *suspiciously clean*, because there was a whole collection of fabric pet collars at the high tide line.

Lorena and I took a decision at that point that we weren't staying on that beach any longer.

Terminally impatient for some kind of reassurance here, Rafe. Chris.

[Image description: postcard showing a lighthouse, at full moon. The picture is a little blurry, as if the photographer's hand is shaking]

Rafe my dear,

I write to you in the knowledge that this may take a while. I spoke to the barmaid at the pub and she said "post can be a bit spotty" because—fill in your own answer about the postal service deeming remote coastal villages unimportant—and commiserated. Feeling like I was onto a winner in terms of actually extracting information, I asked her about the memorial in the gardens; she said she *didn't know about that* and gave such an anxious look stage-left to where her dad was refilling the pumps that I began to fear for her safety. I asked her if it was the people who'd been involved in transforming the "very pretty" gardens and she looked relieved, shrugged, and said "maybe".

It very clearly isn't.

After that I didn't have the guts to bring up the dead dog or the swarm of collars, lying like dead jellyfish on the beach. Lorena certainly wasn't going to; she'd got hold of the local(ish) newspaper and was despairing that the only news reported was that down road by about fifteen miles, where the actual train station is, and the Big Tesco. All the important amenities like secondary schools and doctors' surgeries and so on.

We left before closing this time, while it was still properly light, and didn't linger. Speaking of guts, by the way, the stench from my shoes was so bad even after rigorous washing that I had to leave them outside the cottage when we got back and go to the pub in my flipflops. You can imagine the comments.

And now it's 11:30 p.m., I've read everything in the house barring the bible (I have limits), and I cannot get over the idea that something is outside the cottage, again.

Chris

~~ETA: Rafe there is something fucking squirming on the lawn,~~

~~and I am pretty sure I just saw my fucking, fucking shoes in that mess. My *shoes*, Rafe.~~

~~Absolutely no love until I get new shoes.~~

Chris

[Image description: postcard of two small girls sunbathing on an English beach. Their mother, wearing a knotted hankie on her head, looks faintly troubled]

Rafe,

According to the thing in Lorena's diary, it's the full moon today. She says she knew anyway for mysterious woman reasons which are connected to how many painkillers she was necking at breakfast.

Associated with the painkiller intake and the fact that, despite the weather, she's dug out a hot water bottle, I've been on my own today. I'll see if she's any better this evening but it's probably better that I'm out of the house.

The lighthouse is one hundred percent out of the question now: even if I had some kind of nagging desire to investigate Dead Dog Central, I've only got flipflops since my shoes are??? One with the lawn? Who knows! On the moon. At the bottom of the ocean. Somewhere else, that's for sure. And my toes aren't up for brambles.

That also rules out traipsing uphill to the gardens to have another look at that memorial or just enjoy a pleasant sunny day in the company of some nice flowers, and relax, as originally intended. So it's the beach or nothing. I know, a week ago I'd have said "oh woe is me" sarcastically about that but what with dog collars and climbing fish and midnight swimmers I'm not feeling it, you know?

All the same, I'm writing this to you from an old red beach towel within sight of the pub, the sand is glistening and wet, there's a couple of kids industriously looking for seashells, and the boats are flying flat between the wall and the water, beached. I can't see anything out of the ordinary, and I think my toes are getting sunburnt.

Let's start again:

Having a lovely ("lovely") time. Wish you were here. Wish you would answer me. Wish I hadn't said all those stupid things before I left.

Chris.

[Image description: postcard bearing a hand-drawn illustration of a dancing poodle, which is wearing a little bow]

Rafe, read the other letter first. I know I put two in one envelope but I can't keep sending two letters a day in separates or I really will run out of stamps.

Still on the beach currently, watching the tide creep in with an odd sense of *conclusion*, and the ghost of the full moon is hanging in the big blue sky like a bulb waiting to be lit. I'm tempted to try to cook something in the cottage this evening rather than face the walk back from the pub alone, but I'm sure I don't need to end this sentence: you've seen what happens when I try to cook.

The children who were looking for shells have marched off, and it's just me, the sunshine, and the surprisingly few of the polite seagulls, and the smell of the sea. I definitely have burnt, inconsistently, where the suncream didn't quite reach. You'll see when I get back.

From where I'm sitting, the high tide mark on the path embankment is a dirty green line and the pub kind of looms down, half invisible, with the sign sticking out like the pointy front thing on a big ship. You know, what my twelve-year-old brain still calls the "booby titty lady person". I'd Google the proper term but, you know, no internet.

If I was climbing out of the ocean at high tide, like some sort of sea monster, that would probably be too imposing to take on. But someone walking on the path would be, I think, a pretty easy meal, like shoplifting a bag of crisps.

Not sure I want to hang around on the beach much longer after that. Maybe I'll go and case the garden for my fucking *shoes*.

Love, sunburnt and otherwise,

Chris

[Image description: postcard of a slightly grim-looking white man displaying a tableful of fish by the harbour wall of a perfectly ordinary English seaside village]

Dear Rafe, this one's number 3. Read the others first.

Watched the tide come in for a bit longer, then stumbled off the sand when a wave of indescribable stink poured up ahead of it. You remember when we went to the zoo and they had a Komodo dragon and I was complaining that reptiles somehow have this ability to smell three times worse than any other kind of animal? It smelled a bit like that, but wetter.

I did in fact go back to the house, found Lorena locked in the bathroom having an Anger Bath, apologised on general terms for the existence of the world, tried to find my shoes and only succeeded in finding a slimy, stinking sole which I think probably belonged to one of them . . . tangled in the hedge facing the sea.

Sat in the garden on the inland side reading old newspapers in the afternoon. A lot of notices about missing dogs, in the small ads, I've noticed, but all of the numbers to call for them are out-of-area. ~~Like the locals never lose a dog, or just know not to make a fuss about it~~. Mention of the village in one of the local papers, in passing, in a bizarre article which says it's been voted one of the country's most picturesque seaside towns, but ends with "such a shame" and no explanation.

I think I've made a mistake. It just seemed like such a cheap holiday cottage. If that wasn't a headline for a missing person ad . . .

You would at least write back and tell me if you thought I was going nuts, right?

Only I've been watching the sky trying to will it cloudy, like the moon is the source of whatever . . . weirdness . . . is going on. I'm pretty sure there *is* some weirdness going on. I appreciate the night is not the high point of this town but it is getting weirder the more moon there is. The shoes, the dog collars, even if I imagined the climbing fish I didn't imagine my *shoes* turning up like this.

I'm going to throw this in the post on my way down to the pub.

Seeya soon, I hope,

Chris

[Image description: postcard depicting a picturesque little cottage with roses in the front garden. The name Good Catch is visible above the front door]

Rafe,

I have no fucking idea why I'm writing. I'm just . . . I'll put this in a postbox in town.

On my way to the pub I went to throw your letter into the post. It just stuck out the top of the box and wouldn't go in no matter how much I jiggled it. Because this is the arse of nowhere they don't appear to lock the postbox; I just got it open by thumping it with the flat of my hand.

Whole thing full of letters. Right up to the top. Picked out one of the bottom ones: a postcard addressed to Kevin in Leith. Dated two years ago. Clearly no one is actually collecting these at all. Some kind of practical joke by the villagers that probably wouldn't have been noticed at all if I hadn't been writing to you incontinently.

Took all my letters and a few others off the top, went back to the cottage, and chucked them in my suitcase. At least explains why you're not answering. I rescind my prior remarks, as we keep having to make the clients say . . .

Have returned to the pub to write this, solely because there's no food in the house worth eating. And everyone is just normal, as if they don't have a postbox no one ever collects letters from. I can't start something with them about it if they're not . . . admitting it, right? I have no idea how you even bring it up. (Lorena has retreated to her room with vegan chocolate and will not be reasoned with, I tried to tell her about the post box and received only Italian swearing.)

Very quiet in here. Just me and the barmaid. She keeps looking out of the window. Soup—only thing on the menu tonight—very clearly just reheated from a can. I'm not complaining, especially now, but they are *right next to the sea* where the fish are, you'd think they'd have some.

Occurred to me that this is exactly the kind of place you'd expect a pub dog, and they don't have one.

Also occurred to me that the sea is also full of other, less edible things.

Impatient to come home, frankly.

Love,

Chris

[Image description: postcard of some fishing boats, pulled up onto the sand of a low tide. Barely visible, poking out from behind one, is a bare human foot]

Rafe,

Sun is hanging low in the sky. Barmaid has just anxiously said I should be running along now. Asked me, briefly, if I was a journalist. Looked both relieved and bitterly disappointed when I said no. Muttered something about puppy farms? Postcard image unrelated.

Chris

---------- mailerdaemon: message not sent ---------
From: Chris-Toph-Error <bigbigbigerrorbaby@gmail.com>
Date: Mon, Sep 18, 2023 at 3:16 AM
Subject: help or something I guess
To: Rafe Samuels <rafesamuels@gmail.com>

Jesus Christ Rafe I finally get to the fucking internet and you're not online? I appreciate it's 3:00 a.m. but after all this time I'd hoped you might develop a sense of when something's wrong. Ignore any and all typos.

Left the pub too close to sunset. Was on my way back along the coast path when I heard something go *smack* against the tidal wall and was going to firmly ignore it but then there was a *yelp* and I couldn't help myself.

Turned around and the pub landlord was pulling away a sack with a grim expression. Walked off without looking at me. Down in the water I can hear struggling and thrashing, whimpering noises. Another smack. End of whimpering noses and the feeling you get when you're being watched by something that could kill you. Tiger staring through the glass at the zoo kind of feeling. Something down there wants my blood kind of feeling.

I'm a sensible prison, Rafe—shut up—and normally I'd have just legged it to the cottage and barricaded the door, but you can't bloody leg it in flipflops. So I just kind of froze there on the spot.

Which meant the *thing* that writhed out of the water came up between me and the cottage, instead of directly on top of me, as it squirmed up the steps.

I have no idea why I thought it was a person swimming in the water. It looked **very briefly** human, something hand-shaped gripping the edge of the path, something facelike *staring at me* as I stood there, but mostly it looked like a fractal infinity of squirming . . . squirm . . . shining in the very last rays of light.

A little pink dog collar dropped out of what I can only assume was its mouth. Maybe its anus. Oh, autocorrect gets that word right first time, I see. I don't know and I don't care. I was pretty sure the world was about to drop out of *my* anus at that point.

Currently hiding behind the pub,
Chris

> *(0041-7333-290-108)*
> *Rafe-DO NOT ANSWER YOU'RE MAD AT HIM*
> *Monday, Sep 18, 2023 3:20 AM*

> *Hey ANSWER YOUR DUCKING EMAIL*

> *Please*

> *Answer me*

> *. . .*

From: Rafe Samuels <rafesamuels@gmail.com>
Date: Mon, Sep 29, 2023 at 10:07 AM
Subject: WTF?
To: Chris-Toph-Error <bigbigbigerrorbaby@gmail.com>

Chris,

Just been handed a gigantic stack of unhinged postcards from someone claiming to be you. Has your handwriting and voice down to a T, but I'm assuming isn't you because you don't, as a rule, send hundreds of unhinged postcards when you're sulking. Anyway, it's been a couple of weeks now and I've had a chance to calm down about the job; you were probably right. Hope you're satisfied with that. I assume you're back home now, can't fathom why you're not answering the bloody *phone* but I'd like to see you again. Please.

Rafe

LOVE LIKE THE MOON

TYLER BATTAGLIA

 Their first time was terrifying, yet still strangely beautiful in the intimacy of what passed between them beneath the full moon that night.

The night began when Melissa led Nancy down the rickety, creaking steps to the dark and damp basement. Earlier, she asked Nancy in a frightened whisper, *You're not going to leave me, are you?* and Nancy swore that no matter what happened—or *didn't* happen—to Melissa down there, whatever she *became*, Nancy would stay by her side. Melissa had whispered *It's going to be dangerous* and *I just want you to be sure* and it scared Nancy, but Melissa was safe, and she would keep *Nancy* safe, so even as a million fears raced through her mind about what she was going to find in that basement, she would stay.

Still, the entire way through the house and down the stairs to the ominous unfinished basement with a bare mattress pressed against the wall, Melissa held Nancy's hand tight. If it had been anyone else, Nancy would have run. Anyone but Melissa. But Nancy had no intentions of running, ever. She'd committed to seeing the night through with Melissa and, if luck favoured them, many more nights to come.

Nancy studied the contrasting lines of their joined hands with obsession, seeing where the planes and valleys met and broke apart. Even the differences in their nails, Nancy's bare and chipped, Melissa's painted and perfect. Nancy felt fortunate to be able to touch Melissa in that moment, no matter what came next, a balm for the self-imposed loneliness she had felt her whole life. She would hold onto this memory to get her through the night.

When Melissa let go, it was too soon. Or perhaps not—Nancy checked the time on her phone. The moon would rise soon enough.

"Help me with this," Melissa said, indicating the dirty mattress with a tilt of her head. Her blonde curls bounced over her shoulders, and Nancy wondered what they felt like—*would* feel like—under her fingertips. She also wondered what happened to the beautiful blonde curls and perfectly painted nails on a night like this.

Nancy approached the mattress, digging her hands into the fabric as Melissa gripped the other side with her nails—blue and pink and white. They heaved together and flipped the mattress onto the floor, exposing wounds and tears, spilling polyester batting across the floor like entrails. Nancy noticed a spattering of blood on the floor where the stuffing fell and wondered for a terrifying instant if the blood was Melissa's or someone else's.

In the place where the mattress had rested against the wall, thick chains were bolted into the cement, the kind Nancy saw at auto shops and meant for bearing a surprising amount of weight. They were old enough to have rusted around the welds, probably from the dampness of the basement, and ended in a thick choke collar. A second mattress—just as soggy and tattered—leaned against the wall in the opposite corner. Nancy wondered if an equally disturbing set of chains capable of holding someone or something back—be it girl or wolf or monster—was hidden behind it.

That was the first moment when things started to get a little too *real*. Maybe it was the truth that the choke collar and chains implied. *Something* had happened in that basement, and none of the possibilities seemed pleasant. Even if what Melissa was telling her was true—the chains were meant to hold back a monster—they could hold back something much more innocent, too. *Someone* much more innocent.

"Are these for—?"

"When I turn, yes." Melissa pointed to the other mattress. "My ex and I used to chain each other up, so we'd only be a danger to ourselves. It's a miracle we never tore each other apart, chained down here with nowhere else to go. Maybe Peter was worried we'd get creative and it would happen eventually. Maybe that's why he ran off into the woods."

Faltering, Nancy said, "I'm sorry for your loss."

Melissa laughed, cheerful but burying a tiny, inelegant snort. The sound was divine. "You make it sound like he died. He randomly sends me postcards from whatever town's treeline he's haunting. I think he's living his best life, but I couldn't do it. I'd miss urban amenities. It sort of killed the relationship by necessity, even if he hadn't exactly *meant* to dump me and leave me high and dry. I couldn't do long distance when the boy in question is running around the forest like a wild animal, you know?"

"I know." Nancy didn't. She wasn't sure if she ever could. She hesitated to imagine an apparent monster running around the woods. She also tried not to imagine Melissa, alone in this dank basement, or what kind of threat Peter was worried about. Instead, Nancy looked back to the chains. "Just the one chain holds you—?"

"It's enough."

Melissa walked to a black resin shelf leaning against the wall, crooked and wavering. It looked hastily built, pieces not quite fitting like they were supposed to and the base not flat against the bare floor. Somehow, it was holding up despite the mildewy boxes stacked on top of it. Her eyes landed on one box that had toppled off the shelf, the cardboard collapsing under its own soggy weight—a stuffed animal poked out of the broken flaps, except it had been decapitated with something sharp and ragged, leaving stitching dangling from it like a noose. Like the mattress, polyester gore burst from the seams. The head was nowhere to be found. Nancy wondered what else had been abandoned inside the boxes, never to see the light of day again.

Melissa picked up a key. "We don't have a lot of time left. You need to help chain me up."

Nancy's heart hammered between her lungs when Melissa's

fingers brushed hers to deposit the key into her hands. Everything was suddenly terrifyingly *real* in that moment, in a basement that looked just like one in a serial killer docuseries, lit by the dying rays of sunlight sneaking through the narrow window near the ceiling. In the dark, she was sure it would change into the sort of place that would make her look over her shoulder. But she would be brave, she had to be. Melissa trusted her to be in charge of her safety and she in turn would trust Melissa to not hurt *her*. And Nancy would get to see a secret part of Melissa.

If Melissa didn't become a beast when the full moon rose, she certainly *believed* that she would. Nancy thought about Melissa's hand in hers. She thought of the way they had fit together almost too well. Melissa gripping too tightly, her palm clammy against warm skin. Nancy made up her mind again to stay.

Carefully, in reverent silence, Nancy secured Melissa. Her fingers trembled as she fastened the collar around Melissa's throat, cognizant of the pounding of Melissa's pulse under her fingertips as her fingers brushed her skin. As she hooked the chain through the loop of the collar, she noticed how warm Melissa was against the cool metal of the chain and the padlock. As she latched the padlock into place, securing the collar and chain, she wondered how many people had been given the privilege to see Melissa like this. If she was special.

She held the key in her hands for a moment, feeling the shape and weight of it, memorizing every detail so she would never lose track of it, could identify the exact pattern of the teeth among any number of near-identical keys, before she pocketed it. She was distinctly aware of it close to her skin.

Melissa had enough slack she could sit on the mattress, but she couldn't get to the edge. She crossed her legs, looking up at Nancy with a warm but somehow unconcerned smile. Nancy pictured sharpened teeth under painted lips. Her heart kept racing.

"You can get out of here now," Melissa said. "But please come back in the morning get me out."

Nancy hesitated. "I'll stay. For now."

"Why?" Melissa's smile faltered. "It's not pretty, Nancy."

The use of her name made her heart bloom like the murmuration of a flock of starlings, ready to burst into the night sky. "I just want to make sure everything's okay. I'll stay . . . until you turn," she lied.

"If you think you have to see it to believe it," Melissa's voice was slow with a hint of warning, "then just say so."

It wasn't fair to either of them. But Nancy told the truth this time: "It would make me feel better to know for sure. That it's real—*and* that you're safe."

"Okay. But it's going to get ugly down here, Nancy."

Nancy doubted that anything about Melissa could ever be ugly. "I know."

Walking a few paces toward the other destroyed mattress, Nancy wondered if she should lay it down to sit on, if she was willing to chance whatever vermin might be crawling through it. Instead, she walked a little further, to a pile of boxes to perch on nearer the middle of the room.

"If you're staying, you shouldn't stay too close. Just in case," Melissa warned softly.

Nancy walked further to the wooden steps—a more Melissa-approved distance—and asked, "Better?"

"Better," Melissa agreed with a little sigh of her own.

Nancy sat on the bottom step, shoving her hands into her hoodie pocket as the step creaked beneath her. She fidgeted with the key and waited. It was hard to resist the temptation to check when, precisely, the moon was supposed to rise.

"Thank you for doing this for me."

Nancy licked her lips, her mouth dry from nerves. "Maybe I just owe you a favour," she joked without a lot of conviction. "For all the times you've bailed me out."

Melissa laughed. There was a grainier quality to it now, like her voice was growing rougher around the edges. "We have to stick together, don't we?" she asked. "We're two birds of a feather. Or maybe—wolves of a pelt?"

"How so?"

Melissa's mouth curled into a wicked grin, her glossy lips curling back to show teeth. They looked too big for her mouth now, and Nancy wondered how she could have possibly missed that before. "Girls who *transform*."

It sent shivers up Nancy's spine. The playfully dangerous cut to Melissa's voice was new, and welcome. Pretty, perfect Melissa showing her truth: that she could and *would* bite.

But that wasn't news to her. Melissa mauled anyone who hurt Nancy. When rumours were started, Melissa tracked down the source and made them retract every lie. When some jerk had tailed them while walking at night, Melissa had knocked him to the ground and twisted his arm behind his back until he cried.

Melissa only ever offered one explanation: "Because I've never met a more genuine heart than yours. I worry that the wrong person will eat you alive."

Now Nancy suspected that it all carried more weight than she thought. Melissa's *bite* would be worse than her bark, and perhaps a lot more literal.

"Do you remember," Nancy asked, hoping to lighten the mood, "when we skipped class to find that fallen tree you told me about, in the woods behind campus? The one blooming with mushrooms and moss? I don't think we missed much, but we found a lot."

I thought about us carving our initials into the bark together, she wanted to add. *Not even in a romantic way. It doesn't have to be. Just to memorialize our time together in that old tree, so that anthropologists a thousand years from now would know we were together, we were* there, *in that captured moment. That it happened, and it was real.*

Melissa's reply was a slow, guttural gurgle. Her eyes were gleaming—too bright to look at—but there was clarity there. Maybe she remembered the tree. Maybe she had wanted to carve their initials there, too. Maybe she had just forgotten her pocketknife.

Maybe . . . Nancy had other things to worry about right now.

Melissa's mouth was misshapen now, lips pulled taut, taking the ability to form words. Her skin was stretching, her jaw elongating. She growled through contorted teeth, the enamel grinding until something *cracked*. Dry heaving, Melissa coughed a mouthful of teeth onto the mattress, a few molars tumbling onto the floor with the force of the expulsion. Blood dribbled down her chin, but it quickly got muddled, half-lost, in yellow sable fur sprouting along her throat and swallowing up washed-out skin. Her bones *snapped*, limbs morphing into new shapes as she doubled over, hugging herself until her arms couldn't hold the right shape anymore to comfort herself. A gurgling cry broke from Melissa's misshapen mouth, a haunting cross between a sob and growl.

Clumps of her beautiful blonde curls fell ragged, leaving her scalp patchy as more fur bristled from her skin. Strands of it stuck to her sweat-soaked cheeks and caught on her blackened lips as her eyes bulged and ears forced themselves into inhuman positions. Melissa whined as new teeth burst through her gums, oversized canines at the front of her mouth flashing as the whimper turned into a growl.

The skin of her hands pulled taut across expanding bones, stretching to the point that Nancy thought the elasticity might snap, but instead her palms hardened into paw pads, no longer the supple skin that had fit so well into Nancy's hand. Melissa's perfectly manicured nails split down the middle and the jagged, broken halves collided like tectonic plates and buckled into curved claws, the blue and pink and white nail polish marbling with the surrounding midnight keratin. The vertebrae of Melissa's spine *burst* and rearranged themselves, while her hips shifted back so she could walk on all fours.

Her entire body strained and warped. Splintering, breaking, then rebuilding itself.

But her eyes, her bright eyes, stayed the longest, until even those were lost.

The howl that the wolf—*Melissa*—let out was haunting. Whimpering and growling, she fought the binds for only a few moments before she gave up. The chains must have become familiar, her monthly imprisonment remembered.

And she was a wolf. She was really a wolf.

Nancy let out a choked sob through her fingers, having covered her mouth like it would stop her from screaming. To her credit, it had.

Melissa was a *wolf*.

Nancy would have to re-write her reality in the morning, but for now her best friend, her best friend who she loved more than anything, was a wolf with sharp claws and long teeth, growling softly in a way that suggested discomfort more than aggression.

Nancy would stay all night, until morning, when she had to trust Melissa would be Melissa again.

No matter how long she had to hold in that scream.

Nancy sobbed again, lowering her head to trap it between her knees, until the relentless bestial lament became white noise. Until rhythmic animal noises lulled her to sleep.

The silence woke her. At some point, Melissa had calmed down enough that she, too, had fallen asleep.

But it was still nighttime, and Melissa was still a wolf. Nancy still gripped the key. She hadn't imagined any of it. It had happened, and it was real.

Yet, she looked peaceful. Nancy watched the slow rise of the wolf's breathing in her side, her tail curled around her back legs but her body loose and stomach turned slightly upward, her head pillowed on her paws. Melissa looked almost more at ease as a wolf than as a human, when her eyes were too bright to look at and there was always that hint of bite hiding under the surface, a restless aggression that she didn't quite know what to do with.

Maybe she would look equally peaceful as a sleeping human, and Nancy hoped maybe she would one day be able to say for sure, but as a sleeping wolf, Melissa looked like she was finally finding some solace.

Carefully, Nancy pressed herself to stand from where she was slumped over on the stairs, begging the wood not to creak. Her head spun. Her throat was dry. It made sense—she had cried herself to sleep, after all—but it still felt awful.

She walked to the degraded mattress where wolf-Melissa slept and lowered herself beside her in the polyester nest. Nancy held her breath and held the key tight in her hand. After a moment, Melissa settled, her wolf-shape curling closer to Nancy as if on instinct, surrounding her, straining at her chain and collar to be closer. Maybe she was drawn to a warm body. Nancy didn't dare exhale and disturb the stillness.

Nancy was about to cry again. Lying next to a sleeping wolf had been a risk, but the warmth of the fur against her back was worth it, rough but somehow plush beneath her, enveloping her. Now that she felt safe to breathe again, Nancy inhaled, taking in the rich animal scent of her friend, the woodsy musk that reminded her of rain in a forest. Maybe she was romanticising, but it smelled like a safe haven. Melissa had always protected her. Nancy understood she always would.

When the sunlight streamed through the windows, Nancy knew for certain that the night was over because Melissa's arm, now cradling her, was again human. Her nails, despite it all, still painted blue and pink and white, though the paint had become rough and would need touching-up.

The chain linking her to the wall stretched above them both. As Melissa stirred, the metal clinked gently, a strangely soft noise coming out of the chaotic night.

An exhausted murmur muffled into Nancy's back. "Nancy?"

"I'm here."

"You said you'd leave after I changed." The pause felt like an eternity. "You lied."

Nancy flushed, turning slowly to face her. They came nose-to-nose; it took Nancy's breath away, and with it any excuse, argument, or justification. She wasn't sorry.

Melissa was almost naked, her clothes nothing more than tattered rags, shredded from the transformation, but it hardly mattered.

"How are you feeling?" Nancy asked, opening the hand that still clutched the key. Her palm hurt where the ridges had bit in, leaving sharp red indents in the skin. With careful movements, she leaned over Melissa and unlocked the padlock on the collar, letting the chain fall loose. When Melissa didn't remove the collar herself, Nancy unclasped it, this time letting her fingers brush against Melissa's pulse point again.

Rubbing at a blossoming purple bruise on her throat once she was free, Melissa shared a weary smile. "Tired. In pain. Always am after the moon. Kind of all the time, actually. I guess it figures, my body reshaping itself once a month probably does some hell to the musculoskeletal system."

Maybe that was the real reason for wolf-tears in the night. Not just sorrow, but pain. She wished she could ask Melissa, understand everything she had felt. Had she been scared? Mourning? Or had it simply hurt—and everything else was beyond the wolf? Nancy didn't know if questions about what it was like to be a *wolf* were welcome, even if Melissa remembered. "Do you remember anything?"

Something like pain flashed across Melissa's eyes, and she answered a little too quickly, no pause to search her memory. "No."

Nancy supposed she wasn't the only one who could lie.

The first few months—on the night of the full moon—were similar, then Nancy suggested Melissa roam free. Do what Peter did, explore the woods. Stretch herself out, breathe the fresh air, let herself run free. Although she slept peacefully once she found rest, Melissa was always miserable when night first fell, chained up to a wall in a grungy basement, sleeping on a mattress that Nancy quickly discovered had bed bugs.

"Maybe another time," Melissa kept saying. "It's too dangerous right now." Nancy didn't know what might change to make Melissa think it was safe, but she wanted to find out.

So, they stayed in the basement. The transformation became easier to stomach each full moon, a little less frightening—for Nancy, at least, who had the benefit of not spitting her teeth across the floor or losing unglamorous clumps of hair. They even scrounged up some money to replace the mattress with something marginally less gross, and a little throw the colour of wolf-Melissa's fur to keep warm in the poorly insulated basement as winter approached. It wasn't ideal, but she did what she could to try and make Melissa's time howling at a moon she couldn't see more bearable.

Nancy got a little braver, straying closer sooner each time. Some months, she sat right on the new mattress and read to wolf-Melissa while she was still awake. She wasn't sure how much Melissa remembered, but one day found Melissa finishing the book they'd started while she was a wolf.

It was finally the mail that changed her mind. A postcard from Peter from the same small town as last time. A little woodsy place, a lumber town. Peter had landed a job at the papermill. He was trying to integrate into the community.

Together, Melissa and Nancy looked up the town. There were no sightings of strange wolves, or concerns about townspeople going mysteriously missing. Nothing out of the ordinary. Nothing at all to indicate Peter was some kind of secret menace picking off human prey one by one.

The next time they prepared for their moonlit ritual, Melissa said, "Let's go to the woods tonight."

Nancy's heart sang.

They drove together in silence to the wooded area behind campus. It was off-season, most students went home after finals. It would be just the two of them.

They held hands as they walked through the edge of the trees. Nancy examined the now-familiar planes and valleys where their hands met and broke apart, and Melissa's nails, now painted pink and purple and blue.

This time, Nancy led the way, and Melissa followed, their boots crunching in still-falling snow the only noise disturbing the forest. She hoped this was a memory Melissa also held onto, that it would mean something. When they came upon the fallen tree, bark dried out by winter air and frosted over with a dusting of snow, Melissa grinned playfully. "This place again?" Even with the moss and mushrooms dead for the season, she remembered. The tree meant something. Melissa added softly, "Good choice."

Their hands parted, but with no regret this time because Nancy knew they would find each other again in the morning. Nancy sat on the log after dusting off some of the snow for a drier seat on the dead tree. She didn't mind the cold of the night or the bark, even as her breath plumed out into frosty air.

"Not the best weather for stripping naked in the woods, huh?" Melissa winked as she shed her clothes like a ritual and handed them to Nancy for safekeeping. There was no point ruining the clothes in the transformation. Melissa stood naked in the woods. She stood with her face turned to the sky, gentle snowfall gracing her cheeks, the remaining light of day dappling her skin through the canopy of leaves, beautiful, illustrious. For a moment, Melissa felt too bright to look at, something dazzling about her, a beautiful flower that could kill you if disturbed, her petals bright in warning, but Nancy was not afraid. She had seen terrible things, but her love had only grown. Despite what she knew was coming, despite the cold, she sat straight and would stand guard through the night. If she could survive this, she could survive anything, and she wouldn't be afraid again.

Somehow, Melissa didn't look cold in the winter night, in snow up to her ankles. They spoke softly, so as not to disturb the forest with anything more than the chilled puffs of breath breaking the air.

When moonlight came, so too did the transformation. As always, Melissa's body bent and snapped before becoming something new. She gritted her teeth until she was ready to spit them out, she tugged at her blonde curls, helping shed her hair to make way for the fur. She grimaced through the pain, blood dripping from her chin and splattering red against the snow-crusted forest floor, wiping it from her face with the back of her hand, smearing it in her fresh fur. But this time she was in a new space, where she could stretch her legs and the moonlight could brush her fur. Nancy hoped it made the night easier to bear.

As always, Melissa's eyes were the last to go.

When Melissa was fully wolf, Nancy reached into the backpack to find her book—it was the same one they had been reading the previous month, not having reached the ending herself and intending to read while Melissa ran free, but as she dug in the backpack, she found something else, something cold to the touch.

A pocketknife.

The wolf roamed the forest floor, sniffing at every new smell that came with it, glorying in the wooded haven, leaving deep pawprints in the snow as she trotted confidently across the frozen wood. Her head turned to Nancy when the moonlight glinted off the knife, turning the snow to diamonds.

She padded over, nosing Nancy's hand, then the log.

Nancy remembered.

It felt like a sin to disturb any part of the forest, yet a thrill to become a small part of its grand memory that would outlive any of their footprints. Nancy's heart raced as she carved their initials into the bark. She drew no symbols around them; no cliché hearts, no pluses, no signs. They didn't need anyone to understand. No anthropologist, in a thousand years, needed to know the exact depths of their intimacy. It would be enough to know they were *there*, together, in that captured moment. That it happened, and it was real.

Nancy put the pocketknife back in the bag and looked to her wolf for approval.

Melissa wandered a pace away, standing in a patch of moonlight that glistened off her sable fur, illuminating it, beautiful and free against the backdrop of snowy trees. She lifted her head to the sky that was just peeking through the treetops, and she howled.

It was not in mourning, nor in suffering. It was a howl of adulation and adoration for the forest, for the moon, for her freedom. Nancy lifted her head to the sky, hoping to catch the sight of the glorious moon to which Melissa sang.

And she joined her in song.

IMPACT CITY

CAT McDONALD

TRACK 1—~ insurrection~ feat. LUMINOUS
---
mercurie
LOCATION: OBSERVATORY STAGE

She waits in silence, standing in darkness on the stage. Waiting for the first perfect instant.

Everything is glowing brilliantly, and she knows the crowd can see her, but the last DJ ended their set a little down-tempo so she can afford to take her time. Good, because her chest is pounding—she coughs a little from the anxiety before taking a deep breath and looking out at her audience. The crowd, decked out in neon, are beyond vibrant in the black light, as is the inside of the enormous domed tent that is Observatory Stage, the main stage. She smiles; they're beautiful.

For six years they've tried to wake the creature that came from the stars with annual festivals throbbing with bass and light. The creature's power, its love, its attention is there for the taking. Thousands have arrived for the seventh year of Impact City.

The crowd can't feel it, but she can. The air is pulsing, the earth is trembling. It's stirring.

mercurie is a Summoner, one of dozens performing this year. Grasping at her hard-won chance to be the one to imprint on it.

But more than that.

When her stage lights flare on and ~*insurrection*~ kicks to life, driving an aggressive drumbeat into the air in time with every flash, she can see the sea of people moving like a shoal of luminescent fish.

And she'll imprint on them too.

TRACK 2—ACCELERATE

JACKPOT
LOCATION: LAKESIDE STAGE

Accelerate is an up-tempo number even for him, and he paces against it, arms swinging, completely overcome by nervous energy. It's like this every time he's on stage.

Otherwise, he tries not to think about it.

The Summoner who won at Astral Bounty not only had his wish granted, he became famous. Apex is a household name now because of the power of the meteor child he hatched.

And next will be Jackpot. He stares out through the strobing light, at the way the dancing crowd seems reduced to slow-motion before him. Only he's moving full-speed, and he's going to use that to his advantage.

No one plays Impact City twice.

It's going to be him.

He smiles down at the rowdy crowd in the pit, and they all return his smile.

Who else could it possibly be?

TRACK 3—FATALE

HER
LOCATION: TEMPLE STAGE

Temple Stage is dark, surrounded by trees that block the view of the other stages. No one else is here. No one else's sound can penetrate this place, and even the moonlight seems to struggle to touch a stage that belongs to HER.

She doesn't need flash. She sways gently toward the audience, and in this moment, with the low notes of *Fatale* buzzing in their lungs, they too belong to HER.

She inhales the sound, and swells with the mood and a force that presses against her throat as if trying to escape.

HER, the artist, the performer, the ONLY, has something the other Summoners don't have.

Raw power.

That inhaled note releases, deep and rich and powerful even against the bass of *Fatale*. Some of the dancers freeze, rightly transfixed. She's a sight to behold.

Impact City trembles at the sound of HER. Perhaps even beyond. And this meteor child will be hers, will belong to ONLY HER, and with it anything in the world she could desire. A litany of wishes dance across her heart as she sings, and more and more dancers stop and begin to sway gently in time, all eyes on HER, enraptured.

TRACK 4— DESTINED FEAT. WILDFIRE YOUTH

CONTAGION
LOCATION: HORIZON STAGE

A large mask hides most of the swarm of people from them. It conceals the trees, the brush of the wind, and the starlight above Impact City, but they know Horizon Stage. They've spent every night here since the festival started.

When the sun rises, this will be the first place it reaches. In fact, Contagion occupies the precise spot which will be the first illuminated, hours and hours too early for dawn, and paces. For this track, most of the heavy lifting is done by the projector, bathing Contagion and their costume in shifting light and shadow as the deep, grimy sound seeps into the bodies of the audience. Sparks of light, the energetic and driven rap of Wildfire Youth, lend the track a vile effervescence.

Contagion breathes deep, and the air, even through their mask, tastes like the artificial smoke pumped in from offstage. The stage is flooded in a thick fog that shimmers in the stage light, mysterious, as befits the site of the meteor child's awakening.

Contagion doesn't use a mic. The swarm can't hear them any

more than they can hear the swarm. They prefer it that way. The spectators may as well not be there, except for the thrill of their attention buzzing within the mask.

Contagion was no novice, they'd watched the competition scramble. Jackpot vanished half a year to rehearse something that wouldn't be much unlike his previous work. HER arranged a fresh track for her devastating banshee vocals. Even mercurie, a beginner, had upgraded her stage conjurations.

Contagion did research. And, unknown to the masses, like they always are, they begin to whisper the results of that research, the incantation they found, into the wall of sound, under the beat of *destined*.

TRACK 5—*Radium GIRL*

mercurie
LOCATION: OBSERVATORY STAGE

From the centre of the festival grounds, within the impact crater where the meteor child slumbers, a deep and booming slam stabs through the night. The speakers squeal reverent feedback, killing the music so the tremor has no competition.

mercurie cranes her neck, trying to see over the trees. The brilliant lights of Lakeside Stage and the ominous statues marking the path to Temple Stage are faint through the dark; they too trembled at the sound.

The pause is a breath. A moment.

Then, the world breathes again. The lights return to their pale blue swirling, and *Radium GIRL* takes over the air in a whirlwind, stirring up the stillness with electric energy. This is the song that summoned the dead to her side, this is the song that conjured mercurie into being, the song that forged her from the slag of her old self.

Just like they rehearsed, the ghosts begin to move as the stage lights die down, glowing the same eerie teal in a ballet of death and regrets. The crowd gasps.

That's right, mercurie thinks. You've seen Summoners before, but have you seen a Necromancer?

She joins the dead in their dance, becomes part of the spectacle.

This is who I am, she thinks so hard she can feel her heartbeat piercing the noise, projecting into the centre of Impact City. This is who I am.

Accept me.

TRACK 6—APEX ULTIMATE

JACKPOT

LOCATION: LAKESIDE STAGE

The shriek of feedback startles him just as the last number starts to fade into *Apex Ultimate*, and for a second Jackpot is slammed out of his rhythm. The fans can feel it too, and soon their shocked silence and stillness gives way to eager chatter.

It's happening. This is the year the meteor child at Impact City awakens.

His head starts racing. Who did it? Whose music reached the centre of the crater?

It wasn't his. He'd know if it were, wouldn't he?

Apex Ultimate starts to throb through the speakers and the crowd is still watching him, stunned, as he comes to the realization that he's been frozen in place for almost twenty seconds.

He takes a deep, deep breath to steady himself before he plunges back into the show and flashes the front row a broad, counterfeit smile. If the party ends here, the meteor child will find someone else. But maybe there's still time to attract its attention.

As the first climb in a song full of steep drops begins, he spreads his arms open wide and breathes through the song until he can feel the flare spirits with him, invisibly cranking the temperature on stage. The essence of fire, of sunlight, of raw brilliance, roughly formed into human shapes that can't contain their energy.

And then, just in time for the bass drop, he kicks a switch to turn off the stage light and lets the spirits do the rest in supernatural scarlet firelight.

The crowd gasps, but Jackpot can't feel any more from the crater. He's lost and not even the flare spirits can comfort him.

TRACK 7—SPIRAL*BIND

HER

LOCATION: TEMPLE STAGE

The knocking from the crater didn't shake HER, she couldn't afford to let it. She took in a deep inhale to prepare for the piercing first high note of *Spiral*bind*, an enchanting song meant to snare hearts and sway those dancing bodies laid out in front of her.

She has so much she wants. She is a bottomless pit of yearning and she knows that with this voice, she is deeply, deeply contagious. Her audience wants more, they want more HER, and they want her to be the one that reaches the meteor child.

In wisps like scattered cobwebs, the shadows emerge answering her call, dancing around the penumbra like moths circling a lone porch light. Like the rest of the world, the shadows revolve around HER, desire her, serve her.

But no matter how much power she pours into her voice, the crater doesn't answer. She empties herself into the darkness, spills her limitless desire and formidable soul and nothing answers her.

Her gaze settles on the dancers in front of her, their adoration hers.

Fine, she thinks in the silence between notes. I'll take you all instead.

And it takes a moment, but she does smile.

TRACK 8—Event Horizon

CONTAGION

LOCATION: HORIZON STAGE

Event Horizon looms behind the last song's fading outro like a storm behind a mountain. Contagion can sense the rabble's growing anxiety even though the mask. They're not wrong to be nervous. Impact City always gets chaotic at this time of night, as Summoners unleash everything to awaken the meteor child. The assembled mass in front of their stage are insects compared to the power at play, and in the wrong hands, they'll be crushed. Contagion glances at Temple Stage with a wry smile, knowing what must have happened to the swarm there by now.

Desperation is hot in the air, now that everyone has heard the creature stirring; their invocation worked. Now, Contagion has the undivided attention of the meteor child, and *Event Horizon* is starting, a slow, heavy, brutal track with deep crushing bass.

Contagion is not here to have some idle wish granted. Contagion is here for power.

The meteor child is approaching, so close to being ready to grant the power Contagion desires. The power to destroy and rebuild everything, to reshape the world in Contagion's image and stamp out the world's bloated and rotten governments, great and small.

Only now, deep into the ritual, does their heart begin to race. It will not only be their perfect world. It will be a world with no way to stray from perfection.

The silver-blue light of Luna herself, the iridescent moon spirit, accompanies them on stage, not as any part of the show, but to watch, as she loves to. Her light dissipates in silver layers through the smoke, concealing Contagion further as the ritual continues behind a veil of deception.

Now, Contagion can feel the meteor child's gaze on them.

That's right, they think. I awakened you.

You're like a child to me.

Luna smiles.

TRACK 9—Echo Eternal Feat. Angela and DJ Brickhouse

mercurie

LOCATION: OBSERVATORY STAGE

Another deep rumble echoes from the impact crater, so intense and close that Observatory Stage trembles. For a moment the music yields to silence, enough to throw mercurie off rhythm and make her stumble. A spirit catches her in phosphorescent arms.

Then the music resurrects once more. mercurie and the spirits take their places and rejoin the dance.

It's waking up. It's responding to someone.

She can't feel anything different. Would she know, if she were the one it was watching?

Forget that.

Just dance.

"Everybody! One, two, let's move!" she shouts into her mic. DJ stuff. Normal things, to hype up the crowd. And herself.

The dead aren't her backup dancers. She's theirs.

And together with this painted, glowing audience, they're so much more beautiful than she is on her own.

Everyone has wishes. Every person in that crowd has a wish. Every ghost on her stage has a wish, even those betrayed by the world.

Don't come to me, she thinks to the crater.

Come to *us*. Accept us.

Echo Eternal is dear to her. A close friend's beautiful vocals, another friend's determined rap, her own music, and the dance of the fallen. And now, the eager audience of Observatory Stage, fully alive in the beat. The song has never been more wonderful.

Another crash resounds from the crater and every other stage goes dark.

But the radiant people, dead or alive, that dance at Observatory Stage won't let this moment end. Even when the white light pours into the stage from the crater.

The music can't be stopped.

CORRINE'S CAROUSEL

RICHARD DiPIRRO

 On calm nights, when the air was still and the cackling, chittering insects in the long grass outside her home finally grew quiet, Corrine would wake to the sound of her own screams. Her chest would fill before she was awake, like an imminent explosion emptying the room of oxygen. Then her eyes would open, and the air would burst from her throat in a rending concussion of sound that awoke anyone in hearing range and left them desperate to help her.

It was the stillness in the late hours of the night that wrapped Corrine in dark, silent loneliness which overwhelmed and threatened to smother her in her bed. Stillness of the earth. Stillness of a void, where she lay surrounded by nothing, with nothing to gauge distance or time, nothing to relate to her own existence. To *prove* her own existence. Her nightly screams at once resounded into soundless space and reverberated as if against the inside of a pinewood box.

That poor girl . . .

Corrine had never known a mother. She had never been swept

into that warm, sweet, original embrace. When the screams came and she awoke in a sweating panic, it was one of the rotating succession of haggard housekeepers or nannies who tried in vain to comfort her. Then Corrine's father would caress her damp hair with his callused fingers in clumsy attempts at allaying her fear. He spoke quietly to her in a gravelly voice, night after night, until she fell back into a fitful sleep. Until the next horrifying scream brought him running back to her bedside.

Corrine's father was a farmer. A sweet, quiet man who worked hard and only spoke when words were needed. He was tall and gangling, with hay-coloured hair, mismatched ears, and a rangy gait. His awkward appearance and halting speech led town dwellers to consider Corrine's father eccentric, a bit *unusual*. He had inherited his farm as a young man from a distant, shiftless relation. The farm was tiny and barren when Corrine was born, and over the course of her childhood her father worked it and increased it in size and yield until it provided food and commercial crops for half the county. It grew to a sprawling expanse of stalks and furrows and as Corrine reached adolescence the farm stretched as far as she could see from her second-floor bedroom window. Every year there were more workers—more clanking, cluttering machines in the fields. Tractors and trucks and harvesters. Men yelling and laughing as they worked. The noise soothed Corrine, and she slept easily in the afternoon heat.

Stuck out there with that man . . .

Corrine had never known her father in the company of women. There were tinges of loneliness at the corners of his eyes, which were camouflaged by smudges at the edge of his crooked eyeglasses. After her mother's death, Corrine's father had given up his own pleasures in order to attend to the farm, and to his daughter's terrors. He had lived with Corrine and her nightly screams until they became his screams as well. He tried desperately to help her—he strove to make the evenings quieter for her, in the vain hope that she would find the peace soothing. He didn't know then that the peace was the problem.

She slept during the day, soothed by the noise of the industry around the house and farm. Her father hired tutors, expensive tutors, to come to the house at night to teach his daughter during the hours when she didn't sleep. The quiet hours. He himself didn't sleep at all, and it aged him. He worried incessantly about his daughter, about the things Corrine was missing out on. School and friends. Dances and sports. Church and clubs. But Corrine wasn't troubled by the things she didn't know. She was content with her father, and the noises of the cows and chickens. She slept soundly during the day.

Someone should . . .

Finally, Corrine's father reached out to those in town for help—something he was loath to do. He invited a doctor and a priest from town to examine and interview Corrine, to determine what might help quiet the screams. The doctor found nothing wrong with her and confidently prescribed a sedative which he said would help Corrine sleep. She needed more sunlight and exercise, he said. That, along with the pills, would set her right. She would soon be playing games with the other kids in town.

The priest told Corrine that she was causing her own distress, that the dreams came from her own poisoned psyche. Her fear was caused by sin and demons, and there was no way for her to help herself, and no way for her father to help her. Help would only come from the church, the priest said. Her father had made a mistake keeping Corrine at the farm for so many years. They both were paying for that mistake, and they needed to come into town, where the priest and the others could heal her of the evil she had caused herself.

Corrine's father showed both men the door and went out into the fields to consider what they had said. He didn't like the men. When Corrine's mother was dying, the doctor floundered and stuttered as she bled out in the birthing bed. Then he had stood straight, and with lying eyes he had told Corrine's father he had done all there was to do. That no one could have saved her. The town people had been sad for Corrine's father, had patted him gently on the arm and the shoulder, and told him how sad they all were. They were so, so sad. His wife was somewhere else now, they told him, somewhere better. But Corrine's father could see the dead body right in front of him. He didn't want to hear that her death was part of someone else's plan.

Something wrong at that farm . . .

Corrine didn't go to town. She didn't take the pills. Then, when she was twelve years old, there was a fire in the barn. One of the farmhands had left a cigarette smouldering which lit the hay after the sun had gone down. Corrine had fallen asleep before sunset that evening, and despite the yelling and the chaos of the cows lowing and trucks and men fighting the fire, she slept through the night for the first time in her life. The noise and chaos of the fire dispelled the stillness of the grave and allowed Corrine to sleep untroubled. The next morning, after the last smouldering embers were extinguished, her father finally awakened to the root of Corrine's terror. He understood at last that when the world was dark and quiet, Corrine would awake certain that she was dead. That she had passed away while her eyes were closed, and that she was underground, alone, forever.

The day after the fire, Corrine's father went into town and searched for musicians for hire. He found a man who played the trumpet and another who blew the trombone. Next a fiddle player, and a woman who once played the cello in a big city orchestra. He scrambled to find anyone else who could sit in with his impromptu ensemble, and came across the town's squeeze-box maestro, who agreed to join the group. Corrine's father paid the musicians to sit under her window at night and play. They arrived and argued about seating arrangements until after the sun had slipped below the fields of soybeans and corn. Then, with no practice or rehearsal, they broke into a cacophony of sounds that made Corrine's father wince and made Corrine smile into her pillow before she drifted off to sleep.

The night was too long, though, for the musicians to maintain until morning. After a few hours, the tumultuous riot of sound eventually petered into a noise like an ancient, moth-eaten set of bagpipes, and then only occasional hoots and twangs. And the screaming returned.

They're not like us . . .

A week after the ill-fated concert, a truck arrived at the farm, tightly packed with large wooden crates. Corrine watched from her window as her father and the farmhands unloaded the crates, while others cleared the nearest rows of crops away from the house. It took several days to unpack the crates and sort the contents. The men constructed a wooden wall to screen their activities from view. They worked through the nights with a continuous clamour and the sound of metal ringing upon metal. Floodlights illuminated the yard outside Corrine's window, and she slept well.

On the third evening after the arrival of the truck, Corrine's father called her to her window. The lights were off and the yard was dark. The wooden screen had been removed and Corrine could see there was a structure of some sort in the yard. When her father was sure Corrine was watching, he and the men counted down from three and suddenly the structure blazed forth with light and music. It was a carousel, delivered and constructed and sitting in her yard! Corrine burst into tears of wonder and joy. Fantastical, painted creatures—unicorns and elephants and even a beautiful mermaid—crawled and leapt around an endless circle, encouraged by an invisible calliope. Bright, blinking bulbs encircled the top of the carousel, and the yard and the first few rows of corn tassels danced with coloured light. Corrine was delighted. Her father ran the carousel all night, and Corrine slept as soundly as she ever had before.

... *don't trust them* ...

From that night on, the carousel turned every night. The calliope's whistle echoed to the edges of the farm, and the light from the carousel could be seen across the flat land as a distant, twinkling beacon all the way into town. The gleam of a hundred coloured light bulbs drew curious townsfolk. Parents, children, and those concerned with the safety and propriety of their fellows travelled to the source of the light and late-night music. They found the single, solitary carousel. Corrine's carousel. No other rides or games. The children rode the carousel two or three times around and then asked to go home. Parents and self-proclaimed leaders of the community offered ill-disguised contemptuous glances at Corrine's father as they left. They didn't return and, as owning a carousel outside of town limits wasn't a crime, they weren't heard from again.

The carousel kept turning, and the night got darker, and soon other visitors began arriving. Those who lived at night, who thrived in shadow. People who weren't welcome in town. Some had broken laws. Others were accused of transgressing against small world order and decorum. There were musicians who played forbidden music. Tellers of stories of mysticism and magic. Dancers of unapproved and forgotten movements. Drums arrived and incorporated the calliope's melody into their weird skin-sounds. Strange gourds and hollowed out pieces of wood strung with the entrails of feral animals joined in. The calliope sound was rounded out, smoothed, covered with something rich and old.

Campfires were lit, and the smell of smoke filled the yard and drew Corrine to her window. These visitors didn't come to ride the carousel. They just longed to be in its presence. They carried powders made from brightly coloured flowers and minerals, and they mixed the powders with urine and blood and painted symbols and spells upon each other's bodies. Every night, they danced and sang until at last the music grew quiet, and one of their party began to speak. An older woman with a voice so thick and strong that even the noise of the calliope showed deference when she spoke. She told stories then—stories of the beginnings of things. Why there was time. Where the animals were created. Why there was rain, and drought. Her stories were about magic and giants and forces impossible to write on paper. The tales she told were invisible. They were eternal. The others around the fires listened intently, smoking, and drinking from cups and bottles. Her last story was always about death—walking with death, dancing with death. One story was of death and his lover, and the listeners nodded solemnly as she told it.

She's lost to us . . .

Time passed, as it does. Her father became ill and took to bed, and now Corrine held his head as he passed back and forth between waking and sleep. The commercial crops wilted and died. Corn and soybeans dried up, and other plant life and vegetation began to grow wild in the fields. Eventually, Corrine decided she needed more of the stories than reached her through her second-floor window. She needed to feel the fire on her face.

Corrine crept down to the yard and sat first at the fringes of the firelight, spasmic shadows hiding bits of her between flares. She watched the painted bodies dance, listened to the strange instruments sing and pound their rhythmic moans. But she was drawn most to the stories, the *stories*. Stories of giants fertilizing the earth with their dandruff and sweat, bits of their sloughed off skin compacting, layer upon layer, as they battled with unimaginable creatures. Stories of the black, inky whirlpool spinning in the stomach of a dark giant, at the beginning of time, while he vomited the starlight and celestial bodies.

Her favourite stories, though, were about the thick, pungent First Woman and her love affair with Death. How their thunderous, perpetual coupling was both awful and rapturous. Their insatiable desire for each other took every form, every joining imaginable. As they coupled face-to-face, they rolled across the surface of the world, crushing all who happened to be underneath their sweating forms. As Death took First Woman from behind, her hands pushed up mountain ranges, and when she sat atop him her knees dug deep furrows in the earth that filled with water. His ecstatic cries were thunderclaps, and her sighs pushed the clouds across the sky. Their motion caused the ocean tides and waves that shaped the contours of continents. As she shivered, she gave birth continually. Birds and reptiles fell from her hair as she shook her head. Fish dropped from the corners of her eyes with her tears. And people sprang forth from underneath her fingernails as they raked across Death's back. In their continual orgasm, Death and First Woman moved across the land and sea, destroying and populating forever.

The drums never stopped beating while the old woman told her stories. The rhythm entrained with the heartbeat of the group. It drew them together. Inevitably, couples formed among those around the fire. They touched as they danced, and grew closer and closer until they joined there, around the yard, their moans and cries in time with the drums. Corrine watched from her shadows, entranced. As the couples all reached climax, the drums stopped, and Corrine fell asleep peacefully in the shadow-grass. When she awoke late in the morning, the fire was out, and the people were gone. Until the sun went down again.

By the time her father died, Corrine had stopped screaming. She slept contentedly, day or night, her surroundings peaceful or noisy. She dreamt of carousels, and of giants coupling. She touched her father's lifeless face and felt the gratitude of an adult mixed with the adulation of a little girl.

Her father died on the same day as the old woman storyteller. That night, the people laid both bodies next to each other by the fire. They painted the corpses with red paint mixed with blood, and the blue indigo and ochre paints worn by the giants. They danced and sang songs of reverence, and then, before dawn, they carried the bodies, with some effort, up into the highest rafters of the old, ruined barn. After the bodies were secure, they set the barn on fire and sat in silence watching it burn.

The next night, Corrine came out of the house dressed only in her underwear, smeared with paint she had prepared from her own blood. She walked out into the yard and stood quietly as the fire was built and lit. The drums began their work quietly, but no one danced. No one sang or chanted. All looked at Corrine, waiting. After a moment, Corrine walked across to the silent, still, rusting carousel of her youth and caressed and kissed the worn, faded face of the mermaid. Then she walked back and sat in the old woman's seat and began to tell a story.

THE EDITORS

LESLIE VAN ZWOL

Leslie is nocturnal by nature; the night has always been her calling and her best friend the moon. She's been compared to a magpie, fox, and a raccoon, and feels that tells you more about her than it should. Bios make her uncomfortable, and many of her accomplishments can be attributed to spite.

She's an editor and writer of speculative short stories and poems created with ample dashes of grit, a pinch of darkness, and equal parts love and heartache. She dabbles in theatre, dance, painting (digital and traditional), and due to her ADHD has doom boxes brimming with abandoned dreams.

Her dog Lola is overjoyed the anthology is over so Leslie can get back to her requisite nighttime cuddles and belly-rubs.

She holds firm the belief that stories are magical and anyone can write great things. ***Especially you.***

She can be found on Twitter or Bluesky (and other social media) under @/bobbistyles (spelling varies depending on how quickly she obtained the username; however, dog pictures remain the same).

MEGAN FENNELL

Megan Fennell has been fascinated by night and the creatures thriving in it since becoming obsessed with Charlotte Diamond's reading of "The Imp with Blood-Red Eyes" as a kid. Her long-suffering parents' attempt to give her a nice cassette of children's songs and stories subsequently led to dozens of sleepless nights, a concerned inquiry from a kindergarten teacher about Megan over-using black crayons, and (eventually) several successful decades of writing about misunderstood monsters.

When she's not writing, she fills her time acting, Taiko drumming, painting, and chasing around her tabby terrors and lovable hound. Her writing can be found both under her own name and as one half of the dynamic duo V.F. LeSann.

NOCTURNAL AUTHORS

TERESA AGUINALDO

Teresa Aguinaldo is a retired English instructor and college dean living in Chicago, IL, USA. She began writing creatively later in life; now in retirement, it is her main passion. She is Filipino, born in the Philippines, and came to the US when she was a baby. She grew up listening to the stories of her father, who was reared in a northern farming province. She is always inspired by his tales of surviving in a small barrio, finding safety in the mountains, and minding the elders' stories of the many monsters that inhabited the landscape. "The Tiyanak" (pronounced "cha-nak") is a result of such inspiration. You can also read her short story "Hero" at https://www.thearchipelago.org and follow her on Instagram @manaaguinaldo.

TYLER BATTAGLIA

Tyler Battaglia is a queer and disabled author of horror and dark fantasy. He is interested in subjects that interrogate the connections between faith, monsters, love, queerness, and disability. Tyler also loves a good transformation metaphor. You can find him on social media at @whosthistyler and online at https://www.tylerbattaglia.com, where you can also find a full list of publications to date.

STEWART C BAKER

Stewart C Baker is an academic librarian and author of speculative fiction, poetry, and interactive fiction. His most recent game is the Nebula-nominated *The Bread Must Rise*, a novel-length comedic fantasy from Choice of Games written with James Beamon. Stewart's stories and poems have appeared in *Asimov's, Fantasy, Flash Fiction Online, Lightspeed, Nature,* and other places. Born in England, Stewart has lived in South Carolina, Japan, and Los Angeles, and now lives with his family within the traditional homelands of the Luckiamute Band of Kalapuya in Oregon—although if anyone asks, he'll usually say he's from the Internet.

BETH CATO

Nebula Award-nominated Beth Cato is the author of *A Thousand Recipes for Revenge* and *A Feast for Starving Stone* from 47North plus two fantasy series from Harper Voyager. She's a Hanford, California native now moored in the Driftless Area. She usually has one or two cats in close orbit. Follow her at BethCato.com and on Twitter/X at @BethCato and Instagram at @catocatsandcheese.

BARRY CHARMAN

Barry Charman is a writer living in North London. He has been published in various magazines, including *Ambit, Griffith Review, The Ghastling,* and *Popshot Quarterly.* He has had poems published online and in print, most recently in *The Literary Hatchet* and *The Linnet's Wings.* He has a blog at http://barrycharman.blogspot.co.uk/

TOMMY CHEIS

Tommy Cheis is a Chiricahua Apache (Native American) writer originally from the Dragoon Mountains of Arizona. He is a descendant of Cochise and Naiche. After traveling extensively through distant lands and meeting interesting people, and picking up degrees along the way, he now resides in southeastern Arizona with his wife, dog, and horses. His short stories appear in *Yellow Medicine Review, ZiN Daily, Spirits, Red Paint Review, Pictural Journal, Little Fish, Hot Potato Magazine, The*

Rumen, and *Blue Guitar.* His first novel, *Rare Earth,* is under submission.

JONATHAN CHIBUIK

Ukah Jonathan Chibuike Ukah lives in the United Kingdom with his family. His poems have been featured and will soon be featured in *Atticus Review, The Journal of Undiscovered Poets, Carpe Noctem, The Pierian, The Unleash Creatives,* and elsewhere. He is a winner of the Alexander Pope Poetry Award of *The Pierian* in 2023; The Editor's Prize Choice of the *Unleash Creatives* in 2024, and the Wingless Dreamer Poetry Prize 2024.

DEREK DES ANGES

Derek Des Anges is a multi-genre writer and press cutter living in London, with other horror work published by *Ghoulish Books, From Beyond Press,* and *On The Premises Magazine.* He is horribly, terribly familiar with English seaside towns, and that's why he doesn't live in one anymore.

RICHARD DIPIRRO

Richard R. DiPirro is a disabled U.S. Marine Corps veteran and the author of the novel *Eaten by Wolves.* His work has appeared in a handful of literary magazines and anthologies, including "Tales of the Strange," by Writer's Workout, *The Lindenwood Review, Fiction Reader, Fringe Magazine,* and *Raving Dove Literary Journal.* Richard presently lives in Iowa with his amazing wife and three children and is hard at work on his second novel.

DAVID J. FORTIER

David J. Fortier grew up in Winnipeg, Manitoba, Canada, reading adventure classics, heroic fantasies, and sword & sorcery over the long winters. A proud geek, he loves board games, D&D, superhero movies, LOTR, Star Wars, video games, and Conan comics. He currently resides in Canada, where he writes heroic fantasy, sword & sorcery, steampunk, and other speculative fiction. He's published by *Bards and Sages Quarterly,* Zombies Need Brains, and now Tyche Books.

DAVID JÓN FULLER

David Jón Fuller grew up in Winnipeg, Man., and Edmonton, Alta., and also lived for two years in Iceland where he studied Icelandic language and literature at the University of Iceland. He holds a B.A. (Hon.) in Theatre from the University of Winnipeg.

His short fiction has appeared in *OnSpec* magazine as well as anthologies such as *Leadership Gone Right*; *Kneeling in the Silver Light: Stories from the Great War*; *Swords and Steam*; *No Shit, There I Was*; and *Tesseracts 18: Wrestling with Gods*. He lives in Winnipeg.

CHADWICK GINTHER

Chadwick Ginther is the Prix Aurora Award-winning author of The Thunder Road Trilogy, *Graveyard Mind*, and over thirty short stories, some of which have been collected in *Khyber: Sinister Tales of Sword and Sorcery* and *When the Sky Comes Looking for You: Short Trips Down the Thunder Road*. He lives in Winnipeg, Canada where he writes stories full of skeletons, giants, and dragons. Find him at www.chadwickginther.com

JOSEPH HALDEN

Joseph Halden is a wizard in search of magic, an astronaut in need of space, and a hopeless enthusiast of frivolity. He's shot things with giant lasers, worn an astronaut costume for over 100 days to try and get into space, and made his own soap. A graduate of the Odyssey Writing Workshop and a Pushcart Prize finalist, he writes science fiction and fantasy in western Canada. Find more of his work at www.JosephHalden.com.

RICHARD LAU

Richard Lau is an award-winning writer who is published in magazines, newspapers, and anthologies, as well as in the high-tech industry and online.

JENNIFER LESH FLECK

A past Pushcart Prize nominee for poetry, Jennifer Lesh Fleck has speculative tales published by *The Arcanist*, *MetaStellar*, *Cosmic Horror Monthly*, *Creepy*, *If There's Anyone Left*, and *Radon Journal*, *Gamut*, and forthcoming in *Tales to Terrify* and several fiction anthologies. She and her family live near Portland, OR in a 106-year-old home that's the spitting image of the Amityville Horror House, though repainted a cheery jade green. Her work is often informed by the challenges of lifelong hidden disability from a rare inherited disease. Join Jennifer and her two dedicated demon familiars (who look strikingly like small dogs): @metal.and.mettle (Instagram), @jen_lesh_fleck (Twitter/X)

AVRA MARGARITI

Avra Margariti is a queer author, Greek sea monster, and

Rhysling-nominated poet with a fondness for the dark and the darling. Avra's work haunts publications such as *Strange Horizons, The Deadlands, F&SF, Podcastle, Asimov's, Vastarien,* and *Reckoning.* You can find Avra on twitter (@avramargariti).

THOMAS C. MAVROUDIS

Member of the Denver Horror Collective, as well as the Horror Writers Association, Thomas C. Mavroudis has an MFA from the University of CA, Riverside – Palm Desert under the direction of Stephen Graham Jones. His debut novella, *Bergdorf & Associates,* was released in May of 2021. His short stories have appeared on *Creepy: A Horror Podcast,* the *NoSleep Podcast,* and in *Weirdbook, Cosmic Horror Monthly, Mooncalves, Kelp Journal, December Tales II,* and elsewhere.

CAT MCDONALD

Cat is a decorated podcaster and game designer (the king of PeachGardenGames.com). Cat has been teaching themself calligraphy and digital art, is an award-winning game master, and lives like a medieval monk for the most part.

PAUL MCQUADE

Paul McQuade is a writer and translator originally from Glasgow, Scotland. His writing has received the Sceptre Prize for New Writing, the Austrian Cultural Forum Writing Prize, and been shortlisted for both the Bridport and White Review short story awards. He is the author of the short story collection *Between Tongues.*

VILLE MERILÄINEN

Ville Meriläinen is a Finnish author of fantasy and horror fiction.

TAIS TENG

Tais Teng is a Dutch sf writer and illustrator with the quite unpronounceable name of Thijs van Ebbenhorst Tengbergen, which he shortened to a humble Tais Teng to leave room for exploding spaceships or a clever steampunk lady on the cover of his novels. His drawings range from talking teapots to quite beautiful bat-winged ladies with a naughty character. In his own language, he has written everything from radio plays to hefty fantasy trilogies. One was even a mythos novel with Paul Harland: *Computercode Cthulhu.* To date he has sold seventy-five stories in the English language, while Spatterlight recently published his SF novel *Phaedra: Alastor 824,* set in the universe of Jack Vance. Teng is a great admirer of Clark Ashton Smith and the last years he has been writing stories set in his Zothique, the last continent of Earth, under a dying sun. His Dutch publisher published them as a collection titled *Gekleed in soepel mummieleer (Clad in supple mummie leather)* with 21 interior illustrations. A second Sword & Sorcery series is set in the alternate Arabian Nights universe of the Inland Sea. You can find samples of both of the series in *Swords & Sorceries.* His most recent S & S sales are to *Cirsova, Swords & Sorceries 8,* and *Strange Aeon 2024.*

LAURA VANARENDONK BAUGH

Laura VanArendonk Baugh writes fantasy of many flavours as well as non-fiction. She has summited extinct, dormant, and active volcanoes, but none has yet accepted her sacrifice. She lives in Indiana where she enjoys Dobermans, travel, fair-trade chocolate, and making her imaginary friends fight one another for her own amusement. Find her award-winning work at LauraVAB.com.